"West's first novel is powerful and moving . . . a celebration of the human spirit . . . a heart-stopper, a strong, unblinking deeply human tale."
—*Publishers Weekly*

"This very good first novel . . . is an off-beat tale that features good characterization . . . solid background detail, and a strong sense of the value of human life. Highly recommended."
—James B. Hemesath, *Library Journal*

". . . a first novel of extraordinary impact . . . a work of literature. This novel will warm your heart, lift your spirits and make you feel a certain goodness that we're prone to lose . . . [it is] about life, love, and being close to another person. About mistakes and petty human foolishness, and the senseless hurts we inflict upon those we care for most."
—Paul Bach, *Desert Sentinel*

"West has penned an unusual, well-written novel. . . . The book features some marvelous, descriptive passages that will be remembered long after the last page has been turned. The skillful plotting and the warm human relationships make it exciting, first-rate reading."
—Judy Schuster, *Minneapolis Star Tribune*

". . . an extraordinary book, a powerful story about life, death and man's ability to redeem himself and others through courage, compassion and sacrifice . . . a well-crafted, intricate, heart-stopping suspense story . . . the suspense becomes nearly unbearable. West has developed men and women with full, often bittersweet histories and portrayed them with sensitivity, wry humor and heartbreaking resonance. Stanley

West's . . . *Amos* should be remembered long after the final page is turned."
—Christine B. Vogel, *The Plain Dealer*

"This is a remarkable story. . . . West shows himself to be a seasoned storyteller, offering the reader a variety of emotions. . . . Suspense is built layer upon layer. . . . And holding the story together is a theology that elevates the human spirit to heroic heights."
—Clark Morphew, *St. Paul Dispatch*

"I have just finished *Amos*—an extraordinary book. I read it straight through—literally unable to put it down. . . . it is a celebration of the capacity of the human spirit for compassion and sacrifice and courage. One is inevitably reminded of William Faulkner's speech when he received the Nobel Prize: 'I believe that man will not merely endure, he will prevail . . . he has a soul, a spirit, capable of compassion and sacrifice and endurance . . . courage and pity . . . which have been the glory of his past.'"
—Millicent Fenwick

"The least likely protagonist of the year has to be Amos Lasher, a seventy-eight-year-old resident of a seedy county poor-farm called Sunset Home. . . . Yet West has created a hero in prose that lives up to the promise of the novel's first sentence: 'He was an old man, clinging fiercely to the tattered garment that had once been his dignity.' Comparisons to *One Flew Over the Cuckoo's Nest* and even the film *Cool Hand Luke* are inevitable. In all three stories one man's invincible spirit overcomes the blindness of society and the brutality of its representatives.
—Sally Bright, *The Tulsa World*

Stanley Gordon West

UNTIL THEY BRING THE STREETCARS BACK

Stanley West was born in St. Paul, Minnesota. While growing
up he got around town riding the streetcars. He graduated
from Central High School in 1950. He attended Macalester
College and the University of Minnesota, receiving a degree
in 1955. He moved from the Midwest to Montana in 1964 and
has made his home there ever since. His novel *Amos* was
produced as a CBS Movie of the Week starring Kirk Douglas,
Elizabeth Montgomery and Dorothy McGuire and was
nominated for four Emmys.

Also By Stanley G. West

Amos
Finding Laura Buggs
Growing An Inch
Blind Your Ponies
Sweet Shattered Dreams

UNTIL THEY BRING THE STREETCARS BACK

Stanley Gordon West

LEXINGTON-MARSHALL PUBLISHING
SHAKOPEE, MINNESOTA

Published in the United States by Lexington·Marshall Publishing
15085 Halsey Avenue, Carver, Minnesota 55315

Acknowledgment is made to the following:

Cover photo from the City of Minneapolis Public Works collection, used
by permission.

The People's Chronology by James Trager © 1994 by James Trager,
reprinted by permission of Henry Holt & Company, Inc.

The Electric Railways of Minnesota, © 1976 by Russell L. Olson, used by
permission.

Library of Congress Catalog Card Number: 96-95370
ISBN 0-9656247-6-5
ISBN 978-0-9656247-6-3

Book design by Richard Krogstad
Book production by Peregrine Graphics Services
Author photograph © David Neiman

Printed in the United States of America by McNaughton & Gunn, Inc.
on acid-free paper.

For all of us who attended
Saint Paul Central High School
in 1949
and the special life
we shared there together.

*They never told us
it would pass so swiftly—*

Love the earth and sun and the animals,
    despise riches,
      give alms to every one that asks,
        stand up for the stupid and crazy . . .
—Walt Whitman, *Leaves of Grass,* 1855 Edition

    Well, courting's a pleasure
    And parting is grief,
    But a false-hearted lover
    Is worse than a thief.
    —*On Top of Old Smokey*

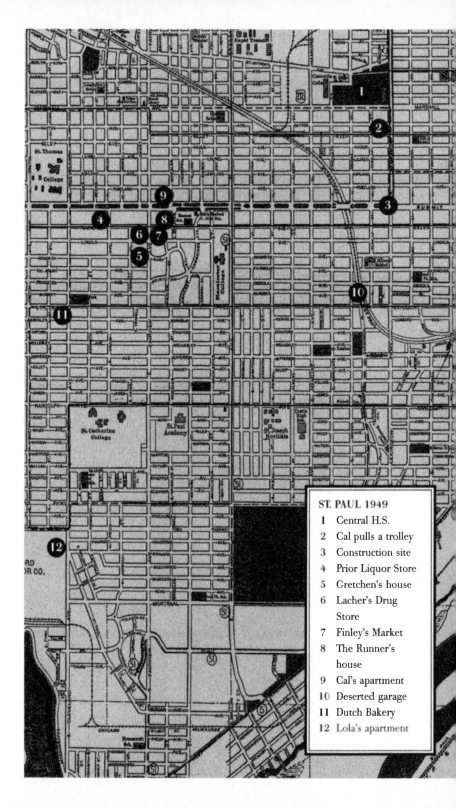

ST. PAUL 1949

1 Central H.S.
2 Cal pulls a trolley
3 Construction site
4 Prior Liquor Store
5 Gretchen's house
6 Lacher's Drug
   Store
7 Finley's Market
8 The Runner's
   house
9 Cal's apartment
10 Deserted garage
11 Dutch Bakery
12 Lola's apartment

UNTIL THEY BRING THE STREETCARS BACK

Chapter 1

If I'd never run into Gretchen Luttermann I wouldn't have landed in that crummy jail. And better still, her father wouldn't be trying to kill me. I know it sounds pretty normal that a girl's father wants to kill some kid, but he really wanted to *kill* me and she wasn't even my girl and it kept getting all mixed up when I tried to explain it.

Criminy, I couldn't believe it, locked up like some lousy criminal or something. If I had to make a list of the places I bet I'd never be, jail would be at the top, ahead of an insane asylum and the moon. It was like the passageway to my old life had caved in and I could never go back, like the laws of nature had changed: wings came off airplanes, internal-combustion engines blew up, and apples fell sideways off trees.

Not just jail, but prison or maybe even the penitentiary. They were probably going to lock me up for a long time and I wanted to tell them they had the wrong guy, but they'd never believe me, it was too late for that, and worst of all, I'd known long enough that I was Gretchen's only chance. What would happen to her now, what good had I done her for all my big talk? At least I didn't have to be looking over my shoulder for her father for a while. I could almost laugh; the only place I was safe was in jail.

When they hauled me to the police station, a cop who looked like he hadn't been to bed in a month asked me a lot of questions and they took my picture and fingerprints like I was Baby Face Nelson or something.

"What's your name?"

"Cal . . . Calvin Gant."

"How old are you?"

"Eighteen."

"Sorry, kid, you're not a youngster anymore, you're into the big-time now."

He had eyes like a Saint Bernard and he looked sad and that scared the willies out of me because I figured he knew how bad it was going to be. It was like I was in a movie and I expected James Cagney to come creaming down the hall with a Thompson sub-machine gun, making a break for it. They locked me in a little iron cell and I felt like I'd thrown up all over myself, like I'd never be clean again, and I was trying not to cry. I sat on the lower bunk, sweating like crazy and gulping for air, and I started thinking about how it all happened.

The first time I met Gretchen was like walking through poison ivy—you don't know you're in trouble until a few days later. I've thought about it four million times. What if I'd been sick that day, or what if my last name was Stubbs or Yarusso and I sat way in the back of the auditorium? Or what if we lived in a different neighborhood and I went to Marshall or Monroe? But I wasn't sick and my name was Gant and I went to Central and I was in fifth period study hall when you're kind of logy from eating lunch and you try not to burp so you don't get that lousy taste in your mouth from the sauerkraut and franks they served in the lunchroom, although I didn't buy my lunch that often; I carried it from home. We weren't poor or anything like that, my dad was a motorman for the Twin Cities Rapid Transit Company, which meant he drove a streetcar, and we did all right, but I usually brought my lunch in a brown paper bag and my mother wanted me to bring the bag home and use it again but I never did because I didn't want kids thinking we were hard up, not having a car and all.

It was my senior year at St. Paul Central, we'd be the class of 1950, and I couldn't believe I hadn't noticed Gretchen in the three years we'd been going to the same school. Jeez, I knew it was a big school, over fifteen hundred kids and all, but it was like I'd never laid eyes on her. I guess that wasn't hard to figure with the plain long dresses she wore and no lipstick or anything like that, and her stringy hair just hung there, and worst of all black socks and those huge brown oxfords that looked like gunboats on her skinny legs. She was skinny all over and she never smiled, so I can see why I never noticed her, like she was a zombie or something.

We had a football game that night, a Friday, the first week of school, and Jerry Douglas, one of my best friends, passed out marbles in front hall just before the bell rang. Jeez, I was sitting there with a marble in my sweating hand like a hand grenade with its pin pulled, wondering if I'd be able to do it. The auditorium was used for a study hall, and we were assigned seats in a checkerboard pattern so nobody had a kid sitting next to him. It was quiet in there, like in church, and the only sound was the squeak from one of the folding wooden seats or the click of the clock high on the wall beside the stage. I eyed the clock and my heart started pounding.

This was crazier than most of the things Jerry pulled, almost like fooling around with the cops or the FBI. You didn't breathe loudly in Miss Whalmen's study hall. Jeez, she could flatten you with just a look, and her nickname, the Prussian General, warned kids for years not to screw around with her. She wore these black silky dresses and whenever you got near her you'd catch a whiff of musty clothes that'd been sprinkled with perfume like someone was embalmed or something.

The hands on the clock moved to 1:18 and you could feel the pressure mounting like you were sitting in the electric chair. In front hall a ton of kids had pushed and shoved to get one of the marbles when Jerry started passing them out, boys and girls, and they went marching into the auditorium to take part in that gang suicide just to be in on anything with Jerry Douglas because he was a popular senior and jock. The clock clicked to 1:19 and I crunched down behind my trig book and looked across the auditorium at Jerry. He had this big sappy grin on his face and I could see he was watching the clock.

When the hands hit 1:20 I laid my marble on the floor and for a hair-raising second it was the only one I could hear, but then they came rumbling from all corners of the auditorium, down the slanting floor, right for old Whalmen where she sat behind a little table in front of the stage. Jeez, it sounded like a herd of elephants on roller skates or something and there were marbles flying all over the place, hitting the metal legs of the seats, popping up in the air, and kids lifting their feet to let them roll by.

With marbles coming at her shins like hockey pucks, Miss Whalmen leaped out of her seat and hopscotched across the floor like Roy Rogers was making her dance with his six-shooters. Gad, I never saw anyone move so fast. Then she stopped on a dime and just stood there with her hands on her hips and I stuck my face in my trig book. When the last marble settled at the foot of the stage, probably let loose by some uncoordinated freshman, she looked at us like nothing happened, like marbles come rolling in all the time. Everybody ducked behind their books and her face never changed expression.

"It would appear that some of you have lost your marbles."

Without trying to be funny she cracked everybody up, a roar like you opened the door on a big cheering crowd for a second and then shut it, and it was deadly silent. She had two kids in the front row take the wastepaper basket and collect Jerry's marbles while she just eyeballed us out of her cold powdered face like she was staring out of her coffin. I felt her eyes sweep over me like a searchlight in a concentration camp and no one dared look at her, no one dared breathe, and the hands on the clock didn't dare move. That's when she finally said what changed my life forever.

"The entire study hall will spend seventh period here today. No excuses!"

"Are you satisfied, you wiener," I asked Jerry and punched him on the shoulder. We did that a lot, punched each other on the shoulder, I don't know why, but we always did. We were

waiting in the front hall for seventh period to begin when all
the other kids were streaming out the front door with school
over for the week and the football game coming up that night
and the sun was shining like crazy and Jerry was beaming
like he'd just had a date with Ava Gardner or something.

"Did you see the look on her face?" Jerry said, "she
thought she was being attacked by an army of gum balls."

"Let's do it again, Monday," Steve Holland said, "with
golf balls."

Steve was one of my best friends, too, although he was a
little wild and you could never tell what he was going to do.
He looked older than most of us, like a college kid or something, and with his wire-rim glasses he looked real smart, and
I think he really was, but he never studied much and had
terrible grades and probably wouldn't even graduate with us.
When he was in sixth grade he got polio and his right leg
kind of shriveled and ended up shorter than his other leg and
it was real skinny, but he was lucky because he didn't die like
a lot of kids did when they couldn't breathe and they stuck
them in iron lungs and things. My parents sent me up north
to live with my uncle Emil the summers when polio was running wild in St. Paul and I never got it. Steve walked with a
limp and the only sport he could play was goalie in hockey
because he didn't have to move very far but we never noticed
his limp anymore like it was just part of him and it wouldn't
seem like Steve if he didn't walk that way.

"You're as crazy as Jerry," I told Steve.

"You probably never dropped your marble," Steve said.

"I did too," I said, "but I don't know why I keep letting you
guys get me in trouble."

"It was worth it," Jerry said. "We couldn't go four years
without getting Whalmen at least once."

We all started dragging through the swinging doors into
the auditorium and the boring hour of pretending we were
studying when we could have been outside and Steve called
out, "Everyone bring golf balls on Monday! Bowling balls!"

When I slid into my seat I saw this tall skinny girl standing beside Whalmen's table and she was staring at the floor in these black socks and big ugly shoes and I could barely hear her saying, "I didn't drop a marble; my father is waiting for me."

Whalmen didn't even look at her and she talked loud enough so everyone in the auditorium could hear her.

"You should address your fellow students. Their childish behavior keeps you here, not I. Take your seat."

The girl I'd never noticed before slunk to the row behind me and slid past a few kids until she sat in the seat off my left shoulder and I could hear her muttering like she was all by herself and didn't know anyone could hear her.

"My father will whip me, he'll hurt me r-e-a-l bad."

I turned halfway around and looked at her up close for the first time, and I thought she was kidding, like when I say my dad will kill me, but when I looked in her face she wasn't smiling or anything, like she hadn't smiled in about eleven years, and she was kind of spooky with her stringy hair and sad hollow face and that terrible dress like they wear in the nut house.

"Aw, Cripes, he isn't going to whip you just because you got seventh period," I said and it surprised her, like it was unusual for another kid to talk to her, and she looked at me like she was afraid and then she stared at the floor and knotted the hem of her dress with her thin hands. I forgot all about seventh period starting and Whalmen spotted me turning around and talking. She couldn't come up with my name and she ran her finger down the seating chart.

"Mr. Gant, do you think this is a recreation period? You will participate in Mr. Kirschbach's seventh period *all* next week. It will be silent in here!"

Whalmen jotted something on the chart like she got a kick out of it and I slunk down in my seat and opened my trig book. Darn, I'd miss an hour of practice every day for a week and because of that I wouldn't be able to play in next week's game, just because of that weird string bean who babbled like she was crazy or something. I was so mad I thought that if her father didn't whale her I wanted my turn, and for the rest of the hour you could've heard hair grow.

Chapter 2

Tom Bradford and Lola Muldoon caught up when I was blasting out of the building after seventh period. They were going together and it was hard for me but I had to get used to it because they were really stuck on each other.

"I almost dropped my marble too soon," Lola said and laughed in a way that made me ache inside. The best looking girl in the senior class, she made boys gulp and whistle silently through their teeth when she'd walk in the hallways and I'd see them take a second look as if their eyes had made her up or something.

"You won't be able to play in the Harding game," Tom said.

"Yeah, just because of that screwball girl," I said.

Ahead of us I spotted her hurrying to a black Plymouth waiting on Marshall Avenue.

"That's her, that's her!" I pointed. "Who is that?"

"Gretchen Luttermann," Lola said as the skinny girl slid into the car and it pulled away into traffic.

"Is she new?" I asked.

"She was in Hilger's social studies with me when we were juniors," Lola said, chewing her gum like mad and snapping it ever so often. "I remember she started late, after we'd been going a few weeks. Some kids called her Gretch the Wretch."

"She said her dad was going to whip her or something," I said, "what a queer."

"My mother would have a cow if she knew I dropped a marble," Lola said.

We crossed Marshall in a dash between the rush-hour traffic and legged it the two blocks along Dunlap, catching a streetcar coming up Selby.

"You coming?" Tom said, hurrying with Lola.

"Naw, I'm going to hitch," I said and I let them run ahead to catch the Selby-Lake.

When I reached the corner, the folding doors swallowed them, and the yellow streetcar rolled away. I caught a glimpse of Lola through a side window and I almost got killed crossing Selby because I wasn't looking at the cars, thinking about how well I'd kept it secret. I'd been in love with her since we were sophomores but I didn't even tell my good buddies Jerry and Steve because I didn't want them kidding me about her; it was too painful.

She dated some big-wheel upperclassman most of our junior year until during the summer when Tom asked her out, and the first thing I knew they were going together. She wore her blonde hair longer than most of the girls, down to her shoulders, and her eyes were some kind of blue—I'm not very hot when it comes to colors, I mean I basically know red and green and yellow and all, but when it comes to the two million in between, I don't know most of their names—but whatever her eyes were, when she'd train them on you it was like getting shot. I was always trying to decide if I'd go out with some other girl, lowering my expectations, or go it alone and dream about Lola.

I didn't have my thumb out for long when a guy with a schnozz like Jimmie Durante gave me a ride in his new four-hole Buick. His hair was all slicked back and he smelled like a barber shop. I liked to hitchhike, not just for the money I saved, but I loved cars, and I got to ride in a lot of new and different ones, and sometimes the drivers would even open the hood and show me their engines; I'd seen a Lincoln V12, a Kaiser inline 6, and an Oldsmobile Rocket V8. I never mentioned hitchhiking around my dad, or anything about cars, because he'd blow a gasket.

When the guy in the four hole dropped me off, I hinted about seeing his engine but he didn't catch on. I walked half a block along Fairview and when I turned up our alley I could hear kids playing in one of the yards, shouting and laughing and having a good time. I looked through a lilac hedge and couldn't believe my eyeballs. Four lousy grade-school boys had snared a cottontail and had it staked out with a string tied to one of its hind legs. The little creeps were taking turns throwing a homemade spear at the rabbit, a long willow stick with an open jackknife tied to one end, and the bunny leaped and jerked like crazy and kept crashing to the ground when it hit the end of the string.

I shot through the hedge and yelled, "You little pricks!" and I scared the crap out of them and they took off in all directions. The cottontail tugged against the string and was flopping all over the place until I kneeled and grabbed it and held it in my lap. While I worked at untying the knot I kept talking to the little bugger, trying to calm it down. Its leg was raw and bloody where the string was cinched and a couple of bleeding cuts showed that those little brats had been at it for a while. When I got the knot untied, I nestled the rabbit in my jacket and zipped it up and after the bunny flopped around a little it settled down. I noticed the lousy spear lying on the ground and I stomped my foot across the jackknife and snapped off the blade.

When I came in the back door with a cardboard box I'd found in the alley and the cottontail sticking its head out of my jacket, my mother hit the ceiling.

"A rabbit!"

My mother hit the ceiling a lot but I could tell when she was really hitting the ceiling or just pretending, which she was doing then because I knew she loved animals and her first reaction to anything unexpected was to hit the ceiling and then figure out what to do on her way down.

"You know pets aren't allowed in our building," she said and I could tell she wanted to touch the little thing but she stayed over by the stove where she was cooking dinner. My dad was the caretaker of the building so we got our apartment for less rent and we all helped with the work, even my little sister, but my parents were real careful not to break any rules so the other five families couldn't rat on us to the owner.

"Can't we keep him just until he heals up?" I said. "Some dirty little kids were torturing him."

I tried to make it sound as horrible as I could because I knew that basically my mother had a soft heart. Peggy, my twelve-year-old sister, must have heard us because she came blasting into the kitchen from her bedroom.

"Oh, a bunny, please, Mom," she said, "please, please."

My mother turned and stirred something on the stove.

"Well . . . just overnight, and then you have to let it go."

I unzipped my jacket and set the little bugger in the box and Peggy kneeled and started to pet it.

"Oh . . . he's all yucky." She held up a bloody hand.

I pulled off my jacket as my mother turned and this time she really hit the ceiling.

"Calvin! Look at your *shirt*, it's ruined, and your *jacket*, it's on your jacket too!"

"It's just blood," I said, noticing the stains for the first time. I don't know why, but I always say *it's just* at times like that: it's just paint, it's just indelible ink, it's just human gore. Criminy, I don't know why I do that; it only makes it worse. She snatched the jacket from me and held it up for a closer look.

"Just *blood! Blood* won't come out! Who's going to pay for this?"

My mother was always stewing about what something would cost, like I'd never be able to buy another jacket until I was fifty-three years old or something. She hung the jacket over the back of a chair and turned to the stove.

"Go take off your shirt before your father gets home, we'll have to soak them in cold water, and don't mention the rabbit; put the box in your closet."

Peggy picked up the box and headed for my room.

"If you'd leave well enough alone, you wouldn't be covered with blood," my mother said.

"Would you want me to let them kill it?"

I pulled off my shirt and waited for her answer, but I knew

I had her, and I knew she wouldn't answer, so while she made a lot of noise rattling pans around on the stove so she could ignore me, I bombed out of there. When my mother wanted to ignore you she could win the North American Ignoring Championship and it was a waste of time to hang around.

On the way to my room I felt pretty good; the cottontail had a safe home for the night. But when I saved the bunny from those little pricks I never would've guessed in seven million years that it would have anything to do with Gretchen Luttermann and her rotten father.

Chapter 3

We ate dinner in the dining room every night when my father got home from driving the Grand-Mississippi line and my mother would have the table all decked out with linen table-cloths and napkins and fancy silverware and we'd say a prayer before we ate and it was one of the only times we were together as a family, except when we went somewhere.

We sat in our God-assigned chairs at the dark mahogany dinner table: my dad at the head, my mom at the other end, closest to the swinging door to the kitchen, with Peggy on my dad's right and me on the left. My dad was a big man and he sat there in his gabardine uniform and one of his crummy Norwegian moods and never said a word. Whenever he was in one of his lousy moods, it was like waiting in the dentist's office when you had cavities to be drilled. I'd sit there and shovel in the food when my stomach was in a knot and the air in the apartment stopped moving.

Could he have found out I'd been rolling marbles down on Whalmen? We never knew what was bothering him and that's what made it so scary, like maybe *you* were the one he was mad at. My mother told me she'd fallen in love with him before World War I and waited for him when his unit went overseas, but she said that as sure as if he'd had a leg blown off, a part of him never came back from the bombardments.

"Pass the salt, please," my mother said to me and she started smiling and nodding and acting like she was happy. She was always doing that, acting cheerful, you know, to make it seem like this was a happy-go-lucky family or some-thing, but you could always tell when she was faking it. I don't mean we weren't ever happy or anything, because we were, we really were, lots of times, but it's just that sometimes she'd try real hard to make things happy when they weren't; sometimes it seemed my mother thought she was responsible for making everybody happy, that it was up to her to make things come out well, not just for us but for half of the civilized world. Peggy and I would try to help her out with the happiness stuff, but it was hard with my dad breathing right there next to us and I'd try to think of something to say and it was like we were ducking through a thunderstorm and trying not to get hit by lightning.

"We have a game tonight," I said.

My mother smiled at me for daring to come up with something and she nodded at me with her curler. She always wore one curler just above her forehead where her hair always stuck out in the wrong direction.

"Don't wash down your food, Calvin," she said. She always called me Calvin, and it wasn't so bad coming from her, but it sounded like I was an old man or something and all my friends called me Cal.

"Pass the potatoes, please," Peggy said.

I handed the bowl across the table and after she took some she stuck the bowl near my dad. Without ever talking about it or anything, the three of us had learned to return all serving dishes to my dad's end of the table so he could reach what he wanted without having to break his silence. Each of us was scared out of our wits that he'd break his silence on us.

"We read in school today that the streetcars used to be pulled by horses," Peggy said.

"They did?" I said, trying to ignore the tension that was sticking to me like humidity.

My mother smiled at both of us, pretending she was happy.

"Dad, did you used to drive a horse?" Peggy asked.

Jeez, she had more guts. My dad wasn't mean or anything; he never hit us or stuff like that, but when he was just sitting there without saying a word it was scary.

"Heavens, no," my mother said, saving my dad from having to answer like she always did. "How old do you think your father is?"

My dad didn't lift his head when he spoke. "Old enough to

see the last of the streetcars; only be pictures in your books before long."

Some of the strain drained out of the room because now we knew what was bothering him; it was something about the streetcars and we were off the hook.

"What are they going to do with them?" Peggy said.

"Junk them . . . the finest streetcars in the country," my dad said.

McCluskey's dog started whining. McCluskey lived across the alley and over a house on the corner and he kept this mangy dog in his backyard that looked like a beagle and a bloodhound had had a head-on collision. The guy had a high wood fence around his yard and he never took care of the scrawny dog and left it out for days at a time, even in winter, and he never gave it water or mercy or anything. Sometimes when the dog was whining you could hear McCluskey come out and beat it and it would cry and yelp and everything and it really made me mad and I wanted to go over and beat McCluskey. My dad said he was a drunken Irishman but that didn't make any difference to me, I still wanted to beat the crap out of him.

"That poor dog," my mother said.

"It's none of our business," my dad said without looking up.

"But he's hungry," Peggy said.

"You learn to stay out of other people's trouble," my dad said and he looked at Peggy. She got the message.

I was glad I had an excuse to leave the table early and I checked on the rabbit in my bedroom when I stuffed some clean socks and a towel in my gym bag. He was calm and wasn't bleeding anymore and Peggy had half buried him in lettuce and carrot tops and grass. My mother came to the doorway and talked as though she didn't want anyone else hearing her.

"You be careful tonight," she said with worry in her frown.

"Do you think you and Dad might come?"

"No . . . not tonight, you know your dad is going through a lot right now."

I zipped my gym bag shut. "Yeah, I know, but I wish he'd see me play sometime."

"Maybe next week."

Oh, Jeez, I remembered Gretchen Luttermann and seventh period.

"Oh . . . not next week."

"Why not?"

"That'll be a lousy game, we'll probably get murdered."

I didn't really believe that but I couldn't think of anything else to say. I started out of the room and my mother reached up and brushed the hair off my forehead. I hated it when she did that and I jerked my head away.

"He'll come, one of these days," she said. "You be careful now."

I pushed past her out of the room and tried to sound sarcastic; I could sound awfully sarcastic when I wanted to.

"You can't play *careful*, Mom."

When we legged it out onto the field like one big herd of red and black everyone on our side of the stadium started whooping it up and cheering and the floodlights lit up the place and gave it kind of an unreal feeling, like when you're at the State Fair at night or something, and it made you feel important.

I sat on the bench as the game started and watched the Central Minutemen and the Johnson Governors bash each other's lines. We were considered the rich kids, the spoiled brats of the city, fair game for all comers because we came from some pretty good neighborhoods, but we were kicking the daylights out of Johnson.

In the second quarter Coach Kascoe stuck me in the game on defense. When I played I left my glasses on the bench, usually with a fourth-stringer named Joe Campbell because I knew we'd have to be ahead by two hundred points before he'd ever get in. I wasn't blind or anything like that but without my glasses everything beyond five yards started to get kind of blurry and I had to squint a lot to try and figure out what was going on.

I was playing in the backfield when this Johnson kid came ripping out like he was going out for a pass so I took off after him and when I glanced back I saw this medicine ball coming through the lights that turned into a football. The kid was ahead of me and the ball hit him on the shoulderpads and bounced off and he fell trying to make the catch but the ball just hung in the air for a second and I picked it off on the run and headed down the sidelines in sweet surprise, hardly able to believe my luck.

I blasted right past Coach Kascoe and the cheering Central bench, right past Lola and the screaming fans, legging it into the bright green field ahead like I was dreaming, lugging the pigskin for good old Central, and in that one second I prayed my father was watching from the stands.

I was digging as hard as I could when I heard someone pounding behind me. I glanced back to see some Johnson kid gaining on me like he had a Rocket V8 under the hood, and my football shoes felt like catcher's mitts, but I could see the goal post and I knew I was home. Just before I crossed the goal line the kid's hand grazed my back, scaring the jock strap off me, and when I twisted away I dropped the ball.

I veered back to recover my fumble but the Johnson kid had already pounced on it at the two-yard line. Jeez! A chance to score a varsity touchdown and I fumbled the ball. I trotted to the sidelines with my eyes on the ground, but before I could hide on the bench between the forty-some other guys huddled there, Coach Kascoe called me over and slapped me on the back.

"Good work, Gant. You just threw Johnson for a seventy-yard loss." He had a big grin on his face so he wasn't mad at me or anything and I was glad about that but I thought Wait until he hears about next week.

Though I played the rest of the game on defense and we whipped the hot-shot Johnson team, 26–7, I couldn't help feeling grateful that my father hadn't come to the game after all. And on the way to the locker room I had one of those crazy thoughts that just show up in your skull out of the blue: I wondered if Gretchen Luttermann ever went to a football game.

Chapter 4

When I came out after showering and dressing there were some parents and bunches of kids still hanging around in the parking lot, yakking about the game and making plans.

"Good game, Cal!" Jerry's dad called and I gave him a wave. Steve spotted me and came gimping over all excited and smiling like he'd scored the winning touchdown or something.

"Hey, Cal, great interception! You guys killed 'em!"

"Yeah, thanks, but I should've had a touchdown."

"C'mon, I got Sandy and Jean, we're going to get something to eat."

We hustled through the parking lot where kids were piling into the few cars and I felt good about Steve asking me along, I really did, because I could never drive since we didn't have a car and it was getting more and more embarrassing when kids were standing around trying to figure out who would ride with who and I'd look at the ground and just stand there but Steve would always bail me out and include me, and Jerry would too when he'd drive, and sometimes I wished I could at least take a streetcar some night and haul everyone around the city.

I started to climb into the back seat of his '39 Chevy when I saw it was already crammed with four bodies. Darn! It wasn't that there'd be eight of us mashed in the car that bothered me, because that was pretty normal, but it was *who* would be in there. Jeez, I wanted to tell them I just remembered I had a dentist appointment or something. Snuggling up in the back seat were Jerry and Sally and Lola and Tom. Up to that point I'd always been able to duck out of doubling with Tom and Lola, but before I could come up with anything I was sitting in the front seat with Jean Daley on my lap.

We bombed across the river into Minneapolis to the Flat-

Top Drive-In where it was big stuff to have a carhop haul the food right out to the car and hang little trays on your rolled down windows. With Jean Daley on my lap it wasn't like we were on a date or anything but just out with the gang. Jean was okay and a lot of fun and she seemed more like a sister than a girlfriend with her plain freckled face and her tomboyish figure and she had a good personality so a guy didn't have to worry about what to say or romance or anything and he could be his normal self.

Everyone was in a good mood after winning the football game and I told myself I'd just ignore Lola and Tom and make the best of it.

"Johnson was supposed to win the City Championship and you guys ran 'em into the ground," Steve said, passing food into the back seat from the tray on his window.

"Yeah, but next week is what counts," Tom said. "The conference starts."

"That was a great run, Cal," Sandy said.

"Don't remind me, gad, I should've had a touchdown."

"You'll get one next week," Jean said.

"He won't get to play next week," Jerry said from the back seat.

"Why not?" Sandy said.

"I got Kirschbach's seventh period all week because of Jerry's marbles and some dumb girl."

"The marbles were great," Steve said. "We ought to bring steelies Monday."

"Anyone got more ketchup?" Jerry asked.

Jean passed the ketchup into the back seat and said, "What girl?"

"Gretchen Luttermann," Lola said.

"Oh, I know her," Sandy said. "She's really strange. She had a sister who went crazy."

"She looks like she died two years ago and is still walking around," Steve said and sprayed us with his machine-gun laugh. Everyone laughed but me. Jeez, I couldn't even enjoy eating fries and malts with my friends anymore without being reminded of that creepy girl.

When we'd eaten everything but the tray, Steve drove along the River Boulevard on the Minneapolis side and I was sure he wouldn't park with Sandy and Jean and all but he was really flying high and I knew you couldn't tell what he'd do when he was like that. It seemed he was either flying high or down in the dumps and he scared the zippers off us by driving backwards for several blocks along the curving parkway where there were hardly any street lights, like he was showing off, but I knew he didn't think of Sandy as a girlfriend or anything so I didn't know why he was doing it. I just about swallowed my tongue when he whipped in the picnic grounds above Minnehaha Falls and parked in the darkest spot in North America.

Cripes, Tom and Lola started necking like the world was coming to an end and I wanted to open the door and run from the sound of their breathing, locked lip to lip six inches behind me. Jerry and Sally were going at it, too, and Steve and Sandy and Jean were talking away and Jean must've thought she was sitting on a zombie's lap or something because I was trying to go deaf and blind. I could've had a penguin on my lap and wouldn't have known the difference and I kept asking myself how I'd let myself get caught in this torture chamber.

Right then I hated Tom for what he was doing with Lola even though he was a friend and didn't know I gave a hoot. I wanted to turn around and shout at him to knock it off. He was a nice enough kid, basically, he really was, although he was so good at everything I could see why he walked around with his ass out of joint sometimes, but then if I was that good at everything, I'd probably walk around with my ass out of joint some of the time too. He got good grades, he was good looking, he played three sports, and he had Lola Muldoon for a girlfriend, and if that wasn't enough, he was going to be a doctor and go to Yale or Harvard or someplace like that where his dad went three million years ago. No wonder Lola went for him; I'd probably go for him too, if I was a girl, but out of all of those big deal things, the only one I envied him for was his girlfriend.

With other cars parked around us, Steve and I were twiddling our thumbs and listening to the muffled sounds and heavy breathing of our friends necking like minks while Johnny Mercer sang "On the Atchison, Topeka and the Santa Fe" and Perry Como crooned "Till the End of Time" over the radio.

"How did Gretchen Luttermann get you in trouble?" Jean said while bouncing to the music on my lap.

"She sits behind me in study hall; I was talking to her."

"Cal's in love with her," Steve said and laughed.

"Real funny, jerk," I said and I was hot and sweaty and I wanted to run down the field again and have another chance at hanging onto the football.

Finally, after what seemed like a week in a dentist's chair, Lola said she had to get home and I vowed that I'd never again let myself be trapped where I'd have to listen to Lola necking with another guy. They dropped me off after Jean.

"Good game, Cal," Jerry called.

"See you in school," Steve said.

"Yeah, see you."

I trudged around to the back of the building and stood in the dark alley and took a gander at the sky. I couldn't stop ragging myself for fumbling the ball and I prayed there'd be no mention of it on the morning sports page for my father's eyes and I was mad that Steve said I was in love with Gretchen Luttermann in front of Lola, mad that my friends thought I had anything to do with that nutty girl.

I realized I was unconsciously locating the north star before I went to sleep like Uncle Emil had pounded it into me when I lived in the woods with him. I had to smile, as if the building and the city avenues would slip off kilter while I slept, yet I knew I trusted the star far more than the surveyors who laid out the streets. When I snapped out the light and curled up in my bed, I thought about the first time I hooked up with Uncle Emil.

The summer I was ten, my parents shipped me off to spend a few weeks with a guy I'd never heard of and I remember wondering what I'd done wrong. My mother said it was for my own good, a wonderful time in the woods with Uncle Emil, my father's brother, who he hadn't said boo about in my whole life. Before I knew it, I was riding a Greyhound all the way to Grand Marais, a small town on the north shore of Lake Superior, way the heck up in Minnesota almost to Canada. When I got off the bus I could see the lake, more like an ocean because you couldn't see across it, and everything smelled like creosote and fish, and seagulls were screaming and flying all over like crazy. A tall, thin, sad-looking guy dressed like a lumberjack or something came up to me.

"You Calvin?"

"Yes, sir." When I was little I said sir a lot whenever I was talking to an adult, which wasn't very often.

"We gotta git."

He turned and started legging it out of there and I hollered.

"I'm supposed to call my mom to tell her I got here okay."

What a lie, but one look at my uncle and the pit of my stomach was telling me to jump back on the bus. In the cafe that doubled as a bus depot I found a phone booth. I closed the door so my strange uncle couldn't hear me and I had no idea what I'd say. With a queasy feeling in my chest I gave the operator our number and when I heard my mother's voice I almost started bawling.

"I have a collect call from Calvin. Will you accept the charges?" the operator said.

"From *who*?" my mother said with surprise in her voice.

"Calvin," the operator repeated.

"Is everything all right?" my mother said.

"Yeah, it's *me*, Mom," I kind of shouted like she'd already forgotten I was her son. There was a long pause on the other end and I could hear my father's voice away from the phone.

"Will you accept the call, ma'am?" the lady said and I could tell she was getting a little sore with us.

"Ah, no, operator . . . we can't accept the call right now."

Jeez, it was like someone punched me in the stomach.

"It's *me*, Mom!" I yelled but she was cut off the line.

"Sorry, young man, you'll have to try another time," the operator said and I was so rattled I couldn't think of anything to say.

Why wouldn't they talk to me? It was like they disowned me or something. I hung up the phone and my eyes were all blurred and I read a telephone number scrawled on the varnished wall with the words MARY JANE WILL DO IT and I wondered what Mary Jane would do and I thought of trying the number to see if *she'd* accept my call. I peered through the smudged glass of the phone booth at the grimy guy waiting for me and I figured the happy life I'd always known had been blasted to smithereens.

In a beat-up Ford station wagon we went banging up this dirt road behind the town, straight into the woods, except you couldn't call it a road because it was nothing but rocks and ruts, and I kept bouncing off the ceiling and my teeth just about rattled out. Jeez, the lousy road went around trees rather than cut one down, and when we had to pass a car coming the other way, one of us had to pull off into the pines. The station wagon had wood sides that creaked like a stagecoach or something and the further we went into the wilderness the more I knew I'd never find my way back home. My uncle hadn't said another word. The Ford was heaped with all kinds of stuff: sleeping bags, blackened cooking utensils, an ax, fishing poles, tents, packs, canoe paddles, and all of it, including my Uncle Emil, smelled like wood smoke and looked like it came over with the Vikings.

All of a sudden we veered off the road and zig-zagged around pines, plowed through brush, until Uncle Emil stopped and got out. Beside my suitcase I was loaded with a Duluth pack on my back and an armload of groceries in a gunny sack and I had to leg it to keep up. We headed into the thick timber and it was getting dark fast and after what seemed like an hour I didn't know if I could walk any farther when Uncle Emil, carrying a ton of packs and stuff himself, stopped in front of me and cupped his hand by his ear. The woods were pitch black when my uncle said another word.

"Listen."

I stood there with sweat pouring out of me, running in my eyes, and mosquitoes diving on me like Jap zeros. I held my breath and listened and I wondered if we were about to be attacked by a bear or something, figuring I'd never make it through the night alive. At first all I heard was crickets and frogs but then from far to our right, I heard it, a scary sound coming out of the dark in a long wail. Another voice joined in, and another, until there was a whole slug of them, howling high notes out there in that spooky forest. I wanted to get down on my hands and knees and start howling myself.

"The wolves are singing," Uncle Emil said and he took off down the trail and I kept stepping on his heels until we finally came to a small log cabin on the shore of a lake. We got our stuff inside and lit a kerosene lamp and I almost died that night sleeping on a mattress on the floor because I was afraid to go outside and pee with a pack of wolves waiting to eat me.

Chapter 5

I hit study hall a few minutes early on Monday and noticed Gretchen huddled in her seat and even though I'd made up my mind to have nothing more to do with her, I couldn't help turning around as I sat down.

"Did your dad punish you?"

She stared into her lap and acted like she didn't hear me at first. I would've thought her a real dog except for something pathetic about her, like when you see a lost fawn standing in the rain or something. A dog tried to look attractive, like wearing the right clothes and fixing her hair but Gretchen Luttermann didn't even try. She glanced at me like she was surprised I noticed her and then looked down like she was talking to the floor.

"Yes . . . he hurt me."

I didn't know what to say. "You're kidding." But I knew right off that she didn't know how, that she was different from anyone I'd ever known. "What did he do?"

"I can't tell you. He'll find out I told."

"How's he going to do that, for crying out loud." I laughed. "I'd never squeal."

She glanced at me and then sat there staring at the floor.

"If I'm not on the curb when he pulls up, he whips me when we get home."

"He *does?* Gosh, what if it isn't your fault?"

"It doesn't matter." She sneaked another look at me and then stared into her lap. "I'm not supposed to talk to you."

"To *me?*"

"To any boy. He forbids it."

Miss Whalmen stood as the bell rang, and I turned in my seat. Maybe she made up stories to get kids' attention or something. Like a spy I glanced across the auditorium to Lola and she was risking seventh period by chewing gum in class and trying to look like she wasn't but I could tell.

Serving my time in Kirschbach's seventh period all week was like walking through a mine field. If it wasn't for D.B. Sandersen, Mr. Kirschbach would win first prize for the teacher who had no idea of what was going on in his class-room. A short, stocky guy with olive skin, dark puffy bags under his eyes, and black oily hair, he taught history and Latin—at least that's what the classes were called—but actually the subject was How to keep a bumbling teacher so distracted you don't have to do any work in his screwball class.

Kids were always pulling something in his seventh period and that's what worried me. He had a torture machine, a big wind-up alarm clock he'd set on his desk that'd divide the hour into bleak agonizing seconds while kids were wasting away. He'd lounge in a magical wooden chair that had rollers and swiveled and tipped back like a rocker, and he seemed to enjoy ramrodding the hour of detention over the school's cutups.

The kids would sucker him out of the room for a few minutes by having someone outside the class call him to the office on the intercom and then they'd hide the clock and set the alarm and five minutes after he was back the alarm would go off at the bottom of the waste basket or buried in one of his drawers and he'd go nuts trying to find it, or someone would loosen the spring tension on his chair and when he'd fall asleep, which he did a lot in seventh period, he'd crash over backwards like a load of coal onto the floor. Whenever he'd realize he'd been bamboozled, he'd fly into a rage and give everyone another week of seventh period and if that happened, I'd be off the football team for good, and all because I talked to Gretchen Luttermann for three seconds.

I sweat it out through seventh period all week and nobody pulled anything and I basically forgot about Gretch the Wretch except a few times when I had to avoid her in the halls. I'd never want her to know I was ducking from her or hurt her feelings or anything, so you have to be good at it and make it look natural like the second you spot her coming you go ninety degrees into the first door as if you have a class there or something. On Thursday I almost ducked into the girls' can.

Mr. Finley, a short, white-haired man, stood checking an order book at the back of the store while I carried boxes of groceries out the back door. He wore wire-rimmed glasses and his eyebrows looked like hairy caterpillars that seemed to move across his forehead when he talked. With his green celluloid visor and his bibbed apron, he reminded me of old Geppetto, he really did, the guy who made Pinocchio.

"You need to stop at Prior Liquor for two orders, Cal," Finley said as I came in from the truck.

"Okay. Anything else for the morning?"

Mr. Finley flipped the order book closed and looked over his glasses at me. "That's everything I can remember. Are you saving your money?"

"Yeah, I am, but I don't dare tell my dad I'm saving for a car. You know how he feels about cars."

"Yes, yes, the enemy of the streetcar, but you must save your money for the future. Do you realize that a nickel you save today becomes a dollar you won't have to earn later on?"

"Yeah, but I feel lousy when I can never drive on dates and things. I always have to get a ride with someone else and pile fifty kids in a car."

I folded one of the collapsible wooden boxes and stacked it with others.

"I think most of my friends think we're too poor to have a car and it's hard to explain. If I told them the truth, they'd think my dad was loony."

"How long have you been working for me now?" he asked.

A woman came through the front door, ringing the little brass bells Finley had fastened to the door frame.

I counted in my head. "Over a year, I started in July."

"Well, I've been thinking I should give you a raise . . . say five cents. That'd make fifty-five cents an hour, but you have to promise to save some of it and not just for a car."

He headed toward the front of the store and I picked up the last box and backed out the door.

"Gosh, thanks, Mr. Finley. Thanks a lot."

I enjoyed tooling around the neighborhood in the '46 Plymouth panel truck when I had extra time because it was the only time I got to drive basically. Steve taught me how in the '39 Chevy and sometimes he'd let me drive when we were goofing around on a Friday night or something and he got tired of me looking under the hood at the Stovebolt Six eighty-horse inline engine. Finley's truck had a straight 6 ninety-five horse that I almost wore out memorizing.

When I pulled up to the corner beside Finley's market, a streetcar came from the west and stopped for a man and woman. It was my father's car. He'd driven the Grand-Mississippi line for ten of the twenty-nine years he'd worked for the company. I honked and waved as the streetcar started across the intersection and my dad, seeing me in the truck, started clanging the bell like crazy and I couldn't help but notice how happy and proud he looked, like what he was doing was awfully important, and it was, it really was, because what would we do without someone to drive the streetcars and everybody would be walking or hitchhiking and crippled people would be dragging down the sidewalk and never get anywhere on time.

I had a regular delivery at 1493 Summit, the fancy boulevard where the rich people lived, but first I had to pick up the orders at the Prior Liquor Store, something Mr. Finley had worked out with Sid, the owner of the place, and for this extra service, I'd get a tip. I pulled in the alley and backed up to the brick building. When I jumped onto the loading dock and slid open the heavy metal door, Sid was standing in the storeroom with a clipboard, checking inventory. He glanced up at me with the stub of a cigarette dangling from the side of his mouth like he thought he was Humphrey Bogart or something and the smoke made him squint through his right eye. Two liquor boxes waited near the back door with yellow receipts tucked into their tops.

"These the two?" I said.

Sid was kind of an undernourished-looking guy with stooped shoulders and crossed eyes. I don't want to sound mean or anything because it's not his fault, but I could never tell for sure where the guy was looking, I really couldn't, and I could never look him in the eye for very long because I'd catch myself trying to figure out which eye was on me.

"Yeah, that's it. What happened to you guys last night; got your asses kicked."

I picked up a case of Chapin & Gore bourbon.

"Yeah, I know . . . I didn't get to play; missed practice all week."

I hauled the liquor to the truck and hustled back.

"Screwing around too much at school, huh?" Sid said and looked at me. At least I thought he looked at me but he could've been reading a calendar on the other side of the room. I picked up the second case and headed for the truck.

"No, talking in study hall," I said, and then muttered to myself, "to a freaky girl."

Though I sat on the bench all night, it irked me just as much that we lost to Harding, Jeez, a team we should've slaughtered, and we all went home with a 6–o loss stenciled on our prats.

In the next couple weeks I managed to avoid Gretchen by getting to study hall just before the bell and blasting out of there the second it was over without looking back. Sometimes, out of the corner of my eye, I noticed her watching me, just staring, like she was sizing me up for something. It was spooky; I could feel her eyeballs on the back of my neck, and even though I pretended to be studying like mad, I was squirming like a worm on a hook and I prayed she wasn't thinking I could be her boyfriend or anything like that. Once, when I got there too early, she touched my shoulder and I turned without thinking and looked at her. She opened her mouth like she was going to say something but the bell saved me and when the hour was over I bombed out the side door.

Chapter 6

On Wednesday Jerry and I were hanging around the hall outside the lunchroom in the sub-basement waiting for the bell.

"Steve is pulling the pins on D.B.'s door," Jerry said. "Some
of the boys are going to jam the stairway so D.B.'ll be late."

"Steve's on probation," I said. "If he gets in any more
trouble, they'll kick him out of school."

"I know, that screwball, acts like he wants to be kicked out."

"Cal," someone said.

I turned and there was Gretchen standing behind me,
holding her books in both arms and staring at the floor. Jeez,
she came out of nowhere, like a ghost or something, because
without really thinking about it I was keeping an eye out for
her. Jerry rolled his eyeballs and I didn't know what to do.

"Hello," I said and I was glad there weren't any kids
around I knew.

The bell rang and Jerry took off and a mob of kids blasted
out of the lunchroom like the sewer was backing up.

"I have to go," I said, and I wedged into the pack, but
Gretchen moved right behind me, shouting above the noise.

"Helga had a baby!"

"Who's Helga?" I yelled over my shoulder, trying to ditch
her, but the stairway was jammed and the jumble of kids
hardly moved.

"She's my sister."

Up ahead one level, senior boys had locked arms, six
abreast, and were taking the steps like Frankenstein.

"Did she go to Central?" I said.

We were moving about an inch a minute.

"Yes, but she's gone now!" she shouted.

As Steve planned, D.B. Sandersen came bombing his way
through the backlog in a sweat to get to his physics classroom
before any of his class.

"Where'd she go?" I said.

D.B. went out of sight around the landing, worming his way through the crowd and I tried to catch up. She stayed on my tail and caught me at the landing.

"She went away, but we still have the baby," she said.

Up ahead, D.B. broke through the log jamb.

"I gotta go; see you in study," I said.

"It's dead!" she said. "The baby's dead!"

I almost ran over two girls getting the heck away from her. Holy cow! She was nuttier than a fruitcake. I made it to the second floor just in time. D.B. rushed to his room and when he yanked the big oak door open, it sprang off its hinges and pounced on him like a gorilla, making him drop his papers and grab it by the edges. I never knew why, but all the doors in the place were big enough for King Kong, they really were.

For a second he stood there, bent backward and straining to straighten the heavy door that was trying to mangle him into the floor, battling the law of gravity he was always yakking about, and nobody offered to help and everyone was laughing like crazy. Two quick steps back, one to the right, three forward, D.B. Sandersen was dancing with the door like Charlie Chaplin, trying to keep it from killing him in front of a hundred students who were basically cracking up. Steve was laughing so hard I thought he'd bust a gut and other kids were hanging on to each other to keep from falling down. I felt sorry for D.B., I mean it *was* funny and I couldn't help but laugh, but it was kind of sad, too, and I always got mixed up on stuff like that, like how I was supposed to feel and I wanted to help him.

The dance went on, three fast steps back, two to the right, until the poor guy finally outwrestled the door and tipped it back against the wall. Without a word he bent to pick up his things and he was puffing and his face was all shiny with sweat. A couple girls helped him with his papers, and he hurried into the room.

Jerry found me and punched me on the shoulder.

"Did you see it? Gad, I though I'd die right on the spot."

"Yeah, but I was afraid he'd get hurt or something," I said.

Kids scattered like chickens and we took off down the stairs, racing to beat the second bell.

"What did Gretch the Wretch want?"

"I don't know, I think she's crazy." I punched him on the shoulder. "Cripes, why didn't you warn me she was coming."

"I never saw her until she was standing there," he said. "She must've been hanging in a locker like a vampire." Jerry laughed his big toothy laugh and we ducked into Whalmen's study hall.

Jeez, except for the unattached door leaning against the wall outside room 203, the classic moment of D.B.Sandersen's door-dancing was over. I figured that if he ever got tired of all that stuff in physics, he could always teach a dance class or something.

With Jerry honking out front, I scrambled to leave, stuffing things in my gym bag while my mother grumbled from the dining room where she was ironing my jock strap.

"I'm hoodooed," she said as she tried to flatten the snarled elastic, one curler in her hair. Believing she was hoodooed had become a philosophy of life for my mother. She had a lot of aches and pains and was sick a lot which only seemed to prove to her that she *was* hoodooed.

I bombed through the dining room. "You're not hoodooed, Mom. I don't need that ironed." I snatched the jock strap from the ironing board and stuffed it in by bag "Are you and Dad coming tonight? It's homecoming and we're playing Monroe."

Monroe was our biggest rival, we hated those guys, but I knew it wouldn't make any difference if we were playing convicts from Stillwater.

"He's working late today and I'm afraid he won't be home in time to eat and get to the game."

"If we had a car he could," I said.

I headed for the door and Jerry honked again.

"That rabbit has to go tomorrow, Calvin," my mom said as she folded up the ironing board. "It's good and mended. It keeps getting out of its box, and it left a pile of its marbles on the kitchen floor this afternoon."

"Okay, okay" I said and I hurried down the front stairs. I hoped my mother would keep forgetting about the rabbit. I'd named him Hot-Foot because he'd be sitting still one second and go blasting across the floor the next as if someone lit a match under him. I knew it was inevitable but I kept putting off letting him go. There were bloodthirsty little grade-schoolers out there and I didn't understand why anyone would want to chop up a little bunny, kill something so lovable and helpless, and it bothered me, it really did.

"I almost died when we missed the extra point," Sandy Meyer said. She was sitting on a folding chair between me and her date, Scott McFarland, along the gym wall, the only girl in the row of stags. "We were ahead the whole game."

"Yeah, a tie is so crummy . . . and with those dorks from Monroe," I said. "Why aren't you dancing?"

"I don't know . . . we did dance once but *I* had to ask *him*."

Scott was pretty bashful around girls and he sat yakking about the game with the stags like old men on a storefront porch.

"I'd dance with you if you weren't with Scott."

"I know, Bean, it's okay." She gave me a hopeless scowl.

Sandy and I had been friends all through grade school and she was the only one who called me Bean. We went to Ramsey and when we were in third grade I got my tongue stuck to the fence one morning. I was just standing there watching some older kids goofing around before the bell and I tried to lick the frost off the pipe along the top of the chain-link fence. My tongue stuck like fly paper. It was about twenty-three below that morning, and when I tried to pull my tongue off, I could tell it wasn't all going to come. It felt like it was frying and I was really scared. I thought I'd go through life without a tongue and end up a beggar with a tin cup or something.

I couldn't talk but I started yelling and I sounded like a sheep. Sandy saw me and shouted, "Don't move, don't move!"

She snatched a small thermos out of her lunch sack and sloshed hot soup over the pipe and my frying tongue and in about five seconds my tongue came loose. Jeez, was I ever happy. It was bean soup with little chunks of ham or bacon and it got all over my face and my winter jacket and it looked like I'd chucked my cookies, but I was so glad to have my tongue back I didn't care. When I rambled into school, kids ducked away from me and screwed up their faces and held their noses. I tried to clean my jacket in the lavatory with paper towels but a lot of the soup just stuck. I knew when my mother saw it she'd hit the ceiling but I felt like kissing Sandy for saving my tongue. Ever since then, usually when she was kind of blue or something, she'd call me Bean.

We gazed across the gymnasium, decked out in red and black to welcome alumni and sweethearts to the homecoming dance.

"If you ever want to get out of a class I can get you a pass," Sandy said as she glanced at her fingernails and then slipped her hands under her dress. She bit her nails all the time, sometimes down to the quick, and she was always hiding them.

"How can you do that?"

"I work in the office first period and I can get blank passes and forge the teachers' names."

"Yeah, but those passes go back to the teacher who signed them," I said. "Steve got nailed doing that."

"I know, but Mary Thompson works in the office sixth period and sorts the passes into the teachers' boxes. She'll just take out the forged pass and tear it up."

"Swell, but I'd be afraid to pull that. With my luck Mary would be absent the day I did it and if my dad ever found out he'd kill me."

"Well let me know if you ever want to," she said.

Sandy was a good friend, I mean, she told you what she really thought, even when you wished she wouldn't, and she wouldn't blab about everything you told her. She was thin and really high-strung but in a nice way, you know, excited and enthused about things, and she acted like she was always behind time and was trying to catch up. When I first got to know her I thought she'd have a big key stuck in her back like a wind-up toy because she always bounced around as if someone had just wound up her spring. She sat next to me in homeroom for three years and was my pipeline to the wacky world of girls.

"How long ago did Gretchen Luttermann's sister go here?" I asked.

"Two years."

"You ever hear anything about a baby?"

"A baby! Whose baby?" Sandy said.

"I don't know. She said some crazy stuff about a baby. I think she's loony."

"Well, it *is* nice that you talk to her, I don't think anyone else does, I'd never know what to say."

"I don't *talk* to her, Cripes, she just talked to me once."

I wished I'd never brought up the subject and I shut up. The band was playing "Dream" and there wasn't much light, you know, to make it romantic and stuff, and I watched Tom and Lola dancing on the crowded floor. They were voted Central's Homecoming King and Queen by the student body. What a lousy coincidence, gad, it was enough to make me go to Monroe or something.

"Aren't Tom and Lola perfect together," Sandy said.

"Yeah, *perfect.*"

I gave it my best sarcasm like I wanted her to know how much I was hurting but Sandy didn't seem to notice.

I tried to watch Lola on the dance floor like Sid, so no one could tell where I was looking. She had grown up over the summer in a way that made me kind of ache inside, and her suntanned smile made me forget to breathe. She had these two upper front teeth that kind of peeked out between her luscious red lips and just about drove me crazy, they really did.

"I think this is the last dance," I said as the band played "Sentimental Journey."

"I know." She sighed. "Don't remind me."

All of a sudden Scott turned to Sandy like he was facing J. Edgar Hoover and his voice sounded like he hadn't talked since he was in grade school.

"Would you like to dance?" he said.

Sandy popped up, and for the final dance, they stepped around the floor like the tin man and the scarecrow in *The Wizard of Oz.*

The sign at the end of the gym, MOP UP MONROE, had come loose on one end and hung limply like our disappointment. Our high hopes for a championship season had gone out with the floodlights on the field. We tied Monroe 13 to 13; the King and Queen danced cheek to cheek as the band played the last song, and I slipped out the side door and hoofed it for home.

Chapter 7

I don't know why but we always sat seven rows back on the right side of Immanuel Lutheran Church unless someone beat us to the punch, but we usually got there early enough to stake out our pew like it wouldn't count if we sat anywhere else. We rode the streetcar four blocks to Snelling, and most Sundays we could've walked it by the time we waited, but riding the Grand-Mississippi was as much a part of our Sunday tradition as the sacraments.

On the streetcar, my dad always rode shotgun and talked with the motorman on the short ride and most of the time it was Andy Johnson, a thin nervous guy who'd lost twin boys in the war—one in Italy, one in the Philippines—and he'd volunteer for every extra hour on the board. My dad said you could always count on Andy to take your run, as though Johnson figured if he drove a big yellow streetcar far enough, his brain would go numb and he'd forget what happened to his boys. I really felt sorry for the guy and I always gave him a big cheery hello.

Pastor Ostrum was a tall rangy guy who impressed me most with the fact that he played basketball in college but he looked as out of place in the pulpit as a giraffe in a phone booth. I'd usually kind of daydream during the sermon but that morning he preached on the meaning of love and I perked up and took notice when he used that magic word. While the six-foot-six minister flipped through his notes like a deck of cards and said things like Love wasn't having a warm feeling but it was a *decision* you make, and Love is not something we wait to have happen to us, but something we *do,* I remembered the first time I saw Lola.

She came strolling past me in the hall, talking with two other girls, and when she laughed, I stopped in my tracks and forgot to breathe. I'd never seen anyone so delicious and as I watched her walk away, I hurt inside because that gorgeously-shaped girl didn't know I was on the planet. Jeez, it was like I'd been run over by a truck or something. It had just happened, I didn't make any decision, I didn't even know her name. Was that love? Or insanity? And what was that ache I lugged around in my chest that only she could stop? If I didn't love Lola, what strange disease made my heart pound whenever I saw her or heard her voice or someone mentioned her name?

When church was over, we'd walk the two blocks home after riding the streetcar and my father always went ahead with my mother while Peggy and I trailed behind, usually ragging each other or something.

"Dad, when did you first know you loved Mom?" I said.

Without turning around and without missing a step, my dad answered, "When she had her knee on my throat."

"Oh, Horace," my mother said and pretended to swat him. So much for romance.

We huddled around the cooler in the drugstore on Dunlap and Selby after football practice, comparing bloody shins and jammed fingers and seeing who could swill the most O-So Grape.

"If we don't beat Mechanic Arts, Kascoe will make us run tackling drills all next week," Jerry said.

"Yeah, and all afternoon I kept getting Fred," I said. "I tried to switch places in line, but every time I looked up, there was madman Walker, ready to break both my legs. Darn it, he tries to kill you every time."

"If I don't get my grades up in English, my dad will break both my legs," Jerry said. "I flunked the last M.R."

Jeez, every Friday we had an English test called Minimum Requirements, and it had all this stuff with spelling and punctuation and grammar, a short test we had shoved at us the minute we showed our face in English and it always took some of the fun out of Fridays because you had to get past the M.R. before you could start thinking about the weekend. M.R.s about drove me nuts, they really did. There were questions like He said lie/lay down to his dog. Everyone knows since the beginning of time that you tell your dog to lay down, but do you think that's the right answer? No, you're supposed to say Lie down according to the M.R.s. Huh! There isn't a dog in the universe that'd know what you meant if you told him to *lie* down. There were all kinds of questions like that and you could never figure them out with logic, and anything below seventy-five was failing. The boys thought it was unfair in English to be graded with the girls because girls were born knowing all that stuff.

Someone shouted that the streetcar was coming, and the place emptied as if a skunk had trotted in the back door. I'd walk over to Summit and hitchhike, saving a dollar a week and hoping I'd get to ride in a Hudson or Packard or something. When the gang boarded the streetcar and it rolled away, I had a clear view up Dunlap where a girl came strolling from school. I'd recognize Lola if she were walking on the moon. I chug-a-lugged my O-So Grape and scrambled across Selby, acting like I hadn't seen her coming.

"Hi, Cal, where's Tom?" she said as she got to the corner. Jeez, she was wearing a gray pleaded skirt and a pink cardigan sweater, and just to see her was like getting hit by madman Walker in tackling drills but in a pleasant way if you know what I mean.

"Hi, they must have caught a streetcar, I'm slow today."

"I've been at a *Cehisean* meeting." She snapped her gum and smiled.

The *Cehisean* was our year book and it was one of those words made with the first letters of other words and I forgot what you called it but I was betting it would show up on an M.R. before long. My throat went dry standing there alone with her, and I nonchalantly fished in my pocket to see if I had eleven cents left after four O-So Grapes and a Nut

Goodie at five cents a crack. I'd take the streetcar home and have Lola to myself for that short breathtaking ride.

"Are you going to the dance?" she said as we peered down Selby for any sign of a streetcar.

She held her books with both arms, snuggling them against her pink sweater, and I felt kind of hot and sweaty and my arms were about to reach out and hug her without even checking with me first.

"Yeah, I better. With Skull and Keys putting it on, Steve would pound me if I didn't."

"Who are you taking?"

"I'm going stag."

A streetcar appeared down the street.

"Cal, there are so many girls who would love to go with you."

It was like she touched me with her eyes and I felt brave.

"Not the right one, though."

"You mean you have a secret heartthrob?" she said.

The streetcar glided up the hill and we found one unoccupied strap to hang onto in the jammed car. She leaned against me as we swayed and bumped together and I could smell her hair.

"Now tell me, who is she?"

She was so close I could kiss her and I felt blood rush to my face and I turned and looked out the window.

"*You* ought to know," I said and my Adam's apple felt like a popcorn ball.

"I don't, Cal, tell me. Does Tom know?"

The streetcar dropped off people at every intersection and little by little the aisle cleared and I lost my excuse to stand leaning against her.

"They took pictures of the cheerleaders Monday," she said. "My dad said he'd watch me cheer sometime, but he never has."

"Aw, that's nothing, we won the city championship last year in JVs and my dad's never seen me play football."

"Why not?"

"He works a lot . . . but he's coming one of these days."

"My dad lives in Baltimore. That's a long way to come, and his work is awfully important."

Sharing confidences in the crowd of the homeward bound, I felt so good I wanted to do cartwheels. Like sweethearts we got off the streetcar together, and the afterglow looked like God had a huge bonfire going somewhere out in South Dakota. I planned to ride as far as St. Clair, which wouldn't be far enough out of the way to make her suspicious, and though it'd be an extra half-mile walk after my body had been a tackling dummy for madman Fred Walker all afternoon, it would be worth ten more minutes with Lola.

Gad, what lousy luck. When we crossed Snelling with a small bunch of people and joined a crowd waiting for the southbound Snelling car, there was the football gang. Lola lit up at the sight of Tom and hurried towards him. I wanted to throw up.

"Hi. I'm glad we caught you," she said, bumping up against him. I hung back and attempted to ignore them.

"Hi. Where have you been?" Tom said, nudging her back.

"*Cehisean* meeting." Lola snapped her gum.

"I thought you were going to hitchhike?" Jerry said and punched me on the shoulder.

"I was . . . but I was too tired," I said, starting to feel lousy and ragging myself for making a big deal out of something that meant nothing to her. Jeez, she could have been riding with the county dogcatcher for all she cared.

"Oh . . . Cal has a secret girlfriend," she said loud enough for everyone in St. Paul to hear, "but he won't tell who."

A streetcar's lights appeared under the railroad bridge at Marshall and moved toward us.

"It's about time," Tom said, "he never has a date."

The waiting transfers began moving up into the car.

"I know who she is," Jerry said. "Gretch the Wretch."

The kids laughed and I took off down the sidewalk. Already up in the streetcar doors, Jerry called after me.

"Cal, aren't you coming? Cal, c'mon!"

I refused to look back until I heard the streetcar cross the intersection. Then I stopped and turned.

The magic of the colored sky faded into darkness, and as I watched the cozy-looking streetcar carry Lola away, the lump shoved its way back into my chest. I pushed my aching legs toward home and wished I could shake Gretchen Luttermann out of my life. She was like a burr in my sock and it irked me the way everyone in the United States knew I talked to her. It was about time I shook Lola out of my life, too, but I didn't want to think about that.

Chapter 8

On my lunch break I parked Finley's truck and sauntered over to a touch football game on the Groveland playground where my buddies were playing four-on-four. The leaves were sloshing colors all over the place, like God was a little kid showing off a new box of Crayons that had eleven thousand shades. I legged it to the grassy bank beside the field and sprawled on my back in the fallen leaves and I felt sleepy and peaceful, stretching out there in the sun, hearing my friends yelling and laughing and roughhousing. I caught a whiff of burning leaves—I loved that smell—and I put my hands under my head and looked off to the north. I don't know why, but I started thinking about the last time I saw Uncle Emil.

The winter Uncle Emil died I was fourteen and I'd spent four summers on the Shore with him. When my mother told me I went in my room and shut the door and cried into my pillow and I think I was the only one in my family who cried unless they went in their rooms and cried into their pillows. My family wasn't real hot on crying. We'd always pretend that we weren't crying when we were and duck out of a room because somehow we'd been taught that crying was something to avoid like ptomaine poisoning so we never got any practice, except for Peggy. She could cry in front of everyone and get away with it. I could remember when I was a little kid and my dad saying Stop that crying or I'll give you something to cry about. Jeez, did he think I was crying for the fun of it? I hate crying!

Uncle Emil left only two requests. He wanted to be cremated and his ashes scattered in the woods, which my parents thought was loony, and he left his land and log cabin to me. Holy Moses, I couldn't believe it; I'd have the cabin in the northern wilderness to go to whenever I could and maybe when I got old enough I'd just live there all the time where I'd never run into Lola. But my father and Uncle Rudy, the brother in Minneapolis my dad *did* talk to, went up north to take care of the arrangements and they found that my uncle owed people money and the cabin and land had to be sold. Uncle Emil died without a penny, and everybody thought that was a catastrophe or something, but I knew he had things that were a whole lot better than money, like animal friends in the woods who listened for his step and recognized his scent, and I thought they'd all look for him and miss him, but not as much as I.

When I said good-bye to Uncle Emil at the end of the summer of 1945, I had this funny feeling that I'd never see him again. Golly, we stood beside the Greyhound like two people who never learned how to say good-bye and with time running out I lunged over and hugged him, pressing my face against his iron chest, and I smelled whiskey and wood smoke and something like loneliness. Uncle Emil awkwardly patted my back as if he didn't know what else to do and I figured it was the only way he knew how to show he liked me.

"Good-bye," I said, wishing I was brave enough to tell him I loved him.

"Good-bye, boy."

I climbed on the bus and found a window where I could see him standing in front of the cafe. When the bus pulled away I flew out of the seat, choking down panic, and I bombed down the aisle and knelt between an old man and an Indian woman on the back seat. With my forehead pressed against the glass, I held my uncle in my eyes until the silver Greyhound barreled over a hill. The window was smeared with tears and I never saw Uncle Emil again. They cremated him and spread his ashes in the woods, but sometimes in my mind it's like he's still standing in front of the cafe, waiting for the lousy bus to bring me back.

After a touchdown, the boys straggled over and flopped on the ground around me.

"Hey, guess who's working at the bakery?" Jerry asked with a sappy grin on his face. Criminy, without thinking I nearly slipped and said Lola.

"I don't know, who?"

"Your girlfriend, Gretch the Wretch," Jerry said and he wiped sweat from his face with his shirt sleeve.

"Funny, Jer, real funny."

I tried to punch him on the shoulder but he rolled away and it ticked me off that Jerry would rat on me for talking to Gretchen, like you couldn't even trust your best friend about stuff like that. Scott propped himself up on one elbow.

"Do you know her?" he asked me.

"Naw, I just sit next to her in study."

"That's a screwy family," Scott said. "My brother was in her sister's class when she cracked up."

"Helga?" I asked.

"Yeah, I think that was her name, Helga Luttermann."

"Cracked up?" Jerry said, rolling back where he could hear.

"Yeah, cracked up right in the middle of the class," Scott said. "The teacher asked Helga to write something on the blackboard, and she went up in front and started to write. Then she just ran the chalk all over the board, like she'd flipped her trolley. The class started laughing before Mrs. Olson noticed. She scolded Helga, and then everyone shut up when Helga just kept scribbling all over the board like a little kid."

"What did they do?" Steve asked.

"Mrs. Olson told the kids to stay in their seats and took off down the hall and when the principal shows up, Helga was sitting in the teacher's chair, rocking slowly, staring at her hands like a zombie."

"What happened to her?" I asked.

"My brother said no one ever saw her again, never came back to school. He heard she went to the loony bin at Fergus Falls."

Jerry grabbed the ball and headed for the field.

"Let's play," he said, glancing back at me. "You better be careful, Cal. That's a weird girlfriend you got there."

"She's not my girlfriend, dumbass!" I yelled.

I stomped to the truck and drove away, steamin' that everyone thought Gretchen and I were buddies or something. Jeez!

After driving around for a few minutes, I circled back and parked a block from the Dutch Bakery. I don't know why, but I did, and I smuggled myself into the little shop that smelled so good my mouth started to water. I bought a glazed doughnut from a large, sweaty woman whose ham-hock arms bulged from her white dress and I couldn't help thinking that we could use her in the line. I nibbled at the doughnut and tried to make it last, loitering until Gretchen finally showed up with a tray of chocolate-chip cookies and slid it into a glass case. She had on this drippy white cap and a big apron over her crummy dress and when she spotted me she stopped in her tracks. She glanced over her shoulder like someone was spying on her but we were alone in the front of the bakery.

"Hi, Gretchen, I didn't know you worked here."

She was planted behind the high glass case like she was trying to make up her mind about something, but I could see that basically she was scared.

"They'll tell my father if I talk to you. I gotta go."

She spun around and darted into the back like a chipmunk while I stood there with half a doughnut in my hand and half a notion to have my head examined. I scrambled out the door, keeping one eye peeled for any of my friends on the way to the truck, because if they spotted me I was a dead duck.

I finished my deliveries and tried to remember what Gretchen said about Helga and the baby, thinking that maybe she hadn't made it up after all. I delivered a box of groceries on Laurel and the thought crossed my mind that Gretchen might be crazy already, making up wild stories like some fruitcake. Did that kind of thing run in a family? Would she crack up one day behind me in study hall or something? Jeez, she was scary and something warned me to stay as far away from her as possible.

In the sub-basement lunch room, I had to swallow the bad news with my baloney sandwich and it didn't go down easy. Cripes, Tom and Lola were going steady. They'd exchanged Hi-Y and sorority pins and wore them like they were already married. When I climbed the stairs from the lunch room with Jerry and Steve, I felt like my lunch had turned to concrete in my stomach, and just when I'd forgotten all about watching out for her, Gretchen showed up like a magazine salesman.

"Hello, Cal," she said.

I glanced sideways at my buddies and stopped.

"Hi," I said and Steve and Jerry drifted away like they owed her money.

"Are you coming to the bakery Saturday?" she asked.

"Oh . . . I don't think so, I just happened to stop for a doughnut."

I kept moving ahead a few steps so she wouldn't get the idea we were going to have this long conversation or anything.

"I eat lunch in back at eleven-thirty," she said with a quick peek into my eyes.

"Oh . . . that's nice."

I edged along but she stuck to me like a wood tick.

"My father keeps me locked up, but I could talk to you on Saturday," she said, and it sounded like it was the last chance I'd ever have to talk to her before the world came to an end.

"I don't think—"

"I don't want to go crazy."

Golly, it was like her hollow eyes were looking out at me from a concentration camp or something.

"Well . . . I'll see, maybe I could come by around eleven thirty."

"I'll be by the back door in the alley," she said hopefully.

"I gotta run. Maybe I'll see you Saturday," I said and I bombed away so she wouldn't tag along to study hall.

It was hard to believe, but for us seniors, it was our last football game at Central. We knew we hadn't done her very proud and we darn well wanted to make up for that a little and everybody was shouting like madmen in the locker room and the coach turned us loose like rabid dogs.

I didn't say anything about the game at dinner that night, like I'd be begging my dad to come, I mean a lot of kids never have their dads see them play, lots of kids don't even have dads or their dads are sick or something. Right in the middle of dinner Peggy piped up and said, "Isn't this your last game, Cal?" and she looked right at my father. I could have kissed her. "Yeah," I said.

It was like she'd learned from my mother how to speak up for someone who didn't speak up for themselves. It didn't work though because my dad started beefing about how the Communists had conquered all of China and Russia had the atom bomb and my football game didn't seem important anymore. My mother tried to make the scary news sound like it wasn't so bad and we could all still be happy.

Wilson would win the City Championship if they beat us but we played like the Minnesota Gophers, scoring the first three times we had the ball, and we ran Wilson right out of the stadium. Boy, I don't know what got into me; I was a maniac out there for a while, like I was mad and happy all at the same time, looking for someone to hit, and it was like sadness drifted down on me from the floodlights and I wished the football season was just starting and I saw how good we could have been and I wished I could have scored a varsity touchdown and I wished my father would have seen me play just once and I knew now that he never would.

It was a good way to wind up our disappointing season and the locker room was a mad house with everyone shouting and laughing and snapping towels and acting like they were trying to forget that they'd never play for Central again. Some kids didn't seem to care, but I was always thinking about dumb stuff like that and I wished I wasn't because it made me sad sometimes when I should be happy and enjoying life.

"You coming with us?" Jerry said. "Tom's got the car."

"Naw, I think I'll look for Steve," I said.

Darn it, I'd never get caught in that meat grinder again, watching Tom and Lola necking. I dressed fast and slipped out of the locker room and started across the parking lot where kids were milling around and I just about bumped into Scott's parents.

"Hello, Cal, you played well," Scott's mother said.

"Thanks," I said and I hustled into the shadows.

When I opened the back door of the apartment building, I hesitated. You could hear McCluskey's dog quietly whining, not loud enough to bring a beating, but like he couldn't quite muffle his awful loneliness.

Chapter 9

I drove in the alley behind the building where the Dutch
Bakery was squeezed between the corner drugstore and the
St. Clair Sweet Shop. Gretchen was perched on the wooden
cover of a garbage-can rack, eating lunch from a paper bag,
wearing that long white apron, that drippy white cap, and
those ugly brown clodhoppers hanging from her skinny legs.
I backed Finley's truck near the rear door of the bakery so it
would look like I was making a delivery or something and I
walked over to her.

"Hi," I said and I smiled. I hadn't really thought about it
but I don't think I'd ever smiled at her before.

"You better sit in the truck," she said without looking
at me.

I opened the back door and shoved several grocery boxes
out of the way. By squatting with my back against the inside
wall and facing her, we could visit with no one the wiser, but
I wondered what kind of fiend we were hiding from and
almost chuckled over this dopey girl's imagination.

"Working hard?" I asked.

"No. I don't mind."

"How much you make an hour?"

"I don't know. Mr. Buehler gives it to my father."

She swung one foot back and forth and I got the feeling I
was talking to a little kid.

"I'm getting fifty-five cents an hour, and I get some tips."

She kept nibbling a peanut-butter sandwich.

"Why won't your dad let you talk to me?"

"He says boys are bad. They do bad things to girls. The
Bible says it's bad. I can't go anywhere without him, except
school and here."

She seemed hypnotized by the motion of her heavy shoe
swinging back and forth, and I caught myself watching it.

"You can't even *talk* to boys?"

"No."

"Jeez, that's terrible. What does he think we'll do to you?"

Right off I wished I hadn't asked and I was embarrassed, but she ignored my question.

"I have to wear ugly clothes. He says if I fix my hair or wear make-up I'm helping the Devil. I look so awful I hate to go to school."

"You don't look so bad."

"Yes I do. I look ugly. I am ugly."

"No you're not, really, it's just the dress, and those shoes. That's not your fault, Criminy, *I'd* look ugly in *those* clothes."

Gad, I kept putting my foot in my mouth, but she seemed to take it like a joke—me wearing her dress and stuff—and she glanced up with a little smile at the corner of her mouth.

"Where does your dad work?" I said.

"Downtown at the post office. Sometimes he works on Saturday, sometimes not."

"Does he really hurt you?" I asked.

She looked away. "You promise never to tell?"

"Yeah . . . sure, I promise."

"He uses a belt on me when I'm bare." She kept swinging her foot. "It hurts bad."

"What about your mother? Doesn't she do anything?"

"When Helga went away my father started coming into my room at night, to *instruct* me. I told my mother once, that he was hurting me. She said she didn't want to hear about it, that my father was a godly man and whatever he was doing was for my own good." She paused. "It wasn't good for Helga."

"What happened to Helga?"

"She went away."

Gretchen folded her brown bag like she planned to reuse it.

"What did he do to her?"

"I can't tell you. He'll find out I told."

"Did she really have a baby?"

"I better go now. Would you like a doughnut. I can have one free."

"No thanks. Does the baker know your dad?"

"He goes to our church. We spend most all of Sunday at church. Do you go to church?" she asked, glancing up for a moment.

"Yeah, we go. Every Sunday."

"We go to the Holy Gospel Church," she said. "I hate it." She slid off the wooden cover.

"Do you go to dances?" she asked while looking at the ground.

"Yeah, most of them."

"I hear kids talking about them."

"Have you ever been to one?" I asked.

"No . . . what are they like?"

"Oh, they're not so hot. Some kids dance and guys sit around and try to get up their nerve to ask a girl to dance and some sit there all night and never dance."

She didn't say anything and I wondered why I made the dances sound so lousy but I think it was because I didn't want her feeling real bad for missing out.

"Will you come back next Saturday?" she asked.

"I'll try."

"Good-bye, Cal," she said and she slunk into the bakery like she didn't belong in the human race.

"Yeah, I'll see you at school," I said to myself.

I climbed in the cab but before I pushed the starter, I just sat there. Jeez, what was it her father did to her when he *instructed* her. I didn't want to know and I really wanted to do something for her. Maybe I could buy her a decent pair of shoes she could wear at school. Or maybe I could listen to my dad who always told me to leave well enough alone and stay out of trouble. I started the truck. Maybe her parents were doing the best they could with their crazy daughter and they *had* to watch her closely.

I pulled out onto St. Clair, off to earn my four dollars or

more in wages and tips and then hurry home to get ready for the powwow. Rather than miss the fun, I'd gotten a date with Jean Daley and all afternoon I couldn't help but wonder if Gretchen had ever been to a powwow or a movie or ever let out of the backyard?

Jerry picked me up and we swung up Summit to get Scott.

"Remember how scared we'd get when we'd knock on that guy's door?" Jerry nodded across the parkway at the huge brick and stucco house. "He'd come flying out after us like he was shot out of a cannon! Man, he could run." Jerry laughed.

"Yeah," I said, "he must have waited behind that door in starting blocks. We'd run for our lives with him right on our tails."

"Through yards, over fences," Jerry said.

"Down alleys—"

"Knocking over garbage cans—"

"Or getting clotheslined," I said, "scared out of our wits. Then we'd meet over at the Ramsey playground and bust a gut laughing and tell each other everything that happened a million times."

We pulled up in front of Scott's house and Jerry honked.

"Do you think he still chases kids?" he said.

"I don't know, if he hasn't died. Maybe the younger kids keep him in shape."

Jerry flashed me that big toothy grin. "Let's do it tonight."

"You mean *right now?*"

"Yeah, only let's get Steve and the girls first and not tell them about the Runner."

"But he might catch Steve," I said, knowing that Steve couldn't run real fast with his shriveled leg.

"Steve can move plenty fast if he's scared enough," Jerry said as Scott opened the door and slid in the back.

"Hi, Jer, Cal."

"Remember the Runner, the guy who used to chase us

when we'd knock on his door?" Jerry said as he pulled away from the curb.

After we rounded everybody up, Steve and the girls couldn't figure out why the three of us were in such a screwy mood, and Jerry and Scott and I had all we could do to keep from giving it away. Scott told them we were stopping to see his grandparents for a minute on the way and no one said a word when Jerry parked on the far side of the boulevard from the house. Summit Avenue had a parkway about a hundred feet wide that divided the lanes of traffic and it was lined with huge elm trees. In jeans and jackets, the bunch of us romped over the boulevard and crossed the eastbound lane and scrambled up the steps of the banked yard like we'd been invited. Ever since the first time I banged on the door of that gloomy-looking house, it gave me goose bumps just getting near it.

"How old is your grandfather?" Jean asked.

"He's over eighty," Scott said. "He can't walk very well."

Jerry choked off a laugh by faking a cough as we moved onto the big open porch and just knowing what was coming from behind that door had me working my way to the back of the bunch. Only a shadowy light slunk through the drapes in the wide front window.

"Knock," Scott told the girls. "Loud, he's hard of hearing."

Sandy was bouncing around as usual and she knocked on the large wood door without knowing she was committing suicide. Immediately the game of chicken went into play or who-could-stay-on-the-porch-the-longest.

Scott couldn't stand the suspense and he stepped through the sheep and banged on the door like he meant to knock it off its hinges. The girls stood sweetly, expecting grandfather to appear, while Jerry and I, hanging on to each other with one hand, were coming right off the floor.

All of a sudden the door blasted open.

"Run!" Jerry shouted. He leaped the steps and landed running.

"He's a madman! Run!" I yelled from the edge of the porch. Scott went past me like he'd stepped on a hornets' nest and the girls' feet were going up and down like they were tap dancing until they got it in gear and went flying off the porch like a Chinese fire drill, banging off each other down the steps and across the lawn. The Runner came out the door and hesitated for a split second, like the shrieking girls confused him, and then, with a wicked smirk on his kisser, he blasted after me.

Jeez, I bombed down the bank and across the eastbound lane onto the parkway with him on my shirttail. Boy, could he run! I ripped around a big tree and headed for the other side where I could ditch him in a yard. I heard him breathing hard and legging it right behind me, and then, all of a sudden I couldn't hear him anymore. I sprinted for another ten yards and then dared to look back. The Runner had veered off and was after Sandy, gaining on her as she ran across the parkway towards the intersection at Wheeler, squawking like a strangling chicken.

"Run, Sandy, Run!" I shouted and I don't know why but I felt close to her right then. She was really pumpin', and as they passed under the streetlight, it looked like he'd catch her. Most of the other kids were hiding behind the elms on the parkway and I could hear them laughing so hard they were coughing and gagging. When Sandy and the lunatic disappeared up Wheeler in the darkness, I held my breath and stared into the shadows, knowing that sometimes he'd double back and come flying out of nowhere.

After a long, scary wait where I thought I saw the Runner in every shadow, Jerry sneaked back to the car, started it, and turned on the lights. I blasted across the parkway and jumped in and Jerry rolled the Oldsmobile along the street. Out of the dark, Scott jumped aboard half a block down.

"Holy balls, we did it," Jerry shouted.

"Did he catch Sandy?" I said.

"I don't know," Jerry said

"Did you see her *run?*" Scott said. "I almost fell down I was laughing so hard."

We cruised around the neighborhood calling out the car windows, scared that the guy would come zinging out of the dark and nail us. One by one we found Steve and the other girls, and finally, Sandy, and Jerry headed out Rice Street for Sucker Lake. Sandy wouldn't talk to Scott or any of us for scaring the daylights out of her.

"How did you get away?" I asked her.

Boy, she was really peeved, but then she couldn't stand not telling us what happened so she tried to sound real miffed.

"We ran into a big dog in the dark," Sandy said, "and the dog started chasing *him.*"

Then she started cracking up and everybody just about split a gut laughing and Jerry almost drove over the curb. We congratulated Sandy on her run, and roared when we thought of the poor guy, a mile from home, still running for his life with a mad dog at the seat of his pants. Before we reached Sucker Lake, both Sandy and Steve were talking about doing it again.

Chapter 10

On Thursday, when I slid into my study hall seat a minute early, Gretchen leaned forward and whispered from behind me.

"Will you be at the bakery Saturday?"

I kept my face straight ahead while I looked at her out of the corner of my eye, like I was imitating Sid.

"Maybe . . . if I can work it in."

The bell rang and I opened my trig book and when I'd forgotten all about her she touched me on the back of my arm. A small folded note slid under my left armpit. I glanced toward Miss Whalmen, who was sitting at her table with her beady eyes trained on some poor kid on the other side of the auditorium, and I slid the note into my book and unfolded it, dreading what it would say.

You are a nice boy Cal

Cripes, that was it. It was embarrassing and I wondered if she expected me to write something back? I crumpled the note and shoved it into the pouch pocket on my GI pants and I couldn't concentrate on anything for the rest of the period and I reworked the same trig problem about six million times. When the bell rang, I blasted for the side door without looking back.

We'd started basketball practice on Monday and by Thursday Coach Mulligan had run our buns off. When I played basketball I could keep my glasses on, taped to my head, and even though we'd shot buckets all summer, I'd never figured how much I'd get to play this year after making the A squad last year and spending most of the time on the bench. But after a week's practice, it looked like I'd be one of the first five, holy smoke, I could hardly believe it, and it made me feel good about myself and pretty excited. It looked like Jerry and Scott would make it, too, which would make for a terrific season with us ripping around out on the floor together and Lola cheering her head off at every game. Tom played hockey and the cheerleaders didn't perform at hockey games.

After practice, seven of us crammed into Jerry's Oldsmobile and rolled down the windows and even though it was already November it was still so warm it was like winter had been canceled. We'd worked hard and my legs felt like tree trunks. The radio blared "On Top of Old Smokey" as we bombed down Marshall and we sang along like we'd just been pardoned from the penitentiary or something.

> *. . . I lost my true lover*
> *by courting so slow.*
>
> *Well, courting's a pleasure*
> *And parting is grief,*
> *But a false-hearted lover*
> *Is worse than a thief.*

The sun dropped somewhere behind Minneapolis and it sprayed the sky with all these incredible colors like it didn't want us to forget it right away. I don't know how to explain it, swinging down Marshall in the afterglow, singing with my friends, but for just a minute or so it was like someone opened a door to all the happiness in the world, like a big crack in the sky, and happiness was pouring down on all of us, and right then it was like everything would turn out okay, Lola and me, my dad with the streetcars, the atom bomb and the Communists, everything. It only lasted a minute and down under the railroad bridge the song ended, the sunlight faded, and in a second it was gone.

"My dad wants to move to Israel this summer," Jerry said.

"Move!" I said. "You mean to live?"

"Yeah, he says we finally have a country of our own. I'm not going. I have a country of my own right here."

I remembered when I found out Jerry was Jewish. I'd

known him about a year and one day I asked him what church he went to. He said his family went to a synagogue and it didn't sound like they went that often and I didn't think much about it because it didn't make any difference to me if he was Jewish or Eskimo. We liked each other right off.

"I'm going to join the Navy," Jerry said. "That way I can stay here. You want to join with me, Cal?"

"I don't know . . . yeah, sure, when we graduate."

"I have to go to VMI next year," Scott said.

"What's that?" Jerry said.

"Virginia Military Institute. My dad went there and now I have to go."

"Jeez, that sounds as bad as moving to Israel," I said.

When I slid out of the car in front of the apartment, Jerry looked over at me.

"Did you know Tom and Lola broke up?"

"No." I tried not to start cheering or anything and I pretended it was kind of ho-hum news. "Who broke up with who?"

"I guess it was Tom. His dad doesn't want him getting serious, with college and med school and everything."

"Yeah, well thanks for the ride."

I hurried for supper and all of a sudden my legs weren't tired anymore and I took the back stairs two at a time and I was humming "On Top of Old Smokey."

At supper the fact that President Truman was speaking at the St. Paul Auditorium that night came up in the conversation.

"I wouldn't walk across the street to see Truman," my dad said. "Gave half of Europe to Stalin and the Communists and did it with a smile on his face."

"Horace, the children," my mom said.

I hated it when she called me *the children*.

Once my mother told me not to be too hard on my dad, that he'd come back from the war half the man he'd been after he'd fought with one of the first American units to see action. "He was a tender man when he went off to war," my mother said, "a romantic man." She kind of gazed off into space when she told me and she was quiet for a minute. "Sometimes, after he came back, he was lost, just plain lost, and then he got a job in the shops. It was as if he gave his soul to the streetcars and the streetcar saved him."

"They're going to scrap the whole thing. The day of the streetcar in St. Paul is over," my dad said over his food.

"You can drive a bus. What's so bad about that?" I said, trying to make things seem better.

"A *bus!* I wouldn't drive one of those filthy machines for love nor money, I'm a streetcar motorman, not a stinking bus driver. Twenty-six years I've driven a streetcar, and now some shysters are going to junk them. Wait and see, things will never be the same without the streetcar."

I didn't understand why my father was so upset and angry. Jeez, all the Company was doing was raising the eleven-cent fare to twelve, and switching to buses did seem like progress. Of course there wouldn't be any trolleys to pull, but I'd out-grown that kind of prank anyway, and besides, my dad was probably exaggerating like he always did when he was mad. I don't know why but that's one thing my family was good at, exaggerating, and I was doing it all the time without even thinking about it and I don't remember when I started but I'd do it about seven thousand times a day.

My dad kept a log of his daily streetcar runs like the captain of a ship and he knew schedules for every line in the Twin Cities and recognized each car like a personal friend. When he first got hired with the Company he worked in the shops, and after he started loving the streetcars, he refused to own a car.

"Calvin," my dad would say, "our streetcars are custom-built right here in St. Paul and finished as nice as your living room. They're mounted on massive double trucks with powerful motors and air brakes, and they run smooth and safe on heavy-duty track. I tell you, Calvin, there are no better streetcars in the world than the big yellow cars of the Twin City Rapid Transit Company. You remember that when you're riding one."

Jeez, I don't know why, but he must have told me that two million times until I could repeat it word for word like the Lord's Prayer. Sometimes I thought my dad was married to the streetcars more than he was to my mom, like they gave him a reason to live or something. After the war everybody wanted to have a car and they quit using the streetcars as much, but my dad wasn't a man to give up on what he believed in and he figured the car was his enemy.

My sister and I did the dishes and cleaned up the kitchen without goofing around too much because we knew that if we did, one of us would be stuck with the whole mess. My mother came into the kitchen when my dad had settled in the living room.

"That rabbit goes out in the morning, Calvin. Not one more day, or I'll let it go myself," she said quietly. "Mrs. Overby stopped by this afternoon and it was dashing all over the place. I was sure she would see it and report us. Your father would be awfully upset if Mr. Shaw heard that we had pets. We could lose our job and our apartment. Not one more day."

She snapped a finger in my direction and slipped back into the front of the apartment and I knew the rabbit was at the end of his visit because when my mother snaps her fingers she's at the end of her rope and she can blow a gasket just like my dad only she does it by making you feel real lousy about yourself, like you should've never done something so bad to her or made so much trouble for her.

Peggy was real sad so I promised she could be with me when I let Hot-Foot go. I figured he'd have a better chance if I let him go at night, so just before bedtime, I got Peggy and we tiptoed down the back stairway. When she opened the outside door ahead of me she called into the dark alley.

"We've called the police! The Police are on their way, we've called the police!"

"What are you *doing?*" I asked her.

"Scaring away anyone who's lurking in the alley to rob you or hurt you."

I laughed as we crossed the alley.

"There's no one lurking out here to hurt you or anything."

"You never know," she said and she followed me closely down the alley.

"Do you always yell that?" I asked.

"Always, every time I come out here in the dark."

Jeez, now *I* was getting spooked and looking behind us and hearing things in the dark like someone breathing.

I found a yard where there were shrubs and a pile of firewood for cover. Peggy and I squatted by the hedge and I set the cottontail on the ground. He crouched there in the shadows for a minute, sniffing the air, and then, like someone pulled a switch, he shot through the hedge and under the wood pile. We waited until we were cold, but the bunny never showed itself again.

"He'll be okay," I told her as we walked to the apartment. I could tell she was feeling lousy and fighting back tears. "He'll be happy with his friends and maybe we'll see him sometimes."

"What if the boys catch him again?"

"They won't," I said, but I could see them dancing with their spear and howling with bloodthirsty cries and I wondered why some people were so mean and why they'd want to hurt someone. And I wondered what Gretchen's father did to her when he *instructed* her and how he could hit her with a belt and all that other mean stuff and it made me mad and sad all muddled together in a lump that stuck in my craw.

When I was undressing in my room, I still hoped that maybe Gretchen just made those stories up, that maybe she wasn't really being hurt like that after all, but if it was all lies, then maybe she was already crazy, like her sister Helga, and maybe she'd end up in the nut house in Fergus Falls no matter what.

Chapter 11

When I pulled in the alley, Gretchen was leaning against the brick wall in that wacky little baker's cap and a long brown coat that looked like the sadness you see hanging on DPs in newsreels. She acted like she didn't notice the truck, but I could tell she was glad I'd come. I opened the back door and sat on an empty grocery box and she stared off into the alley and we could gab without anyone knowing.

"Sometimes I daydream about going to a dance," she said. "I know it's a sin, but I do it anyway."

"There's nothing wrong with that, everybody daydreams."

"I pretend I'm going to a movie or I get asked to join a sorority or I go to a slumber party and I have nice friends. Do you daydream?"

"Yeah, sure, all the time."

"What about?" She glanced at me.

"Oh, I don't know, about winning a football game, scoring a touchdown." I don't know why, but I didn't want to tell her about Lola. "I brought you something," I said.

"What is it?" Her eyes darted towards me for a second.

"Here."

I held out the shoe box. She glanced at the bakery door but it was closed and she took the Schuneman's box and backed over to the wall.

"Open it," I said.

She peeked into the box as if one of those coiled springs was going to pop out at her or something and when she saw the loafers her lower lip almost hit the ground. Crumb, she looked at me like a starving kid I'd just given a burger and fries and I had to look away.

"See if they fit," I said, "go ahead, put them on."

She set the box down like it had a live puppy in it and pulled off one of her gunboats and slipped on a loafer. I hopped out of the truck and felt her toes with my thumb.

"It's too big. I'll change it. The guy at the store said I could."

I backed into the truck while she put her weight on the shiny loafer and inspected it.

"They must have cost a lot," she said.

"Naw, they weren't much."

I felt a rush of happiness and then it got all mixed up with sadness because a pair of seven ninety-five shoes was such a big deal to her, like no one had done anything nice for her since the day she was born.

"I can't keep them, my father would beat me," she told me and I could see how disappointed she was.

"I got that all figured out. I'll bring them to school, see, and you can keep them in your locker. I'll bring some white socks and you can put them on in the morning and take them off before you meet your dad and he'll never know."

She looked at me a second and then down at the loafer, like she was thinking about it. Then she changed shoes and came over to the truck and handed me the box.

"If I take them, will you promise you'll never tell anyone what I tell you?"

I took the loafers, and she backed over to the bakery wall.

"Yeah, I promise."

"No one . . . *ever!* Not your parents or friends or . . . the police, no one. If you ever tell *anyone,* he'll know I told you and he'll kill me."

The way she said it made my throat go dry and I wondered what I was getting into.

"Okay, I promise, I won't ever."

"I've got to tell someone . . ." She hesitated, like basically she didn't trust me or something. Then she looked into my eyes. " . . . and you're the only one I *can* tell."

"I promise, swear to God, I'll never tell anyone."

"My father made Helga have the baby, he did that to her . . ." Her chin was trembling and her hands were shaking and she looked down the alley like she was afraid her father could hear her from downtown. ". . . and he made her do what she did to it."

Cripes, I felt kind of sick and I wanted to slam the back door of the truck and speed away.

"I don't know what to do," she said, "I'm afraid—"

The back door of the bakery swung open and the baker came out all smudged with flour and carrying a pail. She stiffened and stared down the alley like I wasn't there. I started rearranging boxes of groceries in the back of the truck like I was busy working and the guy dumped the heaping pail into a garbage can.

"Done eating, Gretchen?" he asked.

"Yes, sir."

She followed him into the bakery and the door shut.

I drove away and I didn't want to admit it but my bones told me I was being sucked into something I couldn't get out of.

Wednesday night I came home from practice, starving, and I hoped we'd have pot roast or spaghetti and meatballs or something but when I asked my mother what was for supper she said leftovers. Gad, my mother was famous for leftovers; she could grow leftovers, like we could have two regular meals in a week and the other five would be leftovers. Sometimes they weren't too bad, but sometimes it was hard to stomach, like the time she mixed some greasy chicken gravy with the pea soup, Jeez, even my dad couldn't get that down and he usually made us eat whatever she stuck in front of us. She was the only one I ever heard of who could make a two-pound meatloaf without any meat.

About once a year my dad would tell us how he and my mother moved into their apartment when they got married and the first meal she served was leftovers. The next night my dad wasn't taking any chances and he took her out for dinner. After my mother looked over the menu she told the waitress she'd like leftovers. My dad said he knew he was in trouble when the waitress said Sorry, we throw them out, and my mother said What time?

I really shouldn't make fun of my mother because she went through some hard times getting through the Depression and that wasn't easy and she had to be careful not to waste anything and never had much for herself. She wanted to have a big family with lots of kids but the Depression took that dream away from her and when I catch her saving a sliver of soap or eating scraps of food off our plates in the kitchen I don't kid her anymore because she had to make ends meet for so long, she forgets.

At supper, Peggy pulled up her skirt and showed us an oozing scraped knee and she was plenty mad.

"Bobby Overby pushed me down at recess, and the teacher didn't even do anything to him."

My dad glanced at the massacred knee with the rest of us.

"Spit on it," he said.

That was his usual response whenever any of us got hurt. I could see myself coming home with one leg torn off by a truck and my dad glancing at the bloody stump and saying Spit on it.

"What did you do to him?" my mother asked.

"Nothing, I didn't do anything, he just came up and pushed me," Peggy said.

I wondered why it was that whenever something happened to us, my parents always thought it was our fault. Didn't they know that things just happen to you sometimes? I thought I might punch Bobby Overby in the face the next time I ran into him.

Calling Lola was like pouring iodine on a floor burn and I put it off as long as possible. Our Hi-Y was sponsoring a skirt and sweater dance Saturday, and all night I tried to work up the guts while Peggy hung around the kitchen like a spy. Then my father came out for his usual bowl of ice cream before listening to the evening news on the radio. I don't think my parents could sleep if Cedric Adams didn't assure them that the universe was going to hold together for another day. My dad would sit facing our big old Philco and try not to miss a word while my mother ironed his uniform shirt. I had learned never to interrupt when Cedric Adam's booming voice was banging off the living room wall.

In between the kitchen traffic, I'd dial all but the last number and hang up in a sweat. I forced my hand to dial like it was a pirate being prodded off the gangplank or something, all the numbers, and then I stood like I was paralyzed, listening, holding my breath. It rang, and Lola answered.

"Hello," she said.

Jeez, I hung up. I'd wait until I heard if she was going with Tom and I limped to my room feeling really lousy. Cripes, what a chicken. I kept thinking about it and I couldn't fall asleep and I could hear McCluskey's dog whining and I got madder and madder.

I got up and pulled on my shoes and slipped my jacket over my pajamas and sneaked down the back stairs into the basement. In the boiler room I grabbed a rusty crowbar we never used and went out into the alley. It was cold; there wasn't anyone around and I sneaked over to the wood fence and called the dog with a whisper and he started licking my hand like crazy between the boards.

I stuck the crow bar under a slat and started prying. The nails were screeching away as if they were ratting on me but the slat came loose at the bottom. I slid it sideways and was going to loosen a second one when the skinny dog slipped out through the narrow space. He licked my face and whined like he was happy and jumped up on me and his big ears were flopping all over the place and I slid the board back in place and tapped the nails in with the crow bar.

"Okay, fella, you're free now, go on, get outta here."

I pointed down the alley and I figured a lot of nice people would take him in. I knew I couldn't hide him in my closet. He thanked me with his baggy face and wagged his tail like he was trying to throw it away and then he took off around the fence and headed for McCluskey's house.

"No, no, here boy, here boy," I yelled in a whisper, but he

charged right up on the back step and started woofing and scratching at the door.

Gosh, I couldn't believe it. Why didn't he get away when he could?

"Here, boy, come on, here, boy, here, boy," I called quietly.

He came barreling back to the corner of the alley and jumped up on me. I pointed down the alley.

"Go on, now, get outta here. Go on, get away."

I heard McCluskey's back door open and I ducked behind the fence. Sweat was pouring out of me like engine oil and I thought he might have already spotted me. The dog was licking my face and I was glad there wasn't much light in the alley and then McCluskey whistled. The dog hesitated a minute, like he couldn't make up his mind. Then he trotted back to the house and I could hear McCluskey scolding him and I heard the door shut. I peeked over the top of the fence and then hightailed it for the apartment.

When I got in bed I hoped McCluskey couldn't tell someone had pried open his fence and I tried to figure out what was the matter with that poor dog. Maybe he was too scared to run away, like he thought McCluskey was like God or something and could find him wherever he hid.

I started praying for Gretchen but I didn't understand about prayer or how it was supposed to work. I believed in God, I really did, and I'd been praying since I was a little kid. Golly, the prayer my mother taught me to pray when I'd go to bed used to scare the toenails off me.

"Now I lay me down to sleep, I pray the Lord my soul to keep, If I should *die before I wake,* I pray the Lord my soul to take."

Holy smoke, I used to try to stay awake as long as I could because I was scared I'd die when I went to sleep or something.

But I didn't know how to pray for Gretchen. Didn't God know about what was going on with her and her father, and if He did, why did I have to remind him to do something about it? Didn't he care more about her than I did? It was really confusing but I prayed that He'd save Gretchen and throw her father into the penitentiary at Stillwater for about eleven thousand years and even though I didn't understand how it worked, I kept praying like crazy because I didn't know what else to do.

Chapter 12

After a long practice, a Nut Goodie I'd stashed in my locker saved me from malnutrition, but when I got off the Selby-Lake streetcar and started hoofing it for home, I could've eaten a horse. On the way I promised myself I'd bring up the subject without allowing another night to go by. I could smell bacon and waffles in the back stairway and my mouth was watering before I hit the kitchen.

At dinner I loaded up on waffles drenched in butter and maple syrup and I tried to sandwich a word between my own eating and my father's disappointment.

"It couldn't be worse," he said. "Green has taken control of the Company, and all he's interested in is money; not street-cars or people or service, just money, money, money."

"Who is he?" my mother asked.

"Some New York stock speculator, probably never ridden on a streetcar in his life, has no feeling or respect for them. I tell you, Lurine, I don't know what the world's coming to."

My dad slowly shook his head and kept eating, trying to choke down his heartache with the waffles. My mother flopped another one on my plate and I forced myself out on the limb while trying to sound like I couldn't care less.

"Is there some kind of law against parents beating their kids?"

My dad looked at me and raised an eyebrow. "One of your friends getting what he deserves?"

"Don't wash your food down, Calvin," my mother said.

"Well, is there?" I said. "I mean if a father was really cruel and hit a kid with a belt or something."

"I think that's against the law," my mother said and she cocked her head at me. "You know someone like that?"

"Billy Prescott said his dad beat him," Peggy said.

"No . . . I just heard some kids talking," I said.

"Some kids need a whaling," my dad said. "Johnny Qualls had a kid pull his trolley the other night. Said he would have caught the little beggar if it hadn't been for his rupture surgery."

"Have more bacon, Horace," my mother said and she nodded at me to push the plate towards my dad.

"McCluskey's dog kept me awake again," my dad said.

"That man should be reported," my mother said.

I didn't want to give up on it. "Who would you tell?"

"The Humane Society," my mother said.

"No, not the *dog*, if somebody was beating his *kid*."

"The police," my dad said, "you'd tell the police."

"Is it a friend of yours, Calvin?" my mother asked.

"It isn't anybody," I said, feeling like I was getting nowhere. "I just wondered."

I gulped down my milk, but I could tell my mother didn't swallow my story, and I wished there was a Humane Society for kids.

I hurried through the racket in the halls where kids slammed lockers and yakked with friends and I caught Gretchen at her locker.

"Hi, I brought the loafers."

I'd stuck war-time silver pennies in the vamps and stuffed four pairs of white socks in the box.

"Oh . . . thank you," she said and she looked surprised to see me. When she took the box she glanced around like I was giving her counterfeit money or something.

"I'll see you in study. Put them on."

I hurried away, but just far enough so she wouldn't catch me watching her in the gob of kids. After opening the box and gazing at the loafers for a minute, she stooped and put them on. The first bell rang, and kids took off for their home rooms, and when she walked up the hall, I thought they did help, a thousand times better than her clunky oxfords. But with her hair and that terrible dress, the new loafers looked out of place, like a starving girl in a refugee camp wearing a party hat or something.

I turned and admired her loafers before the bell in study hall.

"They look nice. Do they fit?"

"Yes. They're beautiful," she said and she seemed embarrassed with me staring at her feet.

She pulled the brown loafers back where her dress covered them, and I turned around, expecting the bell to ring any second.

"Why did you do it?" she whispered.

Gad, I didn't know, just something to make her feel better I guess, or to look better, but I couldn't tell her that.

"I just felt like it."

The bell rang, and Miss Whalmen rose from behind her table, about to take attendance. I was confused about what kind of a deal I'd gotten myself into? Did she think I wanted to be her boyfriend? Just when I was getting some trig done, I felt her lean toward me.

"I don't think I'll go crazy now," she whispered.

After our Hi-Y meeting Tuesday night, Tom caught me outside the church as we were scrambling for the few cars.

"Cal, have you got a date for the dance?"

"No."

"Are you going to get one?"

"Naw, I'm going stag."

I kept an eye cocked on Jerry's car to make sure I didn't get left behind.

"Would you do me a big favor?" Tom said.

"What?"

"Would you take Lola to the dance?"

I stopped in my tracks in the shadows of the church lawn,

sure that my ears had picked up the voice of God. Jerry honked, but I stood there stunned, expecting to see a burning bush or something.

"My dad won't let me go steady with her anymore, so I'm taking her best friend, Maribee McGinn, to the dance. If you'd take Lola, Lola and I could still dance together some, and you could dance with Maribee. You know Maribee, she's nice and she's fun."

"Does Lola know about this?" I said, starting to suspect Jerry was behind it, but Jerry didn't know how I felt about Lola.

"Yeah, she knows, all you'd have to do is pick her up. We can't double, though, my dad's too smart for that. I think he's got a spy. Will you, please? You'd have fun with Lola."

My heart was doing cartwheels in my chest.

"Well . . . I guess so," I said like I was doing Tom this huge favor. He slapped me on the back and thanked me like I'd just saved his life, and we both beat it for Jerry's car.

Every Tuesday night some of the sleepy neighborhoods of St. Paul looked like they were being invaded. Jeez, all of a sudden six thousand cars'd come pulling up and a ton of boys would pile out and beat it up to some house. Even though the school didn't officially admit the existence of the sororities and frats, all the clubs, including the sanctioned Hi-Ys, met on Tuesday night, the only school night most kids could get out.

Guys would pour into the house and throw themselves into the quicksand with froggy voices and sweating palms to offer girls a ride home or ask them for a date or mingle and flirt in the hope the right girl might notice. Carloads would keep showing up from Hi-Y and fraternity meetings and after death-defying risks of the heart, kids would race off for other sorority meetings, dragging friends to the door and shouting good-byes.

I found Lola in the kitchen.

"Hi, I guess we're going to the dance Saturday?" I said,

holding my breath behind a phony smile, still wondering if this was a practical joke my buddies were pulling on me.

"Yes, thanks, Cal," she said, leaning close to my ear, "I don't think Tom's father likes me. I hope you weren't planning on asking someone else."

"No, not really."

"You can't tell *anyone* about this, okay?" she whispered and I could smell her perfume.

"Okay," I said. Darn, that's what Gretchen was always telling me and I figured I was piling up secrets like cordwood.

I found myself wandering through the packed house with a grin on my face. Saturday night I'd secretly sacrifice myself on the altar of friendship by clinging to Lola Muldoon as if I liked her.

Chapter 13

Steve had honked more than once before I dashed to the car half dressed.

"Don't honk, Mrs. Overby will complain to my dad," I said as I ducked into the front seat. I hated to be late when I always needed a ride and it made me mad that I'd made Steve wait.

"Let's go pound on her door," he said, "maybe she'll chase us."

He gave it the gas and the Chevy whined down Portland in first gear.

"Yeah, with a broom," I said. I pulled on my sweater. "Sorry I'm late. It's my dang sister's fault. I had to clean up the whole kitchen alone because she had to go to some dumb birthday party, and if there's one speck of food in the sink or one crumb on the floor, my dad acts like I robbed a bank." I bent to lace my shoes. "That little twerp never does anything around there."

"Do you love her?" Steve said without looking over at me.

"Do I *what?*"

I wormed my belt through the loops of my yellow cords and wondered if I heard him right.

"Love her . . . she's your sister, for Cripes sake."

"Yeah, don't I know."

"I had a brother."

"You *did?*" I said. "I didn't know that."

"He was born with a bad heart. We slept together in a double bed and he had trouble breathing, always wheezing and coughing. I never slept very good because I was always listening in case he was in trouble. He was six. One morning when I woke up he was dead."

"Dead! Jeez, that must've been awful."

"Yeah, sometimes I still catch myself waking up and listening in the dark to see if I can hear him breathing."

When I went up to Lola's door, she zipped out before I
could ring the bell, like she didn't want her mother seeing
who she was going out with. We had four couples in Steve's
Chevy and I felt awkward and kind of stupid. Jerry had Sally
on his lap next to us in the backseat, and they mangled Lola
up against me, which was a dream come true, except now that
I found myself so close I could smell her Juicy-Fruit breath,
I'd turned feebleminded. Steve had asked Nancy Swanson, a
nice girl, but I knew he loved Katie the way I loved Lola, and
things were getting more mixed up by the minute.

At the dance, I felt like a sorority sister or something,
listening to Lola's tale of woe about how awful it was that
Tom's dad was breaking them up. I wanted to tell her that
Tom's father had just become my all-time hero.

"Tom's dad says he has to date other girls or he can't go
out with me," she told me. What a shame.

I sat there like a stump and couldn't think of anything to
say and we sipped Cokes and watched kids dancing on the
gym floor and I tried to stop the silly grin that kept showing
up on my face. When she wasn't dancing with Tom, she said
we ought to dance a little so no one would catch on. Actually
I didn't know how to dance, but I held my arm around her
little waist, and as we swayed to the music I could smell her
hair and feel the motion of her spine under her yellow
Angora sweater and she was so warm and cuddly I wanted to
pull her closer but I didn't dare. Not only would she wonder
what I was doing, but I'd suddenly gotten hard and I was
afraid that she would feel it if I got too close and sure that
everyone in the gym would notice. I was plenty thankful for
my full-pleated yellow cords and I pulled my sweater down as
far as it would stretch. I never asked my friends if that ever
happened to them; we never talked about stuff like that, and
sometimes I thought I'd be the only kid in my class who'd
go blind.

"What's with Tom and Lola?" Steve said when Lola and
Tom were off in a corner trying to go unnoticed. "I thought
they broke up."

"I guess they're still friends," I said.

"Yeah, and I'm Joe Dimaggio."

"Katie is sitting right over there," I said and nodded.

"Don't look over there!" he said and he stepped in front of me. "She'll see us staring at her."

"She won't see us, go ask her to dance."

"She's on a date, you dork," Steve said.

"Ask her anyway, they're not going steady or anything."

"Yeah, sure, she doesn't even know who I am but I go up and ask her to dance while she's on a date. Boy!"

"She knows who you are; you're a senior wheel."

"Yeah, a senior wheel with a flat tire."

He shrugged and gimped over to a bunch of stags. Jeez, he never said much about his leg or anything and I didn't think it bothered him anymore but maybe I was wrong.

After the dance we bombed downtown to Bridgeman's, and when we'd destroyed some enormous banana splits and other ice cream concoctions, Steve drove the streets of St. Paul like he was lost but never quite came up with the nerve to park. Jerry and Sally were necking away beside us like he was going off to war and I sat there sweating, riding around next to this luscious girl, the love of my life, and I couldn't come up with a single thing to say.

But my nervous stomach was coming up with something and my body was turning into a traitor. My knotting guts were producing gas with the efficiency of Standard Oil, a bulging, expanding balloon that was threatening to explode, and I held off the momentary catastrophe with every muscle in my body.

I could imagine the embarrassment, a gigantic detonation right beside Lola, and the pain was killing me. Jeez, in social studies, Miss Hilger talked about the Hindenburg so much I thought she must have been on it when it went down. Now the ghost of the Hindenburg was turning up in my belly and I tried to think of some excuse to have Steve stop where I could bomb out of the car. My stomach churned and the pressure grew and I was afraid I couldn't hold it back any longer.

"Have you gotten to know Gretchen Luttermann?" Lola said out of the blue.

"Huh . . . oh, no, no, she just sits behind me in study. I don't know her at all."

Jeez, there I was dying in excruciating pain and Lola's talking about Gretchen.

"She seems so strange, I heard her sister went crazy."

"Yeah, that's what I heard, I don't know anything about it."

I rolled down the window in preparation for the inevitable.

Lucky for me, Steve dropped Lola off first, like he could read my mind. Lucky for all of them. I couldn't have gone another block. Like a woman about to have a baby, I walked Lola to the door and said good-night as fast as I could. Then I acted like I was clowning around and I limped across Village Lane and out into a dark vacant lot. When I figured I'd gone far enough, I set the zeppelin free, scaring myself with the horrendous salvo and afraid that I'd scorched my favorite yellow cords.

"What were you doing, you nut?" Steve asked when I got back in the car.

"Don't ask, but I just saved your life."

When Steve dropped me off, I ambled around to the back of the apartment feeling lousy, figuring that Lola was as interested in me as she was in catching polio. I took the basketball from inside the back door and walked past the basket on the telephone pole in the alley. Basketball would be my life. I didn't understand girls or why I ached for Lola and I wished I could forget all about her because I didn't like to hurt that way.

In the shadowed light of the neighborhood I stood eighteen feet from the backboard. My breath showed in the cold night air and I dribbled the ball twice and let it go in a silent arc for the basket. The only sound was the swish of the net.

Someone moved behind me up the alley and I whirled

around and just about jumped out of my skin. Frozen in my tracks, I squinted into the darkness with my heart thumping behind my eyeballs while a dark figure moved toward me out of the blackness and I was ready to blast outta there.

"Cal?" I heard a faint voice. "Cal, is that you?"

When she came through a crack of light, I recognized my little sister, dressed in only her pajamas, bathrobe and untied shoes.

"Jeez, you scared me. What are you doing out here?"

I moved toward her as she reached the back of the apartment.

"I forgot to leave food for Hot-Foot."

"Food for Hot-Foot?"

"Every day I leave a carrot or something for him. I woke up a little while ago and remembered I forgot."

"Does he eat it?" I asked, touched by her thoughtfulness.

"I think so, it's always gone, at least most of the time. I put it by the wood pile where we let him go."

"Does Mom know?"

"No, I sneak stuff for him, he doesn't need much."

McCluskey's dog started whining and the two of us braced ourselves, afraid it would wake our father. I held the door for her and we crept into the back stairway, praying that we'd reach the safety of our beds before the dog wailed again.

When I crawled into my bed, I could remember the way Lola's hair smelled and feel her spine under her soft yellow sweater and I forgot to pray for Gretchen Luttermann.

I got to Finley's Market late on Saturday and my hands were numb after I put up storm windows in a freezing wind. The bigger ones weighed a ton and you had to slide them up the ladder and hook the top corners without flipping over backwards and certain death.

The green celluloid visor rested on Mr. Finley's caterpillar brows as he held the phone in one hand and scribbled in a beat-up order book with the other. I figured he'd die from lead poisoning some day 'cause he always wet his pencil with his tongue before he'd use it.

"Stop at Prior Avenue Liquor," he said. "You sleeping late these days or what?"

He handed me the order slips.

"No, I was putting up storm windows and Mrs.Overby made me wash one about thirty-seven times. I wanted to finish the second story so Dad didn't have to go up the high ladder."

"That's good. How is your dad?"

"Okay, but he's sure they're going to do away with the streetcars."

I picked up a wooden box heaped with groceries and backed out the door.

"I hope he's wrong," Finley said.

At the liquor store the orders weren't ready, and while Sid made them up, I counted the cases of booze in the storeroom, trying to figure how much money all that was worth.

"How's basketball going," Sid said without looking at me, I think.

"Good, really good."

"You gonna play much?"

"Yeah, I'm starting, at guard."

"You gonna beat Monroe?"

"Yeah, for sure."

I finished my first run after noon. With an honest excuse to forget about it, I wheeled into the alley and skidded to a stop behind the bakery. Gretchen was nowhere in sight and I figured I missed her lunch break. After waiting in the truck for a few minutes, I sauntered around the corner drugstore and into the front of the bakery. The woman with hams for arms came from the back.

"Can I help you?"

"I'd like a sugar doughnut, please."

I gave her three cents and nibbled the doughnut, glancing

into as much of the bakery as possible without appearing too obvious. A few customers came and went but Gretchen never showed. When I was left with nothing but sticky fingers, I retreated to the delivery truck, and as I was about to get in, the back door of the bakery swung open. Mr. Buehler came out with a cardboard box.

"Gretchen is home sick," he said to me.

"Who?"

I tried to look like I didn't know what he was talking about.

"I think it's all right that you come and see her. Her father is too strict with that girl. I'll never squeal on her. Stopped this morning to say she was sick."

The baker smiled at me and set the box on a garbage can.

"Thanks." I nodded and slid into the truck.

It was a gloomy, windy day and a strange dread followed me on my second run. I couldn't help wonder if Gretchen was really sick or if something worse had happened to her. When I loaded back at Finley's I tried to find out where she lived, but their name wasn't in the phone book. Didn't they have a phone? Jeez, why didn't I forget about her? More kids than I realized knew she followed me around at school like a mongrel, and now the baker. I wasn't getting the big head with basketball or anything, and it wasn't that I didn't want to be seen with Gretchen, but Cripes, there was something scary about her and her father; I felt danger around her; she wore it like those ugly brown shoes.

Chapter 14

"Mrs. Overby said you left some smudges on two of her storm windows," my mother told me at the supper table.

"That old battle-ax wants them perfect."

"There's nothing wrong with perfect," my dad said. "If it's worth doing, it's worth doing right."

"I can't figure out where the carrots go," my mother said. "I buy them and they just disappear into thin air."

"Maybe there's a giant rat in the building," my dad said and he kind of smiled. Peggy and I didn't look at each other.

Steve and I hoofed it to Jean Daley's slumber party where kids were listening to records and playing cards and dancing, and everybody was eating whatever food wasn't locked up. I managed to talk to Lola in the middle of the hubbub in the basement rec room and I tried to act like it didn't matter if I talked to her or not. We beat around the bush about the upcoming basketball season, and I wanted to ask her to dance but I never came up with the nerve. She didn't pay much attention to me basically, and she goofed off with her girlfriends most of the time.

Steve acted like he'd been drinking, kind of crazy and loud. He was the only one of my friends who actually did drink some, but I think it was mostly three-two beer. Sandy cornered me and wanted to know every word Scott had uttered since the homecoming dance.

"What did he say, Bean, does he like me, just a little, what did he say, what did he say?"

She was bouncing all over the place like if I didn't come up with something fast, she'd be out through the roof.

"I'll tell you, but first, can you find out a kid's address when you work in the office?"

"Sure, in the card file. Whose address do you want?"

"You can never tell," I said, "you have to *promise*."

"I promise, I promise."

"Gretchen Luttermann's."

"Gretchen Luttermann's!"

"Shhhhhh, not so loud," I said. "You promised."

"All right, I'll get it Monday, now tell me about Scott."

"Well, he hasn't said much lately, you know, he doesn't talk about stuff like that a lot, but I think he really likes you," I said, trying to give her her money's worth, and basically I did think he liked her, so I wasn't lying or anything.

"You do? Really? Oh, golly, he's so nifty."

"I think he had fun at the homecoming dance," I said, laying it on thick.

"I'm already worried, Bean." She turned kind of sad. "His dad wants him to go to some military school back east next year and he'll probably meet some dandy girl back there."

"Yeah, I know, but he doesn't want to go. Maybe he won't."

I tried to make her feel better and I wished Scott would fall in love with her. On her twelfth birthday Sandy's parents told her she was adopted, and ever since she was always watching out for grownups and kids who looked like her.

Mrs. Daley shagged us at midnight and Steve seemed down the minute we left the party.

"Do you like Nancy?" I asked as we walked.

"I don't know . . . I wish Katie had been there."

"If she had you'd have hid in the attic or something."

"No I wouldn't, I said Hi to her yesterday."

"I don't believe it," I said. "What did she do?"

"She said Hi . . . and she smiled at me."

"See, I told you."

I punched him on the shoulder and we turned a corner into the wind and I was freezing.

"What would you do if you knew some guy was beating his kid, I mean really beating him with a belt or something?"

"I'd blow up his car with him in it."

Steve sprayed me with his laugh.

"Be serious."

"I am," he said. "Jeez, my leg aches."

Steve bounced with his rhythmic hitch, and I slowed the pace, realizing I'd been legging it pretty fast in the cold.

"When did you have polio?" I said.

"In sixth grade . . . they only passed me because they felt sorry for me."

We walked for a minute and I wished I hadn't brought up the subject we never talked about.

"I was sure I'd die," he said.

"You were too tough for it."

"I don't mean the polio. God was punishing me."

"God? Why would he punish you?"

I caught myself striding again and I slowed my pace.

"Because I killed my little brother."

Jeez, it was like someone punched me in the stomach.

"What do you mean?"

"When they buried my brother, my parents held on to each other and they wouldn't even stand by me. I had to watch them put him in the ground all by myself, and I knew they blamed me."

We walked for a while and the winter wind felt like it was ripping my face off.

"When I found him in bed that morning I didn't call them. I was too scared. I stayed in bed, next to him, and I could hardly breathe and I knew it was my fault."

"Why did you think it was your fault?"

"I should've heard him, I should've heard him and woke up."

"How old were you?"

"I'd just turned eight."

"Well, you can't—"

"I could hear my parents moving around but they didn't come to wake us. Then finally, my mother came in and found him and they went nuts. They kept shouting at me, *Why* didn't you hear him! *Why* didn't you wake us!' Gad, it drives me crazy. He was probably coughing and choking and calling, 'Stevie, Stevie, help me,' and I'm just sleeping away like a lazy bastard."

Steve choked up and his voice cracked.

"God, I wish I'd heard him."

We stopped at the intersection where we'd split up. In the awkward cold I didn't want to leave him alone again, like he was standing beside his brother's grave. All I could come up with was a hand on his shoulder. He turned and crossed Fairview and I wanted to run after him, to say something. He grew smaller and smaller as his gliding hop carried him off into the shadows.

"What if your brother never called you!" I shouted. "Maybe he died in his sleep!"

Steve never broke his gimpy stride.

"You couldn't help him if he never called you!" I yelled.

He had gone too far and I figured he couldn't hear my voice in the swirling wind.

The streetlights were dim against the November darkness and the bare branches of the Dutch elms were clacking in the wind and it was like the world was going to freeze to death. I pulled my collar tight and hunched down into my jacket and slogged the block home.

Tomorrow I'd finish the storm windows and it would be a lot harder with my dad eyeballing each pane. Before I got into bed, I tiptoed down the hall to Peggy's room and tried to open her door quietly but the hinges were screeching away and I wondered why everything in the apartment always made more noise late at night when you wanted to be quiet. I peered into the room and when my eyes got used to the darkness I could make out her form curled under the covers. I listened until I heard her breathing.

"What are you doing?" my mother whispered like a ghost in the hallway, scaring the chicken fat outta me.

"Just checking to see if Peggy's okay," I said.

My mom looked into my sister's room. "Why wouldn't she be?"

"No reason."

"Get to bed, you'll wake your father."

When I got in bed I remembered to pray for Gretchen, and I prayed for Steve, and I wondered if there was anything like storm windows for the heart.

Chapter 15

I met Sandy outside the office after third period and she gave me the address, 1869 Goodrich, and I reminded her she promised not to tell anyone. I watched for Gretchen in the halls all day and she didn't show up in fifth hour study hall and I started getting a bad feeling about it but I kept telling myself that everybody got sick sometime.

I was already late for supper after a long practice but I couldn't resist, and gad, I was surprised that the address was so close to where I lived. Why hadn't I seen Gretchen in the neighborhood in all these years, only six blocks from our apartment? In the darkness I couldn't make out the number, but that had to be the house with that black Plymouth parked out in front. It looked like all the other houses on the block, a two-story with stucco and probably four bedrooms. I walked past the two apartment buildings next to Gretchen's house to the corner and circled around to the alley.

A small, one-car garage sat off the alley that looked unused and you couldn't see in any of the windows in the back of the house because they all had heavy drapes like they were expecting an air raid or something. A window in a dormer on the second floor faced the back and I hadn't climbed a tree in a while, but a large oak in the back yard would get me real close to that window. It wouldn't do any good because it had curtains too, and besides, what if someone in the house saw me? I was hungry and tired and I legged it for home.

When I arrived, my mother was all excited over a picture of me in the *St. Paul Dispatch.*

> *"Cal Gant, one reason why Coach Patrick Mulligan has high hopes for the upcoming season at Central."*

Jeez, in the paper! We hadn't even played a game yet. Had the coach really said that? He'd never said anything like that to me.

"I'm so proud of you, Calvin, but I wish they'd used your real name," my mother said.

I impersonated a kid who took it all calmly, but I was bouncing off the walls inside and I hoped Lola would see it. Peggy made a Federal case out of it and she wanted to take the picture to school the next day. All my dad said was You don't win games with pictures.

I was feeling pretty darn good, and for once, thanks to the *Dispatch*, I wasn't in the dumps when I got off the phone with Lola. She'd seen my picture in the paper and she sounded honestly impressed and we agreed on arrangements for another phony date. I was looking forward to the dance, but whenever I was with her I always tried to be someone else, who she wanted me to be, and then I'd dance to her tune while I felt awkward and out of step. I snuck out of my room three times to look at the picture, like I couldn't believe it was really in the paper. I didn't want to take it in my room like some conceited jackass, but I hoped Peggy wouldn't get jam on it at breakfast.

Gretchen didn't show up on Tuesday, and the way she was always telling me she'd go crazy, I couldn't help but wonder if she had. Steve hobbled up to me in the second floor hall after first period English and waved a yellow slip in my face.

"Wanna cut classes and drive around all day?"

"How did you get out?" I asked, and I headed down the hall for second period trig.

"I put wet blotters in my shoes."

"Wet blotters?"

"Yeah, it raises your temperature about two degrees. I went in and told old Armstrong that I was feeling sick and she takes my temperature and writes me out an excuse for the rest of the day. C'mon, you can do it. I'll get the car."

"How you going to do that?"

"I'll go downtown where my dad parks it and hot-wire it."

"You know how to *hot-wire* a car?" I said.

"How do you think I get it all the time?" He let me have it with his Tommy-gun laugh as we bombed down the stairway to the first floor and I thought Steve was pretty clever. "C'mon, we'll have fun, drive over and see if we can find any good-looking Summit girls."

"Gosh, I wouldn't dare try that with Armstrong."

"What can she say if you have a temperature?"

Jeez, Miss Armstrong, our school nurse, looked like a gal who had grown up on a Minnesota dairy farm and could throw a hog over the barn and I was afraid to pull anything with her. Steve had guts.

"I can't. If I get caught I could get kicked off the team."

"Yeah, you're right, I never thought of that, we need you," Steve said and I ducked into my math class just ahead of the bell.

The Wednesday before Thanksgiving was a carefree day, like a Friday, with the dance that night and the team traveling to Minneapolis Washburn in the afternoon for a scrimmage. I got to study hall a few minutes before the bell and Gretchen showed up and I turned and leaned over the back of the assembly seat.

"Hi, have you been sick?"

"No," she said without looking at me and wearing her big brown oxfords.

"I was worried. I found out where you live."

"Oh, n-o-o-o, you can *never* come to my house, *never, ever!*"

"Okay, okay, I won't. Why weren't you at work Saturday?"

"He wouldn't let me."

"Why?"

"He . . . because . . . he wouldn't."

She nervously picked at a fingernail. I leaned closer.

"Did he hurt you?"

She didn't answer.

"Did he do something to you?" I asked.

She slowly nodded.

"What did he do?"

She pulled her dress slightly above her knee and showed me an ugly-looking bruise. "He wouldn't let me out because the marks would show."

"How did he do that?" I asked and I was fuming at the gills.

"With a cane."

"A cane! Why did he hurt you?"

She twisted one hand with the other in her lap.

"Did he find out about the loafers?"

"No."

"Don't you want to wear them anymore?"

"I'm going to go crazy."

"No you're not."

"Yes I am. I'm going to end up like Helga."

She glanced at me and her eyes blasted me with sadness.

"*I'll* help you," I said, "*I'll* find something we can do. Gosh, there has to be something."

"You can't *tell* anyone, you promised!"

"Shhhhhh, okay, I'll figure out something by myself."

The bell rang, and I turned around and pulled up the fold-out desk top. What on earth could *I* do. Why did I *tell* her such dumb stuff? But doggone it, her father was a mean bastard and I wanted to find some way to pull his trolley.

Chapter 16

Home late from the scrimmage, I hurried to get ready, gulping down the supper my mother kept warm in the oven and almost giving it away that no one was picking me up. On Saturday Mr. Finley said if I didn't mind going in a truck I could use his for my next date, and he winked at me. When I hoofed it over behind the store to fetch the Plymouth, I was pretty excited.

We usually picked up the boys and then the girls, but I picked up Lola first thing, feeling cocky with my picture in the paper and the guy with the car for a change, or the truck.

"Where'd you get the cute truck?" Lola asked.

"My boss, Mr. Finley," I said, holding the door for her. "I use it delivering groceries."

I hurried around and climbed in beside her.

"I like it." She looked over the inside of the truck.

"I don't think your mom did."

"She's always worrying about what people think."

I picked up the other couples and they thought the truck was super. Jerry and Steve brought blankets for the back deck because the truck only had a front seat. I talked Scott into asking Sandy as due payment for services rendered, and with four of them in back, Scott sat in the front with Sandy on his lap, crushing Lola up against me.

God bless Mr. Finley.

"You'll have to do the shifting," I told her.

"I've never driven one like this."

"It's easy, here."

With my hand on top of hers, I showed her how to work the stick shift, and she slipped one of her legs on either side of the stick. When we pulled it into second it rumpled her pleated skirt halfway up her lap and I felt kind of embarrassed, but Lola just laughed and jammed the gears together.

"Grind me a pound," Steve called from the back.

I was having so much fun I started showing off, ripping around corners and flinging my friends in the back into piles like a bunch of kittens.

"Faster, faster," Steve shouted.

"We're not only going to smell like onions and rutabagas, we're going to look like them!" Sandy yelled.

I took a zig-zagging route and we were laughing and bouncing around and acting crazy and no one seemed to care that we arrived at the Turkey Trot in a FINLEY'S MARKET truck or that we smelled like a roadside vegetable stand.

The dance was a roller-coaster of happiness and green-eyed jealousy. Gee, I'd forget I was only Lola's phony boyfriend until Tom would show up like Dracula and snatch her away, and while Tom and Lola were dancing cheek to cheek on the dance floor, I started feeling like *he* was dancing with *my* girl.

After the dance, I turned her loose on the transmission again and I was feeling awfully good until a sadness hit me, and I realized that these phony dates would soon be over and that I might never be happier in my whole life than I was right then with Lola beside me in the grocery truck, holding her hand on the stick shift with the aroma of ripe bananas filling the cab, and I promised myself that I would kiss her if it killed me. After eating at the new drive-in near Minnehaha Falls, I tried to come up with the courage to park, and when I couldn't, I drove half-way around the city on the way home.

On Lola's front step, her mother had an outside light bright enough to land planes. Lola thanked me, and we laughed about her shifting, and I was scared out of my wits, but I swallowed hard and took her by the shoulders and kissed her and I almost exploded when she kissed back! Jeez, after she closed the door, I wandered back to the truck and I could taste her lipstick on my mouth and I started to get in the passenger side.

I dropped Scott last and then drove slowly down Goodrich

past 1869. The house looked scary in the shadows with the black Plymouth moored in front, and I wondered what terrible thing Gretchen's father had done to her. I parked the truck behind Finley's Market and hiked for home and I felt a little guilty that I hadn't told my parents about borrowing the truck because I knew they'd have said No. I tried to convince myself that Lola had enjoyed my kiss, that it wasn't phony, and as I ran my tongue over my lips, I knew that as long as I lived, I'd always have the taste of Lola somewhere in my mind.

Thanksgiving morning we were all decked out in our Sunday best and we hoofed it over to the Selby-Lake line on our way to Minneapolis and Uncle Rudy's. The day was mild and the sky gray and the blustery wind made it feel like fall.

"Enough is enough. I'm calling the Humane Society tomorrow," my mother said.

"It's none of our business," my dad said. "We could get in trouble."

"That poor dog kept you awake half the night," she said as Peggy and I followed close at their heels.

"McCluskey could know someone in the Company. If he found out who reported him, I could lose my job."

"Well someone has to do something," my mother said. "It's a crime."

"Let someone else do it," my dad said.

"What if everyone said that?" Peggy said, having the guts to say what I was thinking.

"I said no! We'll leave well enough alone. I don't want to hear anymore about it."

We crossed Selby and waited for the streetcar and we all knew that the discussion was over.

Right in the middle of the turkey dinner, like he had for the past four years, Uncle Rudy started talking about his boy Neal, my cousin, who was too short to get in the Navy so he

made a harness and hung himself by the shoulders for hours
every day until he was tall enough to get in and then a Jap
Kamikaze dove into his destroyer and blew him to
smithereens. Uncle Rudy got all choked up and the sadness
spilled over on everyone and we all stopped talking and
laughing and having fun. My mother always said Neal
tempted fate and he should've left things alone and stayed
short. Riding the streetcar home, I wondered if I was
tempting fate by trying to help Gretchen and if I should just
leave things alone.

On Saturday I pushed myself through the deliveries, hoping
to catch Gretchen on her lunch break. When I pulled in the
alley, she stood leaning against the brick wall, waiting. I
backed in and opened the rear door, but when I turned and
smiled at her, a car pulled in beside the truck. Gretchen's face
warned me, and I climbed into the back like I was unloading
groceries.

Her father marched from the black Plymouth and stood
face to face with her. I couldn't hear his words from inside
the truck, but Luttermann talked like an officer giving
commands out of a cold, blank face and Gretchen stared at
the ground and didn't say much and I was really mad and I
got out of the truck.

I slammed the back door kind of hard and walked past
Luttermann to leave, measuring him for size. He was a
normal looking guy but kind of cranky, like he was mad at
the world, a little over six foot, thin, a hundred and seventy-
five pounds, with dark sunken eyes and a face that looked
like it hadn't cracked a smile this century. When I started the
truck and drove out of the alley, it wasn't so much how
Luttermann looked as what I felt when I was close to him:
danger, like standing on the porch expecting the Runner to
come creaming out the door at any second. I gunned the
panel truck away and started feeling a little chicken for

leaving, but what could I do? I knew that by saying a word, by letting on that I knew Gretchen or anything about her, I'd get her in terrible trouble.

While I finished the day's deliveries, I made up my mind. I'd call the police—not giving my name—and ask them to check up on Otto Luttermann. But how could they protect Gretchen if they only asked a bunch of questions and went away? If they didn't nail her father, he'd know Gretchen had ratted on him and really get her. I felt my stomach tighten.

During home room on Monday, I made an appointment in the office to see a counselor third period.

"What do you want to see a counselor about?" Miss Hass, the office secretary, asked.

"It's a personal problem," I said.

Third period I felt like a delinquent going up before the principal when Miss Hass ushered me into a back office that reminded me of a dentist's waiting room. The heebie-jeebies I usually got when I'd be waiting to have my teeth drilled kept telling me to bail out of there.

Mr. Rogers, a history teacher, came sweating into the room like he'd come from the tower or something. He shut the door and landed behind the desk. Jeez! *He* was the counselor? The klutzy teacher had been our B-squad basketball coach when I was a sophomore. He had me picking up splinters on the bench while guys who were dribbling off their kneecaps, who weren't even on the A-squad now, played the games. If this guy's counseling was anything like his drippy coaching, I didn't have much hope.

"Hello, Cal. I hear you boys gave Washburn a good going over the other day," the counselor said.

"Yeah. We beat them."

"Now then, Cal, what seems to be the problem?"

"Can you do anything about a father who beats his kid?"

The smile slunk off Mr. Rogers's face.

"Are you having trouble at home?"

"No. It's not about me . . . what if I knew a kid who was being beaten but the kid didn't dare tell anyone. What could you do?"

"Well, I think the student would have to speak up, tell us about it. Is this one of our students?"

I squirmed in the chair and tried to be careful.

"I can't tell . . . I promised." I was thinking. Mr. Rogers waited. "Couldn't you get the police to lock him up?"

"Not just by what you've told me. The student would have to come forward, give evidence, something. They can't go jailing someone on just a story."

"It isn't a story, I've seen h . . . the kid's bruises."

"Oh . . . that's terrible, just terrible."

"If the kid told, would the cops protect him?" I said.

"Well, I don't know. Why don't you tell me who we're talking about, and maybe I can help."

"Are you like a priest, you can never tell anyone?"

"Well, sort of. What we talk about is confidential."

"If they don't protect the kid, the father will kill her," I said and then bit my tongue.

"Oh, now Cal, that sounds a little preposterous. I find it hard to believe that any parent—"

"Do you think the police would do anything if they knew?"

"I don't know. A parent has the right to discipline his children, but if unusual force and cruelty were being used . . . they might give the parent a warning and let him know they would keep an eye on him."

"A *warning?*" I stood up. "I gotta go."

"If you'd tell me who—"

"Thanks, Mr. Rogers."

I opened the door and bombed out of there.

"Any time, Cal, any time," he called after me.

Chapter 17

I was glad to see Gretchen when I hurried into study hall.

"Did your dad know I was there to talk to you on Saturday?" I asked as I slid into my seat.

"No . . ." She gazed into her lap.

"Boy, I was worried. I thought he might punish you if he knew."

"He would."

"What was he doing there?"

"Checking on me. I'm always afraid he'll change his mind and keep me to home Saturdays."

"Maybe I shouldn't come by any more."

"Do come, *please."* She glanced into my face. "I *have* to talk to someone."

I leaned closer as kids filled the auditorium.

"You've got to tell on him, it's the only way."

"No, no, that's what Helga did, and he got out of it, and then he fixed her so she could never tell again. I can *never* tell on him, *never, never,* or he'll do the same thing to me!"

"Well what do you expect me to do, for crying out loud?"

"You can *never* tell, you promised, you *promised me, Cal."*

"Okay, okay, calm down, calm down." I glanced around the auditorium. "I won't tell anyone, I promise."

She started shaking and watched her hands flutter in her lap like they were on their own and she was gulping for air and I thought she was going to have a heart attack or something.

The bell rang and I turned in my seat, afraid she was going to crack up right there in study hall. I kept an eye peeled over my shoulder to see if she needed help and I was mad and all mixed up. I stared into my trig book and wondered what her father had threatened so that she could never tell on him? I peeked back at her out of the corner of my eye in a way that would have made Sid proud, and she was sitting kind of normal like and seemed okay.

I thought of Lola and glanced across the auditorium. She lifted her head and when she saw me she smiled. Jeez, from the world of the crazy to the world of bliss in three seconds.

When the hour was almost over, I felt a tug on my sleeve and Gretchen slipped a note under my left armpit. I kept one eye on Miss Whalmen and took the note, slipping it into my open math book.

Dear Cal,

You are a nice boy. I know how bad and homely I am, but I hope you will come next Saturday. I am afraid I will be lost forever like my father tells me, and I will be burned in the lake of eternal fire. Every day I think something might happen and everything will be all right, but nothing ever does, and I don't think I will be able to go on for many more Saturdays.

I wanted to answer her note but I didn't know what to write and at the bell, I bombed up the aisle without looking back and promised myself I'd do something to help her.

For some unknown reason, we walked home from church on Sunday. Peggy and I followed our parents and we didn't horse around much, holding our coats shut against the blustery day.

"Better get used to walking," my dad said.

"Aren't we going to ride the buses?" I said.

"Ride the buses!" My father snorted without turning around. "I wouldn't get on one of those stinking, good-for-nothing machines if they begged me, belching their filthy soot and diesel fumes all over the city. Humph! I'd walk through hell before I'd get on one of those blasted contraptions."

"Don't upset yourself," my mother said.

I wished I hadn't asked. My father carried on all the way home, and I knew better than to admit I was going to ride the buses when the streetcars were gone. It was progress, and it sure beat walking.

On Monday no one seemed very excited about our first basketball game—the fact was, not too many knew about it. Scheduled right after school at Minneapolis North, there probably wouldn't be any of the student body traveling over there. One of the rumors that hung around our locker room like the odor of stale sweat was that Minneapolis kids were bigger and tougher than St. Paul kids and they all came from roughneck neighborhoods.

I talked with Gretchen for a minute in study hall before we left school early.

"Did you come by on Saturday?" she said.

"Yeah. But you weren't there."

"My father came over twice." She twisted her hands without looking at me. "I ate inside because I was afraid he'd come back when you were there."

Every time I saw her she looked worse, nervous and sad, and so skinny.

"Do you think I'm crazy?" she asked and she looked at me like my answer would decide if she was or not.

"No, gosh, I don't think you're crazy."

With none of our fans to watch the nonconference game, it seemed more like just another scrimmage. Coach Mulligan kept trying different combinations of players, but Rick Powers, a junior center, and I were the bread and butter, both playing the whole game. We beat North, 62–57, and when we dressed we were pretty happy. If we could beat tough kids from Minneapolis like this, who couldn't we beat? Jeez, I felt good about myself when I played—like I had in the woods with Uncle Emil—and I even started believing I was good enough for Lola.

Jerry had managed the car on Tuesday to hit the sorority meetings and I invited Lola to ride home with us. When she accepted, I dared to believe she might ask me to the upcoming formal. The Soko and Deb girls were starting to ask their boyfriends to their annual dinner-dance between Christmas and New Year's, one of the big deals of the year and I wondered if Lola and Tom had fooled his father long enough to be able to go to the formal together, or if the Gant Escort Service would be called into play? Gad, Tom thought his girl was in safe hands and Lola acted like she really had fun with me, and best of all, there'd been no mention of *the kiss;* we had a juicy secret between us.

We parked for almost an hour above Hidden Falls, but most of that time, while Jerry and Sally necked, Lola chattered about her father.

"He's coming to see me at Christmas. Mom won't let me see him or talk to him, but I wait by the phone on Saturdays. He calls right at noon."

"What if your mom answers it?"

"She's usually working Saturdays. If she isn't, I take the phone off the hook, and if it's busy when he calls, he knows she's home. She hates him, says we'll move to another city where he'll never find us if I ever see him or talk to him. She keeps telling me she has to be mother and father to me, but she doesn't, I have a dad, he just lives in Baltimore and can't get back here very often. Darn, I wish they'd get back together."

"Maybe he'll make it to see you cheer at a game."

"Yeah, maybe. I want him to meet Tom, I know Dad will really like Tom."

Cripes, she said it so easily I could tell she never dreamed how it bashed me. I'd thought about telling her I'd loved her for two years but now it was like I'd been drop-kicked into the Mississippi, just a pawn on Tom and Lola's chess board, and I no longer liked the game.

"You have to *see* it," Gretchen said, standing against the wall behind the bakery. "Helga told them everything, but they didn't believe her. They'll have to believe *you*, not just what I've told you, but what you've *seen*."

"See what? for crying out loud. See what?"

"What he . . . does. What he . . . does . . . to me."

Jeez, I scanned both ends of the alley for the black Plymouth and I wanted to get the heck out of there.

"How am I going to do *that?*" I wasn't sure what we were talking about, beatings, torture, or worse?

"I don't know, I don't . . ." her voice trailed off as her eyes caught mine ducking for cover. *"Please."*

"Listen, if you tell them," I said, "they'll remember Helga's story, and now they'll believe you, they'll know your parents are lying, they probably kept a record or something, two sisters wouldn't make up the same story if it wasn't true."

"They won't remember, they didn't pay any attention to Helga. It probably wouldn't even be the same people."

I was thinking like crazy. Part of me wanted to help her and part of me wanted to pretend I'd never heard of her.

"If you're afraid—"

"Oh . . . no," I said. "I want to help you . . . do what I can, but how am I going to *see* anything?"

I knew before the words came out of my mouth, the oak tree in her backyard. The first time I saw it I knew it would become a part of my life, as though I'd seen myself clinging to its branches and peering through the dormer window into the dark secret that was her life.

"I'll find a way," she said. "I have to go in."

She looked into my eyes for a second like she was searching for something she could believe in—bravery, guts, balls? I wondered what she'd found there when she turned away, if she'd noticed my courage tiptoeing down the alley?

Chapter 18

I'd told Tom I wouldn't do it anymore, and when I didn't call Lola by Thursday, she'd caught me in the hall after third period and *she* asked *me* to the dance Saturday night. Holy cow, I melted like grilled cheese when she begged with her eyes and I tried to figure out what color they were and the only word that came out of my spastic mouth was Okay.

Scott had his father's '49 Kaiser with a 100 horse straight 6 and a big ivory steering wheel with a dash like a fighter plane and I got grease on my shirt looking under the hood. I was feeling pretty good because we knocked off Cretin Friday afternoon in their gym and we only beat them about once every thirty-seven years. Scott picked up the six of us before Sandy like he was putting off death, but it wasn't that he didn't like Sandy; he was scared of her.

When we got to the dance the girls acted like they didn't have dates. They danced the lindy hop together because we didn't know how, and it seemed they spent half the night in the girl's lavatory. Lola and I danced a few times and she only danced with Tom once, like they were taking it easy before the big formal. Afterwards we ate at the drive-in and drove around for a while, but with the cuckoo combination of couples and his bashfulness around Sandy, I knew there was a better chance of Scott driving over Minnehaha Falls than parking.

"Let's go knock on that crazy guy's door," Sandy said.

"Naw, it's too late . . . He'd be sound asleep . . . Not tonight," we chimed in.

Steve turned to the girls. "You ever pull a trolley?"

"Nooo, that sounds super," Lola said, "let's do it."

"What if we get caught?" Jean said. "Will we go to jail?"

"No-o-o-o," Steve said and laughed. "But you might get dragged home to your parents."

"If my dad found out I was pulling trolleys," I said, "I'd be safer in jail."

"Does it hurt anything?" Sandy said.

"Naw," Jerry said, "they just hook it up and drive away."

"Let's do it," Sandy said and everyone went for it.

Scott swung over to Grand and spotted a Grand-Mississippi.

"Oh, no you don't," I said. "If we're going to pull a trolley, go over to Selby or Snelling. This is my dad's line."

Scott headed for Selby and the girls acted like we were going to Hollywood or something.

"I don't see why pulling that rope makes the streetcar stop," Jean said.

"It pulls the trolley off the cable," Steve said.

"There's a grooved wheel that runs along the electric cable," I said, "and that's where the streetcar gets its power. It's like unplugging your toaster."

"Then why have the rope?" Sandy said.

"It runs down to a spring-loaded reel that rolls up the rope if the trolly comes off the cable, keeps it from tearing down the cross wires," I said. "They call it a retriever."

"Sounds like a dog," Steve said.

"You really know all about them, don't you," Lola said like she was impressed.

"I ought to," I said, "I've heard it eleven million times."

"Nifty!" Sandy said, "but we're all in skirts."

"You can run faster in skirts than we can in pants," Steve said.

"It sounds kind of scary," Jean said.

"That's what makes it fun," Lola said, snapping her gum.

"Some guys won't chase you," Jerry said, "but others will come like gangbusters."

"My dad chases every kid who pulls his trolley like they were Nazis or something," I said and I started feeling like a traitor.

Over on Selby we found a lonesome-looking streetcar coming from downtown, and Scott barreled ahead a couple of blocks and parked near a stop sign. We all bailed out and crouched behind a parked truck, laughing and roughhousing, waiting for the streetcar to come to a full stop. Then Scott and Sandy dashed out as the streetcar began to move.

"Grab the rope!" Scott yelled, "grab the rope."

They were laughing so hard they couldn't run too fast and Sandy tried to grab the rope as she ran, but the streetcar took off and Sandy couldn't hang on.

"Aw, phooey, I almost had it," Sandy said as we piled into the car.

Scott highballed down to Cleveland, a few blocks ahead of our target. It was Lola's turn, and I hid behind a parked car with her. I grabbed her hand and ran with her and we reached the back of the streetcar as it was starting in motion. Lola grabbed for the rope, barely able to reach it, and hung on for a moment, running along as the streetcar picked up speed.

"I've got it," she shouted.

"Pull!" I yelled, "pull!"

Gee, I wanted to grab it with her, grab it for her, she was so gorgeous—running, reaching up, her arms over her head, straining to pull the rope—like a little girl who needed help and protection. To heck with the streetcar, I wanted to wrap my arms around her and kiss her in the middle of the street.

Lola couldn't keep up and she let go and stopped under a streetlight, panting like she couldn't catch her breath.

"Oh, darn, it wouldn't pull," she said.

"You just about had it, he took off too fast."

I put my arm around her and helped her carry her disappointment back to our cheering friends.

We had to chase the streetcar over the Lake Street bridge into Minneapolis, but Jean Daley did it, the shortest of the girls. She had to leap to reach the rope, and when she got ahold of it, her feet came off the ground and she dangled with all her weight and by accident jerked the trolley from the cable and the streetcar blinked out on the tracks as Jean settled to the street.

"Run," Steve shouted. "Run!"

Without a plan, they ran in opposite directions. Steve hop-scotched it to the left of the streetcar, the safe side, while Jean took off to the right, the side the doors were on. A potbellied conductor bombed out the front doors and spotted Jean ripping across someone's lawn. The guy was so surprised to find a girl pulling his trolley, he didn't chase her. And besides, he probably didn't want anyone seeing him running after a girl in the middle of the night and I was betting he'd never tell the other conductors that a girl had nailed his streetcar.

I went along with the fun and horseplay even though I was feeling lousy about Lola. Some of the time I could forget about it while we went gunning for danger and excitement, but it wouldn't go away, and it came blasting full force when we called it quits and began dropping off the girls. It wasn't any fun anymore, being with her like that, a store-front dummy who she must have thought was so dedicated to his friend that he didn't have a life of his own. Couldn't she tell how I felt about her? The Gant Escort Service was going out of business. I loved her too much to go on pretending that I loved her.

Before I could snap on the light, I realized my father was sitting at the kitchen table.

"Just having a glass of milk," he said.

"Oh . . . hi." There was no glass that I could see.

In his pajamas and robe, my father didn't seem so strong or sure of himself, like he was worn down and his bravery was hanging in the closet with his motorman's uniform. I hardly ever saw him in P.J.s, except when he was sick, and I decided not to snap on the light. I left the back hall light on and I felt awkward standing there alone with him in the shadows.

"You hungry?" he said.

"A little."

I found a bottle of milk among the leftovers in the icebox and fetched a glass in the cupboard and I realized I was moving real slow and careful and it felt like there wasn't enough air in the room. My mother had explained my dad's gloomy moods as the dreads. All Norwegians get them she told me. I always wondered what it was my father dreaded.

"You going to have a carrot?"

"No, just some milk," I said.

"Your mother can't figure out where the carrots go."

My dad had never waited up for me. Could he possibly know that his son had been pulling trolleys on the Selby-Lake line? Jeez, I started growing guilt like mold on old cheese and I stood drinking the milk as the kitchen closed in on me. For my dad to be sitting up at this hour of the night had to be plenty serious.

"How was your date?" he asked.

"Oh . . . okay."

I wanted to tell him how much I loved Lola Muldoon.

"What did you do?"

Cripes, here it came. I could feel the blood rushing to my face and my hands were sweating, and it was lucky the kitchen was dark because with the light on he'd have me dead to rights.

"We went to a dance, but the girls goofed off most of the night. Then we went to get something to eat and—"

"I'm going to lose my job."

I was off the hook; this had nothing to do with me. I drank the cold milk because I didn't know what to say.

"They're cutting eighty cars off the lines immediately and everyone's on probation. There's going to be no more street-cars. *No more streetcars.*"

Cripes, he said it with such a tone in his voice it sounded as incredible as if there'd be no more oxygen.

"When?"

"As fast as they bring in the buses."

"Why are they getting rid of them?"

"It's a crooked business. The streetcars could serve these cities for years to come. Someone's out to make a whole lot of money, and they don't give a damn about the people. We hear GM and Firestone are in on it, and Standard Oil. They're going to rip the soul out of the city."

The lump in my throat I'd carried home slid down and formed a four-pound tumor in my stomach. I almost never heard my father cuss, and that only seemed to make it more terrible, telling me man to man that we might be poor, maybe on welfare. It scared me to see my father so sad and beaten.

"I can work full-time," I said, "I can do lots of jobs."

"They'll probably keep me on until summer. You graduate, that's what this family needs most, getting that diploma. Then you'll be able to do a lot of things, go on to college, learn a profession, do something more than . . . drive a streetcar."

I slid into a chair across the table from him.

"I think I'd like driving a streetcar," I said.

I figured telling a white lie was all right if it helped someone feel better. From the corner of my eye I tried to catch a glimpse of my father's face but I couldn't in the darkness.

"Did you like driving a streetcar?" I didn't mean to put it in the past tense.

He didn't answer right away, stooped in the shadows.

"Yes . . . I always liked driving a streetcar . . . I figured I'd do it until they put me six feet under."

I couldn't believe it because there I was, hearing my dad talk about his feelings, something I'd never heard before, and it was like his dream blew up and I could feel a piece of shrapnel rip into my chest, and I was afraid that his life would end when they kicked him off the Grand-Mississippi line. I wanted to go around the table, over that scary ground that we never dared cross, and put my arms around him and tell him how much I loved him. Gosh, I wanted to do that so badly, but I didn't know what he'd make of it and I was afraid to try.

"You better hit the hay," he said.

I put the empty glass in the sink and felt like a dope because I was sure there was something I should say if I could only think of it.

"Good night, Dad."

"Good night."

I turned for my room like a deserter, leaving him sitting alone in the dark.

Chapter 19

Sandy sat next to me in home room and Miss Lornberg usually let us talk if we kept it down to a roar. With her saddle shoes on the bottom rung of my chair, Sandy made it official Tuesday morning.

"Lola asked Tom to the dinner-dance," she said and I could tell she was plenty mad.

"I know," I said and I tried to hide how much it hurt.

"I think it was real rotten of her, Bean. After all, she's been going out with you for a month now."

I was glad Sandy didn't know how phony I'd been.

The rest of the week I really had to bomb through the hall-ways. With Gretchen coming one way and Lola the other I was ducking into janitor's rooms and lavatories and freshman classes where teachers were looking at me like I'd lost my memory. I hurt too much to see Lola and I wanted to steer clear of Gretchen because I was afraid she'd have figured out a way for me to watch some terrible thing that was happening to her. Criminy, in the middle of my screwball life I wanted to concentrate on the upcoming conference game with Wilson. The games began to count in the standings, and I wanted to win the City Championship more than anything now. Lola would be at every game, and I'd ignore her as we beat the crap out of everybody.

Thursday night my mother called me to the phone and I dragged my sore body into the kitchen figuring it was Steve.

"Hi, Cal, this is Katie, Katie Mills."

"Oh . . . hello . . ." I was clearing my throat like a thirteen year old.

"I'm calling to ask if you'd like to go to the dinner-dance with me?"

Holy Moses! I never thought that when the word was out that Lola wasn't asking me there might be other girls who would. In the sweaty silence, I wondered what Steve would think? Could I suggest that Katie call him? Crumb, Steve was in love with her and I didn't know what to do and I didn't have time to think.

"Sure . . . ah, yeah, I guess so. Thanks . . ."

"That's wonderful, Cal. I'll talk to you at school about it. How was practice?"

"Practice?"

I was still trying to figure out what was happening.

"Your mom said you were late at practice."

"Oh, yeah . . . it was okay."

"I hope you can beat Wilson tomorrow," she said, and I was so muddled by then I'd almost forgotten about the game. After we yakked for another uncomfortable minute, Katie was off the line, and I was really mixed up.

Katie was the kind of girl you wished God made more of, a tall blonde junior with an athletic body and really popular, and I felt pretty good that she had asked me. I'd forget about Lola, but I worried about Steve and hoped he'd understand and wondered if life was always this screwed up.

Friday night Hamline field house was jammed, and when we warmed up at one end of the floor, we gawked at the two overgrown kids at the other end in Wilson uniforms. Jeez, they had Paul Bunyan at six foot seven playing center and Goliath at six foot five playing forward and our tallest player was Scott at six foot three. My mouth felt like sawdust and my stomach was jumping all over the place.

In the first half we stayed with them by using a hustling zone defense and sagging everyone in on the two big kids and we were only down 30–26 at half-time. In the second half the coach had us go full-court press, and though the two big men weren't getting the ball as much, we lost three starters with five fouls; Jerry fouled out in the third quarter.

With three minutes to play, Wilson was ahead 50–47 and everyone in the field house was standing. Jeez, it was like a fire drill with the building burning down and everyone ripping around with their arms in the air and I wasn't even thinking but just doing what came to me. I got a lay-up beating my man off the dribble and another on a give-and-go from Rick and I was fouled. When I tossed in the under-handed free throw we were ahead, 52–51.

Wilson fought its way up the court against our press and tied the game with a free throw. With thirty-seven seconds on the clock the Wilson players were ragging us all over the place. I got a bounce-pass into Rick and he spun around Paul Bunyan and canned a nifty shot off the backboard. Before Wilson could get the ball inbounds the buzzer went off and I couldn't believe it! We'd won!

Everybody went nuts. We hugged and hooted and fans came piling onto the court, shouting and cheering like crazy. I was getting congratulated and slapped on the back by tons of kids and I was trying to spot my dad in the crowd. Then, out of the mob, Lola hugged me with both her arms around my neck.

"You were great!" she shouted. "We beat Wilson!"

"Yeah, thanks," I yelled and I didn't hug her back because I was dripping with sweat and I fought my way into the locker room.

We showered and dressed and the field house was almost empty when I came out of the locker room. Most of the players had a girlfriend waiting, and Jerry's dad hustled over to me.

"Terrific game, Cal, terrific! You really came through when it counted."

"Thanks, Mr. Douglas."

He was a stocky guy with curly black hair who looked like he could play professional football, and when he slapped me on the back, I almost punched him on the shoulder.

"Come on, you can drive," Jerry said, trying to persuade me to go with them in his carload of couples.

"Naw, I'm tired. I'm going home and hit the sack."

I was really beat riding the Snelling streetcar home and I missed being with my buddies. I tried to remember details about the game and a lot of it was a blur, but I could feel Lola's breasts hard against my chest and there was nothing phony about her hug. Gosh, I loved playing the game but I wished my father had been there to see us win.

With school out for the holidays, Mr. Finley kept me busy. But people sure ate more around Christmas, and they drank a whole lot more, too. I stopped at the liquor store and picked up orders and tried to figure out when Sid was looking at me. After our great start, we should've been practicing hard. No practice for two weeks seemed dangerous and stupid and I thought maybe Coach Mulligan didn't want to bother, but the papers had us picked to win the City Championship after knocking off the tallest team in the Twin Cities.

I got into the habit of driving the alley behind the bakery around noon to see if Gretchen was working and on Thursday I caught her out in back in her refugee coat. I pulled in through the wet snow and rolled down the window.

"Hi, has your dad been around?"

She really lit up when she saw me.

"No, he's at work," she told me and she stepped right up to the truck. "I was hoping you would come."

"I've looked for you every day," I said.

I smiled, surprised at how glad I was that I'd found her.

"We're going up north for Christmas, I won't be back until school starts."

"Will it be better for you there, with other people around?"

Her face turned sad.

"No, maybe worse, our relatives have cabins they rent, but no one rents them this time of year; they'll be empty, and . . ."

She stared at the slush around her clodhoppers.

"Oh . . . Gosh, I hope it will be all right."

I was thinking fast about how I could cheer her up and I

spotted the Nut Goodie I was saving for after lunch and its red and green wrapper even looked like Christmas.

"I brought you something," I said and I handed her the candy bar.

She lit up like I'd given her a gold watch or something.

"For me?" she said and she glanced into my eyes. "I'll have to eat it right away."

She unwrapped it and started chomping like a beaver cutting willows.

"I dreamed about you last night," she said with her mouth full.

"You did?"

"Yes, I dreamed you killed my father."

I looked away and I didn't know what to think. Every time she started acting normal she pulled something like that.

"You ran over him in the grocery truck when he was chasing me, and when I woke up I cried because I wanted it to be true so badly, and I know God will punish me for wanting it to be true."

She finished the candy and stuffed the wrapper in a garbage can and looked off into the sky over the roof of the truck.

"I want to thank you for trying to help me." Her voice sounded like she never planned on seeing me again.

"Listen, when you get back I'll–"

"I have to go in now. Good-bye, Cal."

She hurried to the back door like she was catching a train. Then she turned and gazed through the windshield into my face and *smiled*. It blasted me like getting hit by madman Fred Walker in tackling drills and it was like she turned into a different girl with a normal, happy face.

"Thanks for the present, Cal, Merry Christmas," she called and she ducked into the bakery.

I just sat there like I'd seen a smile from a graveyard or something, and even though I didn't know what to make of it, I knew that Gretch the Wretch had more guts than I'd ever have if I lived sixty-three lifetimes.

"Merry Christmas, Gretchen," I said and I started the truck.

Chapter 20

We always opened our presents on Christmas Eve, but before we could, we had to get through a meal of oyster stew and lutefisk. Gad, have you ever seen lutefisk? It looks like King Kong blew his nose on your plate and it smells like a wolverine crawled under our davenport and died a month ago. And the oyster stew was kind of a milky soup with butter floating on it and it looked like leftovers from the sewage plant and I always expected something to poke its head out and spit at me.

I didn't know how Norwegians could eat lutefisk or why they ever invented it but they must've run out of food crossing the ocean and forgotten about a barrel of fish they had stashed somewhere, and when they found it, the fish had rotted, but they were starving so they gobbled it up and thought it tasted pretty good. Jeez, why couldn't we have been Chinese or something so we could have chop suey on Christmas. My mother made lefsa and that was good, but you couldn't soak up any lutefisk to get rid of it with lefsa. We always had to eat what was put in front of us so I was pretty good at smuggling stuff like Lima beans or Brussels sprouts into my napkin and then into a pocket, but you sure couldn't sneak a gob of slime into your pocket.

I'd look at my sister and we'd both make a face like we were throwing up. I don't know why my parents did that because we didn't do anything else Norwegian, like ski to school or raise Norwegian elk hounds. I don't like to complain, but I never knew why we had to eat rotten fish on Christmas Eve.

After the meal it was basically a pretty happy time and we were all having fun unwrapping presents around the tree. I got a package I knew was from my dad because my mother put in a lot of time wrapping hers but my dad just rolled his in Christmas paper and slapped on a little Scotch tape. It was a box but it was too heavy for clothes. When I ripped off the paper I couldn't believe it; a carton of Nut Goodies. How did he know I loved them? My parents didn't let us eat much candy and I never let on when I did. I couldn't figure if he just made a lucky guess or if he knew more than I thought. I slipped when I thanked him and told him they were my favorite although we'd been taught to say any gift we got was our favorite, even if it was orange underwear. Then my father unwrapped a crescent wrench imprinted with those words that made him boil: MADE IN JAPAN. I was afraid the happy mood would drain out of our Christmas Eve.

"If I've told you once, I've told you a thousand times, Lurine, don't buy *anything* made in Japan!" He held the wrench out and shook it. "They don't know how to make anything but junk and never will. You might as well throw the money away."

An American-made wrench like that would cost four times as much, and she'd given in to her depression-years habit and gone for the cheapest.

"I can take it back," she said. "I kept the slip."

My dad took a deep breath and set the wrench on the floor.

"Well, we won't hear McCluskey's dog tonight," he said.

"Why not?" Peggy said.

"I suppose that brute lets him in the house at Christmas," my mother said, still looking glum over the wrench.

"He doesn't have the dog anymore," my dad said. "I called the Humane Society."

"Oh, good, Daddy," Peggy said.

"I thought you didn't want trouble," my mother said. "You said you could lose your job if we stuck our nose in."

"I know, I know, but I couldn't let that dog suffer anymore."

"What did they do?" I said.

"They took the dog. They called me back and told me they'd found a good home for him. He's probably curled up under some Christmas tree right now with his belly full."

"That's swell, Daddy," my sister said and she ran over and hugged him and I could tell my dad was happy. He'd blasted one of his bad moods before it got a grip on him and when my mother gathered up a bunch of wrapping paper to save for next year, she snatched the crescent wrench and got it out of sight like she wasn't taking any chances. Even though no one said so, we probably would've all agreed that the news about McCluskey's dog was the best present of the night and what my dad did, risking his job and all, convinced me that I had to do the same for Gretchen, no matter what, that I couldn't let her suffer anymore.

We always went to the midnight candlelight service and in the dark sanctuary, when all the candles were lit and we sang "Silent Night," I prayed that somehow I could forget about Lola. I'd tried, usually making it about three minutes before some word or thought would make me remember her. I wanted to cut down to only thinking about her eleven million times a day.

My parents gave me a phonograph, and the first chance I got I bought a bunch of records, mostly Frank Sinatra. With the phonograph next to my bed, I'd put on a stack and listen while I fell asleep and every song seemed to be about Lola and me.

The big night came and Katie and I rode to the St. Paul Hotel for the dinner-dance with Scott and Sandy. All the guys wore double-breasted suits and wide ties and most of the girls looked terrific in formals, though some of the dresses were kind of drippy, like one girl looked like she was in a big lamp shade and another looked like her mother made the dress out of the living room drapes. Some jackass put Katie and me at the same table with Tom and Lola and even though there were ten people at each of the round tables, I knew I wouldn't last two minutes sitting by Lola.

Jeez, she had her hair up on top of her head with a white

orchid and she wore a white strapless formal and when I first saw her I could hardly breathe and we switched places with Jerry and Sally at a table across the ballroom. The strapless gowns on some girls looked like they might slide right down to their waist with nothing to stop them, but not Lola's, Criminy, not Lola's.

The ritzy ballroom was all decorated romantic and everything, and Katie looked terrific in a light blue formal with bare shoulders and I knew busloads of boys would have pulled eyeteeth to be with her and there I was feeling like I was on a chain gang.

I did everything I could to stay as far from Lola and Tom as possible, but in the hall, on the way to the men's room, I almost bumped into her when she came out of the ladies' room.

"Hi, Cal, I'm glad to see you here tonight."

"Why?"

"You miss out on so much, not having a girlfriend."

"What do you care?"

"I just mean you ought to have more fun . . . it's our senior year and everything."

"You seem to know all about it," I said and I could tell she was surprised at my attitude.

"I've gotten to know Katie in Debs, she's a swell girl, you ought to latch on to her."

"Who made you the expert on romance?"

"No one. I just thought—"

"You don't know anything!" I said. "You don't even know when someone's in love with *you!*"

Gosh, I could feel the blood in my face and we both stood there and looked at each other like we didn't believe what we just heard. Then I stomped into the men's room.

After that I was kind of numb and I faked it through the rest of the dance. We ate at the Rainbow Cafe, half-way across Minneapolis, and I thanked Katie at her door and almost kissed her I was so mad, and I hoped she didn't notice what a dork I'd been. When Scott dropped me at the apartment, I felt I'd been left out of the human race and I told myself I'd forget about her.

Spit on it! A lot of people walk around with a big hole in their chest. I could do it with the best of them. Look at Steve. Somehow I thought that having polio would be easier than being hopelessly in love with Lola Muldoon.

Chapter 21

Thursday night I bombed over to Goodrich to see if
Gretchen had come back. I really missed seeing all the kids
with school out and it was like the world stopped or something. I shoveled a lot of snow and delivered groceries and
some of the team sneaked in the old gym at Fort Snelling to
play basketball a few afternoons. I thought I ought to ask
Katie out at least once to be polite, but I didn't want to make
Steve feel bad.

There weren't any lights in Gretchen's house and the sidewalk wasn't shoveled so I went around through the alley and
walked into the backyard. The big oak tree was the kind that
kept its dead leaves until spring and I grabbed the lower
branch with my leather mittens and pulled myself up the
trunk, climbing until I was level with the second-story
dormer. I peered into the window and I couldn't tell for sure
but it seemed that the curtains were open and I was staring
into the darkness of Gretchen's life.

Like a little kid I sat in the crook of the tree and I realized
that no one in the house would be able to see me behind the
thick trunk and leaves but I could see whatever went on in
that room. Shivers ran down my legs when I thought about
what that might be and I remembered Gretchen's words You
have to *see* it. I perched in the big oak for a while, trying to
come up with some way I could help her, but I started
freezing my buns off and I slid out of the tree and took off
for home.

New Year's Eve my parents went to bed around ten as if my
father dreaded the coming year. Tom was having a party at
his house, but I still felt pretty lousy about not going to the
dinner-dance with Lola and I sure didn't want to start the

New Year watching those two together or be reminded of what a sap I'd been. I made Peggy beg me about seventy-three times before I said I'd play rummy with her. Darn, I knew all my friends would be at Tom's and I'd be sitting at home with my little sister!

Peggy and I made popcorn and drank root beer and played at the kitchen table while we waited for midnight and she could tell I wasn't about to bust out singing.

"Are you feeling sorry for yourself, Cal?"

"I don't know . . . I guess so."

If anyone else had asked, I'd have denied it, said I was fine. She picked up a seven and stuck it in her hand.

"Mom says we aren't supposed to feel sorry for ourselves, just for other people."

"I know," I said and I discarded a queen.

"I feel sorry for myself sometimes," she said. "You know what I do?"

She picked up the queen and laid down three of them.

"What?"

"I just say Spit on it!"

Around eleven someone knocked on the back door. When I opened it, Steve stood there, out of breath and his hair mussed like he'd been gimping pretty fast.

"Jerry said you were home," Steve said in his booming voice.

"Yeah, but not so loud; my parents are asleep."

I guessed he'd been drinking.

"What are you doing?" Steve asked, all excited.

"Playing rummy with my sister." I backed into the kitchen. Steve stepped in and shut the door behind him.

"Oh, swell," he said. "Hi, Peg."

He seemed to calm down a couple notches when he saw her.

"Hi," she said, "do you want to play rummy?"

"That'd be hunky-dory."

Steve planted himself at the table next to Peggy and I could tell she was proud that he wanted to play with her and she shuffled the cards with a big smile on her kisser.

"Where did you see Jer?" I asked as I sat with them.

"At Tom's."

"Are there many kids there?"

"Yeah, the house was jammed."

I could tell that neither of us wanted to talk about Tom's party and I guessed that Katie must be there with someone, too. We played for almost an hour and Peggy was thrashing us and I figured Steve was slyly discarding whatever Peggy was saving.

"Does your leg hurt you much?" Peggy asked.

"No, only if I run around too much."

"I sure hope I don't get polio," she said.

I wanted to tell her to pipe down.

"You won't, you're a good kid," Steve said. He studied his hand. "I quit hockey."

"Quit!" I said. "How come?"

"The coach plays me 'cause he's afraid people will think he's a bum if he doesn't. The players don't say anything, but I'm losing games for them. Hermanson's a better goalie than I am."

"I'll bet you're the best goalie they have," Peggy said.

"Don't *quit,"* I said. "It's not just the goalie that loses games. Maybe he can use both of you, switch you around."

"No . . . as long as I'm on the team he'll think he has to play me. I'm tired of hockey anyway."

I knew he was lying; he loved playing hockey.

"I wish you'd keep playing, Steve," Peggy said and I sure liked my little sister right then.

When it was about eleven forty-five, Steve bounced up like he'd just remembered something.

"I gotta go."

"Aren't you going to stay till midnight?" Peggy said.

"Naw, I gotta go. Thanks for the popcorn and stuff."

He ducked out the door and was gone.

We hung on until the stroke of midnight and 1950 came in quietly for us.

"Cal . . . 1949 can never come back, ever," Peggy said.

She went to bed a few minutes later, thinking it was a pretty big deal to welcome in a new year, and I felt like hugging her but I didn't. Just as I snapped off the light in the kitchen I heard a knock at the back door. Steve? I went to the door in stocking feet and my shirt pulled out and all unbuttoned. Sandy was standing there like she'd just fallen off a bridge.

"Hi, Bean, can I talk to you a minute?"

"Yeah, sure."

She stepped into the kitchen, her face streaked with tears.

"What's the matter?" I said, and she slumped into a chair.

"You're my best friend, Bean, you've always been, and I feel so bad. I was at Tom's and Scott showed up with *Katie*."

"Oh, gosh . . . I'm sorry . . . maybe *she* asked him."

"No, I found out, *he* asked her. I thought we had so much fun at the dinner-dance together, and then, just four days later . . ."

I sat at the table, and when she pulled off a new leather glove and saw her chewed fingernails, she slipped it back on.

"Remember how your tongue was stuck to the fence?" she said.

"Oh, golly, yeah, I'll never forget how—"

"That's how it feels, only it's my heart. I need someone to pour bean soup over my heart so it won't be stuck on Scott."

"Boy, I wish I could, Sand."

"I wish you could, too, it really hurts, it really hurts."

I sat there like a door nail and couldn't come up with any happiness stuff and I felt like waking my mom. Then Sandy perked up a little.

"When I was downtown last week I saw a lady who looked just like me and I went up to her and told her I was adopted."

"What did she say?"

"She said that was nice, that she and her husband thought of adopting once, but then they had four kids of their own."

I wondered if she'd ever thought that her real mom and dad might be dead, but I didn't say anything.

"Do you think there's something wrong with me?" she said.

"Heck, no, there's nothing wrong with you, what do you mean?"

"Why didn't my real mother or father keep me?"

Jeez, people were always asking me questions I couldn't answer and I felt like I was flunking Life, and she must've thought Scott didn't like her because there was something basically wrong with her like a big ugly wart or something.

"I don't know," I said, "maybe they were poor and couldn't feed you and buy you clothes and things and they wanted you to have a good life or something."

"I wouldn't have eaten much, Bean, I didn't need much."

It got so quiet in the kitchen it was like the world had run out of answers and I couldn't look at her.

"I've got to get home," she said and she was gone.

Lying in bed, I wished I could have done something for her and I was feeling pretty lousy and I worried about the coming year, the year we'd graduate and scatter, the year Jerry and I would join the Navy, the year when everything would change. The papers kept blabbing about the tidal wave of Communism conquering the world and it was always saying that an atomic war was going to wipe out the whole human race like the guy writing it was happy about it or something. Sometimes I tried to imagine what it would be like to get fried by an atom bomb and it was scary. With my father's job hanging by a thread, and Gretchen more and more scared that she'd go crazy, it was no wonder I worried sometimes. But even with all of that, I still kept thinking about Lola. In a roundabout way I'd told her I loved her at the dinner-dance and I couldn't help wonder what she'd do about that.

I felt good when I scrambled in the door at school and heard everyone yakking and slamming lockers and laughing like life had started again and everything was okay. I wanted to see if

Gretchen made it back and I zipped into the basement and shoved my way through the hallway where kids were stuffing coats in their lockers and hanging around for the first bell. Up ahead I spied her standing by her locker, staring into it while a bunch of boys were looking at her and laughing. As I got closer it looked like most of them were freshmen or sophomores.

"Hey, Gretch, wanna go to the dog show with me? We could win," I heard one of the kids say, showing off for his buddies, and they hooted and poked each other. In the hubbub of the crowded hallway, no one noticed me and I stood there for a minute like I couldn't believe it.

"Where do you buy your clothes, cutey, in Poland?"

Gretchen just kept looking into her locker.

"Arf, arf, arf. Here, Gretch, here, girl," one boy said and patted his leg. That did it!

I curled a fist and was ready to give the kid a fat lip, but on the spur of the moment, I shoved my way through the circle and acted like I hadn't noticed them.

"Hi, Gretchen, ready to go?"

When she heard my voice, she turned and looked at me like I'd dropped in from the moon.

"Hi," she said, and she glanced at the kids around her like she was ashamed to have me see what was going on.

"Let me carry your books," I said and I held out my hand.

She was as blasted as the little pricks who were picking on her, and she handed me her binder and social studies. The kids stood there with their mouths hanging open and I knew they recognized me. They'd probably cheered their guts out at the Wilson game and I remembered how I looked up to a senior athlete when I was a freshman. They glanced sideways at each other like they'd been caught with their pants down and none of them knew what to do with his hands or face. Gretchen closed her locker, and the circle opened for us to pass.

Some of the jerks slunk away into the crowded hall and

others began making excuses to each other, and I got a bang out of it because I could see in their eyes that they were wondering how in the heck a dog like Gretchen Luttermann could have one of the jocks of the senior class carrying her books. I took her arm and escorted her up to front hall where she'd be safe for a while.

"Does that happen often?" I said.

"Sometimes."

I was surprised that anyone at Central would be that mean to her. Golly, I knew that behind her back some kids called her Gretch the Wretch, but no one said it in front of her, did they? None of the kids I knew would.

"How was it for you up north," I said, "with your dad and everything?"

She didn't look at me. "Oh . . . I don't know."

Jeez, the way she said it scared me, like she'd given up and she was thinking about going crazy. Right then I knew I couldn't put off doing something any longer. I'd let it slide, hoping for some big miracle, hoping some adults would notice her and step in and do something. What was wrong with everybody? Were they all blind? I watched her head off for her home room and then I hustled for mine, thinking about how close I came to hitting that kid and realizing I could have been kicked out of school.

That afternoon practice was lousy and we tripped and fumbled all over the gym and I knew we should've been practicing like mad all through vacation. Only two more practices before the Washington game and we were being touted as the team to beat for the City Championship and Mulligan kept us running twenty minutes over as if that would make up for laying off for two weeks. It was late when we finished showering, but I had Jerry drop me at Lacher's Drugstore and I was dead set on making the call before I went home.

From the phone booth in the drugstore—in case they could trace the call—I dialed the police and I couldn't keep my hand from shaking.

"Police department, Sergeant Thompson," a man's deep voice answered.

"I know a man who beats his daughter."

"You want to make a complaint?"

"Yeah, sorta."

"Just a minute," Thompson said and went off the line.

I waited and my stomach was squirming.

"Sergeant Riley speaking. Can I help you?" a younger, gruff voice asked and I almost hung up.

"I want to tell someone about a guy who beats his daughter."

"Okay, go ahead. Who am I talking to?"

"I can't say."

I was scared stiff and I started feeling like *I'd* done something wrong just talking to the cop.

"Well, who's the man who beats his daughter?" Riley said.

"I can't tell you."

"Listen, if this is a prank—"

"No, please, it isn't a prank. I can't tell you his name unless you promise you'll lock him up. Otherwise he'll hurt her real bad."

"Okay, okay, tell me about him."

"He beats her, but she's so afraid of him she'll never tell anyone, and he's careful not to leave bruises, or to keep her home until they heal up. I've seen some of the marks on her legs."

"Anything else?"

"I think he does bad things to her."

"Like what?"

"Bad things, like, touching her and . . . and, you know, sex things."

I had my hand on the lever, ready to hang up in a second.

"How do you know, did she tell you this?"

"No, not exactly, but she's afraid she'll have a baby."

I couldn't think of anything more to say. Darn, it didn't seem like much on the phone.

"Listen . . . what did you say your name was?"

"Ca . . . I didn't, I can't." Riley was clever.

"Okay, whoever you are, I know you want to help, but you've got to give me this guy's name. I promise, we'll just keep an eye on him. If what you say is true, we can nab him and lock him up, but from what you've given me, we can't do anything. Can't lock a man up and then check into it, you can see that. Get this girl to come to us. Can you do that?"

"No, she'd never dare. Even if you lock him up for a while, she's sure he'll get her when he gets out. I've never seen anyone so scared." I didn't know how far I dared to go. "Her sister told the police once, but they didn't believe her. Then he did something real bad to her, and she went crazy, ended up in an insane asylum. I won't give you his name unless you promise you'll protect her."

Darn, the more I thought about Gretchen the madder I got, and I wasn't as scared to talk to the cops.

"Listen, fella, you think about it. My name's Sergeant Riley. I'm on from three until midnight, Tuesday through Saturday. Give me his name and we'll check him out, quietly. He'll never know it unless we have something to arrest him for."

Riley sounded like a good guy and I wanted to trust him, but it was Gretchen's pain I was gambling with, and maybe, I was starting to believe, her life.

"All right, I'll think about it, thanks a lot. Good-bye."

I hung up and hustled out of the drugstore. Did Riley keep me on the phone to trace the call? I pulled my jacket collar up against the cold and ran along Fairview for home, expecting squad cars to come screeching up to the drugstore with cops piling out. I kept looking back down the street to the intersection in front of Lacher's, but when I turned up the alley two blocks away, no cop cars had showed up.

Chapter 22

A blizzard blasted into St. Paul on Tuesday and my mother
drummed me out of bed early to shovel the walk. I caught a
ride to school before the worst of it and all day, as snow piled
up on the window sills, I racked my brain for some way I
could help Gretchen, not only to get her away from her
father, but something quick to keep her from giving up and
going crazy. The only time I could do anything with her was
school time, and what could I do during classes? Then
Sandy's genius popped into my head. If she could get me out
of class anytime, that had to go for Gretchen too, and if I
could talk Gretchen into it, I'd take her out of school, go
downtown, no, that would scare her, too close to her father.
Downtown Minneapolis, that would be like the other side of
the world.

I brought up the idea in study hall before the bell, like it
was just something I was thinking about.

"You'll be back in plenty of time to be waiting for your
father on the curb, an hour early if you want."

"Oh, no, I wouldn't dare." She shook her head. "No, no, I
couldn't, I couldn't."

"Just think about it, that's all, just think about it. We'll go to
Minneapolis."

"Oh, but what if he caught me?"

"He could never catch us, he'll be at work. There's millions
of people in Minneapolis, and we'll have fun."

The city shoveled out and the team showed up at Hamline
field house Thursday night, but so did the Washington Rice
Streeters. We played them even for three quarters and took
the lead, 30–28, but with the long lay-off, it seemed we'd lost
the toughness we'd shown in the Wilson game, like the team

didn't want to win as much as Washington did, and in the fourth quarter we missed shots and didn't rebound and they beat us, 45–40.

When I tried to get to sleep that night I felt terrible and I kept thinking about how rotten we played. We should've beaten those dickfaces by ten points or more. I tried to look at it like I was growing up or something. Cripes, what difference did it make if we lost one lousy basketball game compared to what Gretchen was going through every day. But as I lay there wide awake and Sinatra crooned "I'll Never Smile Again," I recognized how much I hated losing. I hated losing the game and I hated losing Lola and I hated that my dad might lose his job, and darn it, I'd find a way to help Gretchen because I wasn't going to lose at that.

I met Gretchen outside her home room on Tuesday before first period and walked to her locker. When she opened it she froze, panicked, and I could see in her eyes how afraid she was.

"He'll find out, he'll beat me."

She scared me because she could be right and I'd be to blame and I just about gave up, but I knew if I could get her out of there it would be good for her, so I blackmailed her and I felt lousy about it.

"If we don't go now, we *will* get in trouble," I said. "All the passes have been delivered, you can't go to your classes, we have to get out of here or your dad *will* hear about it."

She looked at me and bit her lip like we were going off to war or something and then she pulled on her coat and tied on an ugly gray head scarf like she'd made up her mind. I figured we better leave the building one at a time in case a teacher glanced from a window and recognized us taking off together. I sent her first and watched as she crossed Marshall and I knew she'd be scared to death, expecting her father to come wheeling out of the traffic at any second. When she turned up Dunlap, I beat it across the parking lot and caught up to her and we piled on a Selby-Lake streetcar.

She hunched down in the seat like I hadn't paid her fare.

"I've never been to Minneapolis," she said.

"You'll like it."

We crossed the river into Minneapolis and little by little she gazed out the window at the sights and I hoped she'd forget herself. In that awful coat and scarf and with her starving face, I noticed people looking out of the corner of their eyes like they were Sid's relatives. Even though she wore the penny loafers she still stuck out like an oddball.

Sandy had distributed the phony passes and it seemed the most logical to forge Coach Mulligan's name on mine so the teachers would think it was something to do with basketball. Sandy promised she wouldn't tell anyone and I knew I could trust her, but she looked at me like I was a little nutty that morning when I was actually going through with it, cutting classes all day and taking Gretch the Wretch on a holiday to Minneapolis.

At Hennepin we'd transfer onto a streetcar going downtown. I held her hand as we crossed the street to wait, not like I'd hold Lola's hand, but more like you'd hold the hand of a kid who might get lost or step into the street and get run over. Rolling downtown in the cozy streetcar, with its faint electric smell, she started taking in everything around her like she felt safe, rocking gently with the motion of the trolley, hearing the thump thump thump of the air-brake motor like it was a friendly heartbeat. She looked at the other people, the Burma Shave sign overhead, and the buildings and sights we passed. She pointed out things with some excitement, and I smiled and nodded. I was feeling pretty happy about the way things were working out, and I thought it was as good a time as any to bring up my latest idea.

"Have you ever thought about running away from home?"

"Oh, nooo, he'd *find* me, he'd *catch* me. He'd have the *police* on me!"

"I'd help you. He'd never be able to find you, and if he couldn't find you, he couldn't hurt you anymore."

"Helga ran away once and he found her. He'd find me. I can never run away, *never*."

Her voice got louder with each word, and I was afraid everyone in Hennepin County would hear about my plan.

"Okay, shhhhhh, okay. I was just trying to think of something. Forget running away, I'll think of something else."

We got off downtown in the dirty snow and the streets were crammed with people and cars. I led her into a big Woolworth's Five & Dime and we wandered up and down the aisles. She stopped and looked at everything and picked up stuff like she'd never seen it before—sparkling jewelry, a pearl-handled mirror, ribbons in tons of colors, nail polish, lipsticks, bright metal compacts with rouge and tiny mirrors, and glimmering bottles of perfume, dirt cheap and pretty as punch.

She smiled and glanced at me now and then and I let her take her time. At the candy counter she couldn't make up her mind, and I bought a little of everything, but I had over six dollars with me so we didn't have to worry. She had a licorice twist in her mouth like a cigar when I led her across the street to Dayton's, the big cheese department store of Minneapolis, and I figured she'd forgotten about her father and her lousy life for a little while.

We browsed through the women's clothes department and once she glanced over at me, holding the sleeve of this beautiful yellow coat with a fur collar, not like she wanted it but like she just wanted to make sure I saw it. I couldn't believe how everything made such a big impression on her like she'd never been in a department store before, and when we wandered into the toy department she went bug-eyed over the dolls and stuffed animals and rows and rows of toys.

"Look at this, Cal . . . oh, Cal, look at this . . . listen, Cal."

I was having a ball spinning tops, cranking music boxes and popping up jack-in-the-boxes. A sour-faced saleswoman

watched us like we were shoplifting or something, but after
she saw the little-girl happiness that lit up Gretchen's face,
she backed off and left us alone. I wanted to buy her something but I knew she couldn't take it home. She hung on to a
boy doll with little overalls and a shirt even though she kept
on inspecting all the others. We slowly moved up and down
the aisles and she cuddled the chubby little doll and wouldn't
put it down.

"Would you like that?" I said to her and nodded at the doll.

"Oh, yes . . . but I can't . . ."

"You can keep it in your locker, like the loafers."

There was hope in her eyes and I bought the doll for a
dollar seventy-five and the saleswoman put it in a bag. With
time going like crazy, I had to drag her out of the toy
department.

We came out on Seventh Street and there was a cafeteria
where Gretchen pushed her tray along the chrome rail and
couldn't decide what to take with all the choices, about to
take one dish and then reneging for another. We loaded our
trays, not only with hamburgers and fries and onion rings
and Cokes, but with four different desserts. The lady cashier
raised her eyebrows when she saw our heap.

"We've been in Antarctica for a year," I said.

The woman acted like she believed me, and Gretchen
laughed! Gretchen laughed, and I felt like grabbing her and
twirling her around in front of the whole cafeteria. We carried
our trays to a table by a large window where we could watch
people hurrying through the noon hour, little puffs of frosty
breath sailing in front of their faces like cotton candy.
Gretchen ate a chocolate sundae and a piece of ice cream pie
before touching the other food, drank two bottles of Coke,
and after stuffing herself, came up for air and looked at me.

"Why did you tell her Antarctica?"

"I don't know, she thought we were starving," I said, and I
thought it was true. From some frozen and lifeless place,
Gretchen was starving.

"Why are you doing this?" she said.

"Doing what?"

"This . . . taking me to Minneapolis, all of this."

"Are you having fun?"

"Yes . . . more fun than I've ever had."

"That's why, you deserve to have lots of fun. Let's go."

I took her by the hand and we wove through the idling cars that jammed the street and bombed back into Dayton's where we rode the escalator on our way to the record department. She was a little surprised and afraid of the moving staircase and she giggled at the idea of it. I found "I'll Be Seeing You" by Frank Sinatra in the rack, and we settled into a booth to listen.

"Do you like his singing?" I asked and she nodded.

When the record ended I said, "What would you like to hear?"

"I don't know . . . love songs."

I picked out a stack, and she listened while she hugged the doll and stared at her loafers like she was thinking about something real hard. I wished I could know what she was thinking behind those skittish eyes and ducking face. Gad, she was kind of old for a doll, but maybe she never had one when she was little, maybe she was never allowed to be with other kids, and still she wanted love songs. We listened through the stack without talking, but time ran out on us and we had to get moving. After we used the rest rooms, we hit the elevators and she held her breath and gasped quietly when we stopped at each floor and we fell all the way to the basement. We got two chocolate malts from the cheerful lady tending the malt machine, ten cents apiece, and we boarded a Hennepin streetcar long before rush hour.

"How long has it been bad for you?" I said.

"Mostly since Helga went crazy. He didn't pay me much attention when Helga still lived with us."

She took the doll and held it like it was alive.

"Do you ever see Helga?"

"He took me up to Fergus Falls to see her once, said that's what would happen to me if I ever told anyone about him."

"Do you believe that?"

"Yes . . . that's why I made you promise . . . you can never tell anyone, Cal." The fear had come back into her voice.

"I promised, don't worry."

"Helga tried to tell on him. It was her word against his. My mother lied and told them Helga just made up a story. I wish my mother had told the truth, but she's too scared. If she was stronger, she could stop him, tell on him. The police told Helga if there were no witnesses, they couldn't do anything about it."

"That's terrible."

"Then he fixed her so she couldn't ever tell again."

Her voice trailed off, and when we crossed into St. Paul, she turned to look at the Mississippi, covered with ice and snow.

"How did he do that?" I said.

"He made her kill her baby, Little Jacob, only she wouldn't do it, so he made her hold him under water." Tears were running down her face and for the first time I could see that she was mad. "He put Little Jacob under water in the bathtub and held Helga's hands around him, and the baby fought and splashed and waved his tiny little hands and kicked his little feet. He wanted to live *so bad*, but he couldn't breathe, and then he drowned in Helga's hands." She knotted her fingers in her lap. "I *hate* my father! I know it's a sin, but I can't help it, I *hate him*."

She started crying and wiping her face on her coat sleeve.

"He said if Helga ever told on him, he'd tell them *she* killed the baby, and they'd hang her. After a while, she went crazy."

I sat there like I'd been kicked in the stomach and I couldn't understand how this awful stuff could happen right next door to my safe and normal life. It was so awful I still didn't know if I should believe her, but if Luttermann murdered a baby, there had to be a way to nail him, and it scared the bug juice out of me to think I might have to be the one to do it.

The closer we got to school, the more nervous she got.

"I want to tell you something else, but if he finds out I told anyone, he'll get me like he got Helga."

"I'll never tell anyone, I swear to God."

She glanced into my eyes. "The baby's in the freezer."

"In the *freezer!* Holy cow . . . why?"

"He said he'd keep it and if I ever told on him, he'd tell the police *I* killed the baby and they'd hang *me.*"

"Have you seen it?"

"No, I'm not allowed in the freezer, but I know it's there."

"Where's the freezer?"

"In the back entry, but you can *never ever* tell anyone."

"I promise."

After we scrambled the two blocks to school, Gretchen changed her shoes and socks at her locker and then she hugged the doll and set it in the locker real careful.

"I'll see you tomorrow," she said to it and shut the door. We waited for the bell and I stuck with her until she left the building with the rush of other kids.

"Thank you, Cal." She headed for the street.

I watched her walk away and I could hardly believe what I'd heard—a baby in the freezer! I could see her standing at the curb, waiting for her father, and I felt awful. I didn't know if the trip to Minneapolis made it easier for Gretchen or harder. Maybe by showing her a little of what she was missing it would make it worse for her. But at least I hoped it would keep her from going crazy until I could find a way to nail her father and dump his wagon for good. Until I did, Gretchen had to go home to a slaughterhouse.

Chapter 23

When I showed up for practice, coach Mulligan called me into his little office just off the gym. Shoot, what crummy luck. Miss Bellows had talked with Mulligan in the teachers' lounge and asked why he'd taken me out of her precious English class like the world would come to an end if I missed ten seconds of that stuff.

"I didn't think you were the kind of kid who'd pull something like that, Cal," the coach said. "I'm disappointed in you. Where were you?"

"Oh. . . just over at the drugstore."

"Who were you with?"

"No one."

Jeez, Mulligan looked at me like I had the word LIAR tattooed on my forehead and I hated lying to him, but how could I tell him where I'd been?

"You'll have seventh period for a week on the days we don't practice. Now get changed."

When I dressed for practice I felt lousy, knowing the coach would think I was some kind of a hood or something. I always wanted his respect and now I'd lost it, and it seemed to show in the coach's attitude during practice. I hoped none of my other teachers talked to him in the next few days and I prayed that my parents wouldn't find out. With my father in a lousy mood more and more, he'd make a federal case out of it while my mother hit the ceiling. I'd earn back Mulligan's respect by playing great basketball.

On my way home after practice, I thought about Little Jacob and the freezer and on the spur of the moment I cut over Snelling to the church and caught Pastor Ostrum in his office getting ready for some meeting. He was sprawled in his chair behind his desk.

"I met a family awhile ago and I wondered if you'd call on them," I said. He was an easy guy to talk to. "I don't think they have a church."

"Are they in our neighborhood?"

"Yeah, just down Goodrich, 1869."

"How did you meet them?"

"Oh, ah, when I was delivering groceries, but could you just stop like you were making routine calls, without saying anything about me? You know, with my job and everything, my boss might not like it."

"Sure. I'll drop in on them one evening this week." He jotted down the address. "1869 Goodrich?"

"Yeah, that's it."

"What's their name?"

"Luttermann, Mr. and Mrs. Otto Luttermann. I think they have some kids."

"Well thanks for your concern, Cal. I'll pay them a visit."

"Good, and when you're there, could you notice if you think everything is all right?"

He leaned back in his chair and put his hands behind his head, and I wanted to tell him to look in the freezer.

"What do you mean?"

"Oh, I don't know, but I got the feeling that there was something wrong in the family, you know, like they had a problem or something. Could you see if anything seems peculiar?"

"I'll do what I can."

He stuck a pipe in his mouth and held it with his teeth.

"Thanks a lot," I said and I hurried out of the church.

Golly, with all his experience, maybe he'd recognize Luttermann for the lunatic he was and bring in the police. That's what the church was for wasn't it, to save people? Well, Gretchen needed saving more than anyone I ever knew. I legged it for home with a little hope kind of jingling in my pockets.

Wednesday night, instead of getting to bed early as my
mother thought, I was sitting in the oak tree behind
Gretchen's house. In study hall that day she dared to show
me what her father had done, shyly moving her dress above
one knee to uncover two ugly welts. It embarrassed me and
really ticked me off. In a hurry, she had forgotten to take off
the loafers Tuesday and only noticed them when her father
pulled up to the curb. She told him a girl let her wear them
for the day and he punished her for trying to look pretty and
attract boys. She wouldn't wear the loafers again or keep
them in her locker, and I put them in mine. She asked me to
hide her baby doll, too, in case her father checked hers. Jeez,
now I had a doll in my locker and I was sitting in a tree in
someone's backyard in the middle of the night and if my
buddies found out they'd think *I'd* gone loopy.

Slowly, the lights in the house went out, one by one, room
by room, and I hadn't been able to see anything. Maybe, if
Gretchen knew I was out here, she could part the curtain a
little without her father noticing. I had no idea what I was
doing there, but the sight of her bruised leg made me plenty
mad. I gave up hope that God was going to help her and I
figured I had to start *doing* something.

I sat there in the cold as the house gradually got dark, and
I thought about the strange stuff that went on that week. I
took a shot when I should've held the ball at the end of the
game and Harding tied it up and beat us in overtime. Gad I
felt terrible; I thought I could can the shot; instead I lost the
game. Then I'd gone to the Deb sorority meeting Tuesday
night with Steve and Scott, and Lola had come up and talked
to me like I was her long-lost husband or something, but I
wasn't going to play their game any more.

"Could you give me a ride home tonight?" she said.

I usually think of the words I wish I'd said a year too late,
but for once in my life I said the right thing at the right time.

"I don't do that anymore."

"Do what?"

"Live for Tom."

"Neither do I," she said. "I miss seeing you, talking to you. Gosh we had fun together, pulling trolleys and goofing around. All Tom ever wants to do is park."

Jeez, that's what *I* wanted to do with her.

"And this has nothing to do with Tom's father?"

"No, it has nothing to do with Tom," she said.

"Golly, I'm sorry, I don't have a ride, we walked tonight."

I could have taken Lola home on the streetcar, but I didn't know what to think, and I didn't mention it to Scott or Steve on the way home.

Luttermann's back door squeaked, scaring the toenails off me, and Gretchen's father stepped out and the door creaked shut. He just stood there below me for a minute and I could see his little puffs of breath in the frosty air. I didn't dare breathe, and I knew he could easily see me if he turned his head. I wanted to inch around the trunk, but I didn't dare swallow or blink an eye. When I felt my lungs were about to explode, he took off, walking quickly out the alley and back south on the side street.

I waited a minute and then shinnied down the tree and sneaked out the alley to the street. A block up I could barely make out the shadow of a man fading and appearing in the circles of streetlight. I decided to follow him, see where in heck he was going at ten o'clock at night. He turned left on St. Clair, and I ran between the shoveled snowbanks to catch up, but when I peered down St. Clair, I couldn't find him any-where. I legged it a block to Fairview, searching the yards and houses on both sides of the street, but there wasn't a living thing in sight. While I was standing at the corner it hit me like a ton of bricks. What if he'd spotted me and was laying for me in the shadows. The hair on my head stood up under-neath my cap.

Jeez, I froze on the spot and I could feel his eyes on me. I pulled a Sid, keeping my head pointed straight ahead like I was just hanging around, but I scanned the doorways and

shrubs and fences out of the corners of my eyes. Then I
broke loose and hoofed it down Fairview and tried to whistle
and I didn't dare look back and I expected him to step out
from behind every tree I passed. I began to run, hearing footsteps crunching in the snow behind me and I almost went
down on the ice a couple of times and I sprinted past Finley's
Market and across Grand. When I was on the other side of
Summit, I found the nerve to turn and look back. Nothing. As
far as I could see, Fairview stood empty except for the snowbanks and the trees and the silent streetlights. Otto
Luttermann had disappeared like a weasel in the night.

I knew my goose was cooked when Sandy showed up in
Kirschbach's seventh period Thursday afternoon. With a
game that night, there was no practice and I was serving my
time for getting caught skipping school the day I took
Gretchen to Minneapolis. If I got any more detention, I'd be
off the team for good. When I spotted Sandy over a couple of
rows, a boulder rolled into the pit of my stomach.

About fifteen minutes into the hour, Sandy got permission
to go to the lavatory. When the intercom rang, I knew who
was on it and what she'd tell Kirschbach. Sure enough, he
told us to stay in our seats and study quietly and he beat it
down the hall. Ron Lyman jumped up and bolted for
Kirschbach's desk and kids yelled their suggestions.

"Get the clock!"

"Fix the chair!"

"His glasses!"

Sandy showed up and slipped into her seat. Ron had
Kirschbach's thick horn-rimmed glasses in his hand when we
could hear Kirschbach's heavy steps charging up the hall. In
the panic of the moment, Ron stuffed the glasses into the soft
leather briefcase that was lying on the desk. He'd barely
made it to his seat when Kirschbach burst into the room,
knowing he'd been bamboozled into going to the office

again. We pretended we were studying like mad while he stormed around the room like a puffed up gorilla, trying to figure out what we'd pulled while he was gone. His big alarm clock was ticking away on his desk, he checked his magical chair, and then he noticed his glasses were missing. He stood at his desk scowling at us.

"*Where* are my glasses?" His voice thundered.

We all cringed and slid down in our seats.

"*Who* has my glasses?"

Gad, his voice boomed and the blood vessels in his face were bulging and the kids in the front row were cowering and I knew right then I'd never play basketball for Central again.

"Where are my glasses?" he shouted and he slammed his fist down on top of his *briefcase.*

We cut loose with a blast of laughter you could've heard downtown and Kirschbach stopped in his tracks like he was confused. He hadn't done anything funny. We had his glasses and we were making fun of him and he was really steaming and with a clenched fist he pounded the briefcase with each word.

"Where (*smash*) are (*pound*) my (*whack*) glasses (*thump*)?

By that time we were laughing so hard some kids were about to cough up their tonsils. I couldn't help but laugh though I knew I was doomed. Kirschbach squinted at us out of his dark paunchy face.

"If you don't tell me where my glasses are this minute, you'll all have another week of seventh period, two weeks!"

The room went deadly silent; no one would squeal, like shipmates going down with the ship. About then it hit Sandy and she looked over at me with horror in her face, her hand over her mouth.

"We're going to sit here until the guilty party confesses," Kirschbach said and he settled in his swivel chair, staring at us like an enraged ape at the Como Zoo.

Without taking his eyes off us he reached into his briefcase for something and came out with a bow of his horn-rimmed glasses. When he saw what he had, he got this dopey expression on his face like he'd just had an accident in his pants. We sat there deadpan, never letting on. Without looking he slyly slid his hand back into his briefcase and felt around, discovering the other pieces of the glasses he'd just pounded into smithereens. By the look on his kisser we could tell he was trying to figure out how that could've happened.

Just before the hour was up he announced sheepishly, "None of you will have additional seventh period. It seems my glasses were misplaced."

When his alarm clock announced the hour was up, I'd made it through the mine field one more time.

I was having trouble paying attention to the pastor's sermon on Sunday because the little Jorgenson kid was sitting right in front of me and he kept turning around and staring at me like I had fangs or something and he kept wiping his running nose on the back of the pew.

The pastor was preaching about how the disciples were telling the little kids that wanted to see Jesus to scram, like they weren't important or something, and Jesus told them to knock it off because the little kids were the most important people in his kingdom and they should let the children come and see him and sit on his lap and all that kind of stuff, and I wanted to stand up and ask what I should do about a guy down the street who holds little kids under water until they drown.

I didn't want to think about our lousy game on Thursday night when we lost to Humboldt, but it kept coming up in my head. Jeez, we stood around flat-footed and played like our I.Q.s had dropped below fifty and we'd all come down with St. Vitus's dance, and a lot of it was my fault; I wasn't leading the team the way I wanted to, like I should be, and we were flushing our season down the sewer.

I wanted to concentrate on basketball but Gretchen and Lola kept clogging up all the space in my brain and when I was thinking about one, the other would elbow her way in. Lola was acting like she liked me and it was throwing me for a loop and I figured it could still be just to fool Tom's father, but I wasn't sure. After the game she was waiting for me with the other girlfriends, standing around like worried miners' wives waiting to hear if their man had been buried in the cave-in. Jerry drove, and we went right home. Lola and I snuggled in the backseat and I think she was feeling as lousy as I was, and I just wanted to hold on to her. I hated losing.

I dragged my heels after church and let Peggy and my parents shuffle ahead as we filed out with the congregation. I waited until Pastor Ostrum had finished shaking hands with everyone so no one would hear me.

"Good morning, Cal," he said and he shook my hand.

I didn't want to give him a chance to ask about basketball.

"Good morning, did you get a chance to call on Luttermanns?"

"Yes, I stopped the other night, met the whole family."

"Did you go *in* the house?"

"Oh, yes . . . had a nice long visit. They have three girls."

I wanted to tell him he missed the boy in the freezer.

"Did you notice anything . . . anything peculiar?"

"No . . . not really. They're a little somber, but they seem like a solid Christian family, go to the Holy Gospel Church, and boy, our kids don't memorize scripture like those kids do. No, they seem like real fine folks."

I couldn't believe it. Luttermann had not only invited the pastor in, but he'd convinced Ostrum that he was a nice, normal father. Dang, the wolf in sheep's clothing had pulled the wool over the preacher's brain. What a backfire. The pastor sounded like he'd support the lunatic for mayor, for crying out loud.

I was really disappointed. I'd hoped Ostrum would see that Luttermann was crazy and have him hauled away in a straitjacket but I was right back where I'd started, nowhere! So much for evangelism.

I hustled to catch up to my family because my dad was always in a hurry and looking at his watch like God was timing him, that if he stood in one spot too long, lightning would blast him. We headed along Snelling and I began to realize how hard it would be to get Luttermann without Gretchen telling on him.

I had sneaked into the oak tree and waited on three freezing nights without seeing a blooming thing through the dormer window. Gretchen had told me that it was her room and said she'd try to part the curtain, but so far she hadn't got it done. I slid around to the far side of the big oak when the lights went out in the house because I didn't dare risk leaving until Luttermann came out and took off on his nightly walk. I pretended I was a great horned owl, like those Uncle Emil taught me about, sitting on the limb and slowly turning my head from side to side, blinking my eyes and feeling cunning like that feathered hunter who could see in the dark and bring down it's prey without a sound.

Like he was punching the clock at the post office, Luttermann left the house every night at ten o'clock, but I hadn't dared follow him again. While I perched in the tree I was half freezing to death when a plan to save Gretchen showed up in my head, just like that, and it sent shivers down my legs. Like a jigsaw puzzle, not all the pieces fit yet, and some were missing, but I could see what the puzzle was supposed to look like, and I thought it could work. It scared me to think about it, but it also made me happy, that one night I'd swoop down and sink my talons in Luttermann's back.

Gretchen's father came out and hiked off into the freezing night and with my heart going like sixty I shinnied down the tree and hightailed it for home. I had a plan, and if I could pull it off, I'd nail his ass to an iron cell in Stillwater.

Chapter 24

On a night when no one had a car and kids stayed home with a lot of flu and colds going around, I hiked from Hi-Y to the Deb meeting at some girl's house on Juliet. Tired from a long, hard practice and not getting enough sleep, I'd have stayed home if it weren't for the bright surprise in my life. I walked the six blocks with my heart singing, not used to having Lola wanting to see me as much as I wanted to see her. When I thought about how she'd be watching the door, I ran the last block.

Some cars arrived and left, but with only a handful of kids at the house, I had little hope of catching a ride. Steve showed up with a bunch from Skull and Keys, and I buttonholed him.

"Would you teach me how to hot-wire a car?"

"You mean right now?"

"Nooo, not now . . . but sometime soon."

"You don't have a car."

"I know, but I'm saving up, I'm going to get one this summer."

"In the meantime you going to start stealing cars?"

Steve riddled the room with his Tommy-gun laugh.

"Finley's truck, so I can use it once in a while. Is it hard?"

"No, it's simple." Steve cocked his head at me. "I never figured you'd pull anything like that. What if he catches you?"

"Oh, Finley wouldn't really care. I'll probably only do it once or twice. Will you show me?"

"Yeah, sure, when?"

"Saturday, when I have the truck."

Lola came from the back of the house wearing a white Angora scarf and mittens and she leaned up against me and I felt a big sappy grin show up on my face.

"You want to go with us?" Steve asked us.

I looked at Lola.

"Let's walk," she said and she took me by the arm and I could feel myself growing three inches taller.

"Okay, we'll walk," I told Steve. "Thanks anyway."

I pulled Lola towards the door.

"Don't steal any cars," Steve hollered as we bounced down the steps together.

"What did he mean by that?" she asked.

"I don't know. He's a nut."

It was a mild night, around twenty degrees with a slight breeze. We walked hand in hand under the streetlights in the nippy night air. We tried to see the stars through the skating clouds, she pushed me into the snow, and I pulled her into my lap. I was so happy I wanted to jump over snowbanks and ring doorbells and wave at strangers, but as we walked down Cleveland, I kept wondering about Tom and I had to find out what was going on. If I was going to die, kill me right then and get it over with.

"Are you still going out with Tom?" I said.

"No," she said as we walked, "and my mother's having a fit. She wants me to marry someone who's going to be a doctor or an architect or something like that."

"She does?"

"Yes . . . she's awfully bitter about my dad and she doesn't want me ending up like her, having to scrimp and work all her life. She says she got fooled by high school romance and look where it got her, that it's all a bunch of bunk and that I have to be practical."

"Doesn't she care if you love someone?"

"She says that's not important."

"What do *you* want?" I said, afraid of her answer.

"I thought about what you said at the formal, that I didn't even know when someone loved me. You were right, and I realized that Tom doesn't love me. He wants me, wants to neck and everything with me, but he doesn't love me. That's why I want to go out with you, Cal. I can tell you . . . like me."

Jeez, I couldn't believe it.

"What about your mom?" I said.

"She doesn't know everything. I want to be in love."

We played and laughed and hung on to each other and it was like nothing else mattered as long as we were together.

When I turned for home the soreness came back to my legs as I ran down a Randolph-Highland Park streetcar. I still couldn't believe that she might be falling in love with me, but even though she had me going around whistling all the time, I hadn't forgotten about Little Jacob and Gretchen. Steve had promised to show me how to hot-wire a car, and no one in the world would ever guess what car I had in mind.

At supper, the mystery of the disappearing carrots was solved once and for all. I passed the Lima beans from my father to my mother without helping myself.

"Take some beans, Calvin, they're good for you," my mother said.

"Last night I saw a carrot walk out of the kitchen with Peggy," my dad said without looking up.

I spooned only four beans on my plate and my mother was so distracted by the carrot report that I got away with it. My sister gulped silently.

"Peggy?" my mother said.

"But Cedric Adams was on," Peggy said, like she couldn't believe my dad had left the living room during that hallowed time.

"Where was the carrot going with you?" he said.

"I take them for Hot-Foot, he's a rabbit."

My mother turned somber at the mention of the cottontail, like she was in on it with us.

"That the rabbit Cal had in his room last fall?" my dad said with a slight smile drifting onto his face.

"You knew about it?" my mother said.

"He used to visit me in the bathroom when I was shaving in the morning. Nice little bunny."

While the rest of us cringed at this astonishing thunder-bolt, my dad seemed to be enjoying himself and he let a full-blown grin pitch camp in the stubbled furrows of his Norwegian face.

"I'm trying to help him live through the winter," Peggy said.

"That's good," he said.

"But that's good food," my mother said.

"From now on we'll keep a dish by the sink for all the left-overs Hot-Foot would like," my dad said.

Peggy and I smiled at each other but she couldn't let well enough alone.

"I used to help McCluskey's dog, too," she said.

"You did?" I said, amazed at my little sister.

"Yeah. I'd throw half a peanut-butter sandwich over the fence to him."

"That was good food," my mother said.

"Good for you," my father said.

It sounds kind of dopey, but I could tell that my father was having a hard time, you know, like feeling things were kind of hopeless, and right then he was doing everything he could to keep from going under.

"How did he like peanut-butter sandwiches?" my dad said.

"Oh, swell, he loved them, and Hostess cupcakes too," Peggy said.

"Hostess cupcakes!" My mother kind of gasped.

"Yeah, he liked 'em."

"What did you eat for lunch?" my mother said.

"I wasn't as hungry as he was."

I felt like jumping up and hugging my little sister. Jeez, lots of times I felt like doing something like that but I was always afraid it would look corny or something.

"Well, we'll get the bunny through the winter," my dad said, "but in the spring, he'll be able to take care of himself."

We ate supper in a cheery atmosphere, like everyone was feeling good and everything was going to turn out okay.

We beat Johnson on Thursday night and we were all feeling pretty good with the long overdue win. Steve had the car and a date with Kay Reynolds and he acted his usual fruitcake self when he was with a new girl. We hit the White Castle on Lake Street and eight of us sat in the car and gobbled about forty *gut bombs* and the aroma of the little steamed hamburgers and minced onions reminded me of the log cabin and Uncle Emil, and I don't know why, but I thought he'd have come to see me play if he'd been around.

When Steve had dropped everyone off but me, I wanted to tell him about my plan. I'd worked it out pretty good in my head and I knew I could trust him, but I realized that for every person who knew, the chances that Luttermann would get away went up. I couldn't tell *anyone,* not even Gretchen.

"Do you think it's all right to break the law to help someone who's in trouble?" I said.

"What do you mean?" Steve said.

"I don't know, like you break the speed limit if you're driving someone to the hospital who's dying, or you steal food to feed someone who's starving."

"Yeah . . . that would be all right . . . why, what are you planning to do?"

Steve pulled up in front of the apartment.

"Nothing. It was some stuff we had to read in social studies and I was just thinking about it."

I opened the door and got out.

"Good game," Steve said.

"Thanks."

I waved and walked around to the back of the apartment.

Son of a gun, we could win, but it riled me when I thought of what we should have done in our senior year and it reminded me that I was in a lot more than a game with Luttermann, and there would be no room for what I should have done. Like the basketball season, I'd have just one chance, and I figured it would be Gretchen's only chance.

Chapter 25

Jeez, I was really jumpy at work on Saturday because I knew I had to quit stewing about my plan and *do* it. When I stopped at the liquor store there were two cases setting out and after I loaded them in the truck I sneaked to the door of the salesroom, ready to ask Sid if there was anything else. Sid was waiting on a customer and I hustled back through the storeroom, lifted a case of Old Fitzgerald, and loaded it like it was a regular order.

I slammed the door and drove away and my heart was pumping like a tom-tom and I had a hard time breathing. I'd thought about the right and wrong of it for days, ever since I came up with the idea while sitting in the oak tree. I put off doing anything all winter, hoping that somehow, something else would happen, and I wasn't sure that I could really do what I'd have to, but I had to start. Gretchen was hanging by a thread, every day trying to stay alive, so sure she'd go crazy that she probably would, while I played basketball and necked with my girlfriend. I figured getting Gretchen free would make it right.

I'd never stolen anything, except a comic book once from the five-and-dime on Selby and Snelling. It bothered me so much I decided to sneak it back into the store, but I didn't dare. I went in and pretended to find a dime on the floor near the cash register and I handed it over to the spindly lady, figuring that would make it even. She raised an eyebrow and I wondered if she could see a reformed shoplifter in my eyes. But a case of whiskey, that was serious crime. Would Sid notice the missing case on some balance sheet? That was what I had to find out.

I stopped at a deserted garage across the railroad tracks off St. Clair. It was perfect. I'd found it driving the alleys in the delivery truck. The house was boarded up, and I hoped no one would see me stashing the liquor. In a sweat I set the Old Fitzgerald in the garage, hid it under the rags and junk that covered the floor, and shoved the jimmied door closed. When I drove off to make my deliveries, the hairs on the back of my neck warned me: I was out on thin ice, and I could never go back to Sid with thirty or forty dollars and tell him I found it by the cash register.

I finished the first run around noon and I was glad I found Gretchen behind the bakery. I was excited and I wanted to somehow let on that I'd started. I'd been feeding her Nut Goodies whenever I could in hopes that they'd fatten her up some but she was thinner than ever. Standing near the open door at the back of the truck she nailed me.

"Do you think it's my fault, what my father does to me?"

"What do you mean?" I said, squatting inside the Plymouth.

"Maybe it's because of the way I am or look or something, that makes him do those things."

"Criminy, no, it's not you! Your father's a stinking pervert."

"Maybe it's my fault because I don't fight him anymore, I just let him do what he wants."

Jeez, I hated talking about this; I didn't know what to say.

"I used to fight him, at first, but he hurt me bad and I don't want to be hurt anymore . . . When he tells me to take off my clothes, I just do. He used to tie me, but he doesn't much anymore and when he—"

"I did something today," I half shouted to drown her out, "a little while ago, that's going to get you free, honest, just hold on a little longer, please."

I didn't want to hear anymore of that stuff and I was relieved that Gretchen had to get back to work. Sometimes I'd think about what her father was doing to her and I'd catch myself and really be ashamed and I'd remember how terrible it was for Gretchen and wonder if *I* was some kind of a pervert.

When I'd finished for the day, I bombed home from

Finley's Market to eat and get ready for the dance, and I ran fast, toward the sound of Lola's laughter.

My dad ate supper in a quiet mood, like he was giving up or something. My mother was in bed with a cold and her back out of whack, something that happened a lot during the winter months. Peggy had become good at filling the gap, and she'd served up wieners and baked beans.

"They've canceled the rehabilitation program," my dad said.

"What's that?" Peggy said.

"Overhauling the cars every eighteen months, regular as clockwork. We tore them down and replaced anything that was worn or shoddy, turned 'em out like new. Now they're going to let them wear out and fall apart right on the line. It'll be sad to see."

"Will they fall apart while I'm riding on them?" Peggy said.

"Maybe the people won't let them," I said.

"The *people!* They're the ones giving up on them. All through the Depression, when they couldn't afford a car, they rode them, and all during the war, when they couldn't buy gasoline, they rode them. Now, in the good times, they're too fat and sassy to ride a streetcar. They're starting classes for *bus* drivers. Think of it!" My dad kind of growled. *"Bus* driving!"

"You'd make a good bus driver," I said.

"Bus driver! I wouldn't drive one of those filthy, two-bit contraptions if they tripled my salary. Those stinking beasts will ruin this city. To hell with all of them, to hell with their driving lessons, to hell with the Company."

Jeez, we weren't used to hearing my dad swear and we knew when to be quiet and allow the storm to blow itself out.

I was nervous when Jerry picked me up for the dance, thinking the cops were already out looking for me. Everyone must've got the car that night because Jerry and I were just doubling and Lola and I would have the whole back seat to ourselves.

The Jalop-Hop was perfect and I hardly noticed who was there. Lola and I danced almost every dance and sometimes we realized we were still dancing when the music had stopped. We danced so close I was afraid she'd ask me if I had a flashlight in my pocket. Rock hard against her belly, she had to notice, but we could've been dancing in the middle of Wabasha and Seventh during rush hour for all we knew, and I only remembered the case of Old Fitzgerald once.

Jerry and Sally weren't getting along too hot and when he parked above Minnehaha Falls, she got out of the car and walked off. He went after her, and we had the car all to our-selves. Sinatra sang one of my favorite love songs, "How Deep Is The Ocean," and I don't know what got into me but while we were kissing, I touched her lips with my tongue. When she didn't flinch, I moved my tongue along the edge of her lip and then slowly slipped it into her mouth, and she just kept on kissing me and I was breathing like a locomotive and I thought my heart would bust out of my chest. Holy smoke! I'd French kissed her.

What had sounded gross when an older kid named Marvin Rust explained it to me turned out to be the most exciting thing I'd ever done. When I heard about such things, sexual things, I always figured it would be awkward, that I'd be clumsy, and I was really surprised at how easy it was and how scary and delicious her mouth was. I didn't want to act like a sex fiend so I kissed her a couple of times with a regular kiss and then I slipped my tongue in again and kind of felt around and all of a sudden it met *her tongue!* Holy cow, our tongues were touching and teasing and tasting each other, and I thought my ears were going to blow right off my skull. I slipped my tongue in and out of her mouth a couple of times and then I caught my breath before I died.

Jerry and Sally showed up, lovey-dovey, and he headed for St. Paul. I hardly noticed we were moving and just as we started across the Ford Bridge, she nearly blew my socks off when she slipped *her* tongue into *my* mouth!

Half-way across the bridge, Jerry hit the brakes and we just about ended up in the front seat.

"Look!" he said.

There was Steve, sitting on the concrete railing of the bridge with his legs hanging over the side. Jeez, one slip and he'd fall a mile onto the frozen river.

Jerry stepped out of the car and called over the roof, "Hey, Steve, what're you doing?"

Steve looked over at us for a minute like he didn't know us.

"Hi, Jer, I'm going for a swim," he yelled and I could tell he'd been drinking.

I got out and walked towards him and I wasn't sure what to do and the wind was blowing and it was freezing out there.

"Don't get too close; I might lose my balance," he said.

Lola and Sally came and stood beside me on the sidewalk about ten yards from Steve.

"I've got to move the car," Jerry said and he drove across the bridge and I thought the rat was deserting us.

"Why don't you get down," I said, "you could get hurt goofing around like that."

"Get down, Steve, please," Lola said.

I tried to inch forward in hopes that he wouldn't notice.

"Don't get any closer!" he shouted, and I backed up a step.

"C'mon, Steve, get down, it's cold out here."

"It's cold everywhere," he said.

"What's the matter, why are you doing this?" I said.

"Because no one in the world gives a damn if I'm dead or alive."

"*We* do," I said, "all your friends do."

"And your parents do," Sally said.

"They'd be glad I was out of their hair," Steve said.

"Come down, Steve, please, *I* care about you," Lola said and the way she said it *I'd* have come down.

Then I saw Jerry. Cripes, how did he get back to the other side of the bridge? He was moving towards us along the railing, bent low and walking like Groucho Marx. I looked at my shoes so Steve couldn't see my lips moving and I whispered to the girls.

"Don't look at Jerry, keep staring right at Steve."

As long as Steve turned and looked over his left shoulder at us, he'd never spot Jerry coming from his right.

"C'mon, Steve, quit fooling around," I said, trying to keep his attention. "You've got tons of friends who care about you."

"Please, Steve," Sally said, "come down and–"

"No, no!" He waved his hand at us. "Go get Katie and bring her here. If she cares if I'm dead or alive, I'll get down. Go on, get her." He patted the railing. "I'll wait right here."

Jerry was almost there.

"Okay, I'll get her," I said, "but what if you slip while I'm gone? Get down on the sidewalk until I get back and then–"

"YEEEAH!" Jerry yelled as he grabbed Steve around the waist and Steve blurted a shout of surprise.

I ripped over and grabbed Steve's arm, and we dragged him off the concrete railing and flattened him on the sidewalk.

"Let go!" Steve yelled. "Just leave me alone!"

"Don't you ever do that again, you dumb bunny!" I shouted in his face and I pounded him on the chest. "Don't you ever . . . !"

Jeez, I was hitting him pretty hard and I let up but I was mad enough to kill him and I was crying and I wiped my face and the girls were crying and we all kind of piled on top of Steve and hugged each other and I could smell beer on his breath and everyone was laughing and crying in a big hog pile.

"How'd you get back to the other side?" I asked Jerry.

"I hitchhiked, rode right past you. The guy wondered what was going on and I told him we were just goofing around."

"Great move," I said and I punched him on the shoulder.

"You scared the crap out of me," Steve told Jerry like he was really mad. "I almost jumped into the river."

"We better get out of here," Jerry said. "Someone might have called the cops."

We helped each other off the cold concrete and piled in the car at the end of the bridge and we drove around for over an hour talking with Steve and trying to show him that we cared about what happened to him and then we dropped him at his house. When he got out and went in, I realized *we* couldn't keep him alive if he wanted to die. Ten minutes later he could walk back to the bridge. I didn't know if Steve would ever have the guts, or enough pain, to jump, but it made me feel bad that he even thought of such a terrible thing. I took Lola in my arms and I didn't think about French kissing. I thought about Gretchen and Little Jacob and I clung to Lola like one of us was about to fall off the Ford Bridge, into the icy river below.

Chapter 26

Saturdays I'd stop to see Gretchen behind the bakery and give her a Nut Goodie, but I'd only stay for a minute, so I wouldn't tip her father that she had someone on her side. There was no chance to swipe another case of liquor on Saturday because Sid stood around in the storeroom like he was lonesome.

"You guys won another one Friday night," Sid said.

"Yeah, we beat Marshall."

"What's the matter with Central? You beat the tough teams and lose to the bums."

"I know, Jeez, we could have won the city title."

I stalled as long as I could and left before Sid got suspicious but the day wasn't wasted. I met Steve in a parking lot at Highland Village, and he showed me how to hot-wire the Plymouth truck. I studied every step like it would show up in an M.R. sometime and when Steve finished I asked him to do it again from the beginning. All I'd need was a screwdriver and a length of wire and I would practice on Finley's truck until I could do it in the dark, because that's exactly how I'd have to do it.

I drove Finley's truck to the Valentine Dance, tripling with Jerry and Steve, and in the hope that Steve might never put two and two together later on, I hot-wired it, even though Mr. Finley gave me permission to use it.

I gave Lola a mushy Valentine and a two-pound box of chocolates on Valentine's Day when I took her home from the Deb meeting, and she'd given me a funny card in school that only hinted at love. When the dance was close to over and we were slow dancing to "Time After Time," I put my lips against her ear.

"I love you," I whispered.

The words had just gone out of my mouth on their own, and suddenly it seemed like the whole world was standing there listening for what she'd say: birds stopped flying and rabbits turned their ears and dogs stopped barking. She didn't say anything for a minute, like she was trying to come up with something that wouldn't hurt my feelings, and my heart held its breath and plugged its ears like it knew she could break it with one word. Then she tilted her head back and looked into my eyes.

"You make me feel different . . . when I'm with you," she said.

"What do you mean?" Oh, Jeez, it was going to be something polite and kind.

"I don't know, happy . . . safe . . . like you'd love me no matter what, whole hog."

"What's wrong with whole hog?"

"Nothing, but it's kinda scary, I've never had that before. I love it, and I love *you*, Cal. I *love* you."

Holy cow, I was home! I kissed her right there on the dance floor in front of everyone. She loved me! The world was happy and beautiful and I wanted to fly. We'd go steady and then we'd get engaged and then we'd get married, and I'd have all the rest of my life to figure out the color of her eyes.

On a cold, quiet night, I roosted in the branches of the red oak, pretending I was an owl, when all of a sudden the curtain winked and a slit opened where I could see into the bedroom. I stared through that sliver of light until I was half hypnotized but I couldn't see anyone. Then something moved, but I couldn't make out what until finally I figured it was a person, probably Gretchen, standing with her back to the window, naked. She stood there for a long time and my eyes ached from staring so hard.

After a while she moved to the side like she was climbing onto a bed and for a minute I couldn't see anyone. Then I caught a glimpse of a man's body with his clothes on, and he was holding something in his hand but I couldn't figure out what it was and then the curtain whipped shut and I was leaning so far toward the window I almost fell out of the tree.

Jeez, I was breathing hard and I was steaming mad and I stared at the curtain for ten or fifteen minutes and my imagination was going wild about what Luttermann was doing to her until I almost blew a fuse. When the room went dark, a crazy thought bombed into my head: Snatch the baby right then, just do it! It would be quick and simple and Gretchen would be free. I waited until ten, trying to work up the nerve and my heart was going like sixty.

When Luttermann came out and walked off into the night, I slid down the rough trunk and wiped out my tracks from the tree to the alley like I did whenever there was new snow. I sneaked to the street and waited until the rat went out of sight a couple of blocks down Howell. Then I hustled back to the porch and gingerly opened the storm door. Darn, the spring squawked like a strangling chicken and I held it still while I slowly turned the knob of the inner door. It opened.

My hands and forehead started sweating as I thought about doing it right then, nailing that lunatic before he could ever touch Gretchen again, but I was scared outta my wits and I talked myself out of it, figuring that I needed to carefully think it over first. I slowly pulled the inner door shut until the latch snapped in place. Then I eased the squeaking storm door closed and got the heck out of there. Tomorrow night I would do it!

"Yeah, this is Sergeant Riley, what can I do for you?"

"I talked to you a month ago, about a man who beat his daughter, and I have a question."

I was calling from Lacher's Drugstore after practice and I tried to disguise my voice.

"Oh . . . yeah, go ahead," the sergeant said.

"If I brought you a body, would you—"

"A *body!* A *dead* body? My god, are you serious?"

"Yes, a dead body. Would you—"

"Have you *seen* this body?"

"Well . . . no, but I think I know where it is."

"Where?"

"I can't tell you. If you go there and it's not there and you don't lock the man up, he'll know his daughter told me about it and he'll really hurt her."

"Tell me where and I'll take care of the guy," Riley said.

"You promise, if I bring you the body, you'll lock the man up, and keep him locked up until there's a trial or something?"

"Listen, I don't know if this is on the level, but if you show us a body, and the person you believe did the killing, we'll lock him up, but we'll need proof."

"Oh, there'll be proof, an eyewitness. I'll bring you the body tonight."

"Hold it, hold it! If you've found a body, don't *touch* it, for god's sake! You'll destroy evidence. Tell us where it is. You could screw it all up."

"I won't be destroying any clues. How late do you work?"

"Wait a minute, you could get in serious trouble for interfering with police work. Don't go near the body, just—"

"Do you want the body or don't you?"

"You tell us where it is, don't go near it, you *hear* me!"

Jeez, he started sounding like my dad.

"How late do you work?" I said.

"I'm on until midnight, but you let me come and get the body with you. Then you won't mess up the evidence, and besides, you'll be safer. You could get yourself killed, you know."

"You don't understand, I have to do it this way. By the time you do it legal, there won't *be* any body."

"Tell me who this is, in case something goes—"

"I'll see you tonight," I said and I hung up.

Chapter 27

When I didn't eat much supper my mother asked if I was
feeling all right and I was so jumpy on the phone with Lola I
could hardly talk. We yakked about stuff that seemed kind of
silly compared to what I was planning, and when I hung up, I
said good night to my parents and went to my room as usual
while they waited for Cedric Adams and the evening news.
I'd give old Cedric some news that'd sprout hair on his teeth.
I waited about ten minutes and then sneaked out the back
door, leaving my blankets looking like I was in bed and a
stack of Sinatra playing softly. I had to get into the tree
before Luttermann came out. After running the six blocks, I
climbed into the oak at nine fifty and I couldn't catch my
breath. Gretchen's room was dark and I jacked myself up by
telling myself she wouldn't be sleeping there tomorrow and
that creep would never lay another finger on her as long as
he lived.

Then the squeaking door told me Lutterman was there, in
the dark, a shadow. He stood there, like he was listening for
something, and I thought sure he'd hear my heart pounding.
Then he hiked out through the alley and headed south on
Howell like always. I caught my breath and slid out of the
tree and sneaked over to the enclosed porch. When I slowly
opened the storm door, the spring started screeching and I
held it like I was strangling a snake, cringing there on
Gretchen's back step. I tried the knob on the inner door,
almost hoping that it would be locked. It wasn't. I slid in,
easing the storm door closed, and Criminy, it sounded like
the opening of "Inner Sanctum."

There was the usual junk and a chest-type freezer. I
listened for a minute and let my eyes get used to the darkness. Bony fingers of light from the neighborhood poked in
the windows and there wasn't a sound from the house. I crept

to the Kelvinator and swung open the top. A dim light came on and the packages of food looked as normal as pie. With my heart hammering, I dug through the frozen food toward the bottom. There wasn't much room to shove packages around in the freezer, and one slid off and hit the floor like a brick. I was bending over the freezer and I didn't move a muscle, straining every cell in my body to hear. Nothing.

Cripes, I started to panic and I dug like crazy for the bottom until I found a wrapped bundle I figured was it, what I prayed I'd never find. I pulled it to the top and saw it was stamped ROAST BEEF. My hands were numb and I fumbled to unwrap it, to be sure; I couldn't bring Sergeant Riley a beef roast or a leg o' lamb.

I peeled back two layers of waxed paper, until, in the frosty light, Little Jacob stared up at me like he was still gasping for air. His frantic, drowning face shocked me and I hit my head on the freezer lid. All of a sudden *I* couldn't breathe and I was gasping for air like *I* was drowning. I had to get out of there! I rewrapped the package and grabbed it and closed the freezer. The sound behind me from the house didn't register until I had my hand on the knob of the storm door. I glanced back and saw Luttermann looming out of the inner doorway with a butcher knife in his hand.

I almost tore the storm door off its hinges blasting out of the porch. I plowed through the snow, headed for the street, and I heard the storm door bang again behind me. With the baby under my arm, I bombed out onto Goodrich and almost went down on the ice. I glanced back and saw him coming from between the houses, and Jeez, the guy was really flying.

I took the middle of the street, ripping past streetlights and sleeping families and I started shouting bloody murder.

"Hey, help! Help, somebody! Call the police!"

But I couldn't keep it up; I didn't have enough breath. When I was almost to the corner, a car showed up on Fairview.

"Hey, stop! Help!" I shouted, but its side windows were all frosted over and it went sailing by.

I looked up and down Fairview as I crossed but that was the only car in sight. I was losing my wind and I ran into tangle town, where the streets curved and circled all over the place.

In the silent cold, I heard his crunching footsteps behind me, like the Runner, but this wasn't some prank. If I didn't outrun him, it wouldn't be trouble with my father. I was running for my life and if I didn't run fast enough, my blood would be smeared all over Goodrich or Amherst. I could feel the blade driving into my back any second and I was ripping as fast as I could. The frozen baby was getting heavy, like a stone out of Helga's belly, and I switched arms holding it. I kept praying that a car would come along, maybe even a cop car, because basically Luttermann was gaining on me.

At the five-cornered intersection with Cambridge and Princeton, I cut to the right down Princeton, almost falling on a patch of ice. My chest ached and I couldn't breathe and I had a fist of pain in my right side but he was relentless, step for step behind me, and I couldn't shake him, and it made me mad. I'd run the basketball court for months, I was in great shape, but I'd never run for my life before and an older guy with a butcher's knife was catching up. I thought of cutting through yards the way I ditched the Runner, but I might fall in the snow or be trapped by a fence in a neighborhood I didn't know so I stayed out on the icy streets. By the time I knocked and someone came to a door, they'd find my body with a carving knife stuck between my shoulder blades.

I don't know why, but I started thinking all kinds of crazy stuff, like what was Lola doing right then and what if Uncle Emil could be here now and take his ax to Luttermann. Then I heard a streetcar over on St. Clair, a little more than a block away. I wondered if I could make it that far.

Luttermann was only a few yards behind, puffing, his feet pounding the packed snow and ice. The sounds of the street-car came closer, and I figured it hadn't crossed Wheeler yet. I was afraid my legs were going to buckle under me and then something grazed my back. I yelled and lunged away and the frozen package slipped from my arm and slid along the icy street beside me like a curling stone and I couldn't stop for a second to pick it up.

The streetcar headed downtown, crossing in front of me from right to left. Luckily, the motorman was holding back so he didn't outrun his schedule in the lazy night hours when there were hardly any riders. I ran with everything I had left and I knew if I didn't make it I was dead. When I pulled even with her, stride for stride, I leaped onto the cowcatcher.

I looked back and saw the maniac stooped and stumbling under a streetlight, gasping for air. In one arm he held the frozen bundle and in his other hand he held the butcher knife. The St. Clair streetcar saved me.

When the motorman stopped for the traffic light at Snelling, I climbed off the cowcatcher and beat it out of there. I didn't want to be tagged for some stupid prank when minutes before I'd escaped being murdered by a lunatic.

A block away, I slowed into a fast walk but my heart and head were still going full throttle. Son of a gun, I'd blown it. I dropped Little Jacob and lost the evidence that could have set Gretchen free; I'd fumbled the ball again. Luttermann would get rid of the baby now, and I hated to think of what might happen to Gretchen.

Riley was waiting, and I had nothing to bring him but fish stories. If I told him what happened, that Luttermann chased me with a butcher knife and I saw the frozen baby, would that be enough to put him in jail? But if it wasn't, even though the police went and asked Luttermann a bunch of questions, he'd still be able to get Gretchen. I had to protect her no matter what, I was the only one she had.

For the life of me I couldn't figure how Luttermann had circled back and ambushed me at the freezer. Could he have spotted me in the tree and set a trap? Just the thought of it made it hard to breathe and made me sweat.

On gimpy legs, I stumbled up the back steps like I'd been in a train wreck or something. When I was safe in my room I felt weak and sick to my stomach. After undressing I climbed under the covers, but the chills rattled my bones and even with an extra blanket I was still cold, my teeth chattering, and I couldn't believe what had happened. Criminy, I must have been nuts to try it. I couldn't get to sleep; in my mind I was still running from Luttermann.

Had he recognized me as the kid he saw behind the bakery? Would he think Gretchen had anything to do with it? I couldn't quit worrying about her and I got up twice to call the cops and tell them to go roaring up to her house and save her. I could never stop at the bakery again to help her through the day or go near the house until her father was put away. I felt like I was coming down with the flu and it made me wonder if I'd be able to go through with my plan, something I should have stuck to in the first place and forgot about that half-baked stunt that almost got me killed.

One day when Uncle Emil and I were hiking through the woods we found a dead great horned owl, its wings spread, the ground around it beaten and thrashed in a wide circle. Riddled with porcupine quills, it was rotting and maggots crawled all over it. Uncle Emil kneeled and counted the quills sticking in its head and wings and body. There were forty-three. I remembered how sad I felt for the owl. My uncle looked at the huge bird for a minute.

"Bit off more than he could chew," he said, and then he pulled out a large tail feather. He handed it to me, and we kept hiking through the pines. I still had that feather stuck in the mirror over my dresser, and I could hear Uncle Emil warning me, You've bit off more than you can chew. One thing I knew for sure. I could never let Luttermann catch a glimpse of me or find out who I was or I'd be worse off than the owl. Could he make Gretchen tell who I was? Would she? I was probably the only one outside of his family who'd seen the baby and that meant that now *he'd* be after *me*. Around five I fell asleep, praying that Gretchen would be all right.

Chapter 28

When my mother shook me, I leaped out of bed ready to run and she almost hit the ceiling. I forgot to set my alarm and it felt like I hadn't even been to bed and now I was late and my shoulder ached where I'd bashed it on the streetcar. I had to concentrate: what day was it and what would be expected of me.

At the breakfast table, Peggy put her ear to her cereal bowl, nearly dipping a pigtail in the cream.

"Yep, they're all here."

Halfway through my Rice Crispies, I didn't give a hoot if Snap, Crackle, and Pop were there or not. I knew Banana was. Jeez, at breakfast my mother sliced bananas on anything that wasn't moving, and I knew that some day I'd go to pick up my books or tennis shoes and they'd be covered with sliced bananas.

At school I felt safe, protected by all the kids, but I had trouble staying awake in class. Little Jacob's gasping face kept showing up in my head like a bad dream. Lola yakked about usual things as if the world weren't a place where murdered babies got stuffed in freezers and you weren't chased by madmen with carving knives.

I watched for Gretchen all day but she never showed. Jeez, what was she going through? I wanted to call Sergeant Riley but I had no idea what I could tell him. I found a dead baby in this guy's freezer and he chased me all over tangle town with a butcher knife? Where's the baby now? I don't know, I fumbled it when I jumped onto the cowcatcher. Cripes, Riley would hang up on me. If Gretchen were a dog, the Humane Society would take her away and protect her, but for kids who were treated worse than dogs, they didn't have a lousy thing.

I hitched for home after school and I asked my mother to wake me for supper. Then I buried myself in bed and slept like a log. It was hard to come around when she called me and it seemed I'd been sleeping about twelve seconds. We were playing the best team in the city, and I felt numb, like my blood had turned to oatmeal.

"Bobby Overby was running on the stairs again," Peggy said as we ate around the dinning room table.

"You take care of yourself," my mother said.

"Do you think you could come to the game?" I said to my mother like my dad wasn't in the room.

"Well, maybe we could, if your father has some time to rest after supper. What time does the game start?"

"Eight-fifteen," my dad said, and I just about swallowed my fork. I didn't think he even knew there *was* a game. We all kept eating and no one said anything more about it.

Hamline's field house had standing room only, and Monroe only had to beat us to be champs. It would make up for a lot of our crummy season if we could knock them off, and once the game started, I forgot everything else and became a maniac out there; so did Jerry. Jeez, I'd never been in a game like that where we fought over every inch of the floor from start to finish. A stocky kid guarding me started lipping off, said he was going to pound me after the game and he probably could have, but I almost laughed. He should've seen the guy who was after me the night before.

We played like they'd hang us if we lost and our swarming zone defense rattled Monroe. With seconds to go, we were hanging onto a one-point lead, scrambling on defense, and everyone in the building was standing. A Monroe guard tossed up a frantic shot that banked off the backboard, hit the rim, and bounced off. We had a ten-man scrimmage going for the loose ball. Jerry had it for a second but a Monroe kid slapped it away and then Scott snatched it in his big hands and held it above his head as the buzzer blasted over the racket.

Central kids swarmed onto the court like we'd won the City Championship, shouting and hugging and I was carried along with the mob and someone was trying to rip the jersey off my back.

"Cal! Cal!" I heard in the uproar, and I managed to turn and look down. Peggy was hanging on with both hands like she was being left behind on a sinking ship. I stood my ground and wrapped an arm around her and shouted above the pandemonium.

"What are you doing here? Is Dad here?"

"No, I came by myself. You won't tell on me, will you?"

We were getting mangled and I looked at my sister and I got all choked up and it wasn't because we'd beaten Monroe.

"Of course I won't," I yelled, "where do they think you are?"

"Staying overnight with Anita. You were wonderful, Cal."

"You're the one who's wonderful."

I hoisted her onto my shoulders and we whooped and shouted with the happy fans. It ended our season on a sensational note, beating the arrogant Monroe jerks who had acted like all they had to do was show up. Steve and Jean let Peggy sit between them and he taught her how to shift when the four of us gave her a ride to her friend's house. I wouldn't let her take the streetcar alone, and she became the big cheese in the crowded Chevy.

"Remember, don't tell anyone I was there," Peggy said as we pulled up in front of the house.

"Don't worry," Steve said, "none of us will ever squeal."

"How about Anita's parents?" I said from the back seat.

"They're out."

"Why didn't she come with you?" Lola said.

"She was afraid to."

Peggy puffed up like a winter sparrow when Steve said he'd walk her to the door, and I wanted to punch him on the shoulder.

"I can't wait for that kid to grow up," Steve said as he got in and drove off.

Jean laughed. "She's already too grown up for you."

Being with Lola made me feel that everything would turn out okay and I was so tired it felt like a dream. Steve drove around and I cuddled with Lola, but I couldn't get Gretchen out of my mind. I prayed she'd survived my stupidity, and I wanted to tell my friends about the terrible stuff that was going on in our neighborhood, but I knew I never could.

Chapter 29

Saturday morning the paper had a picture of Central fans whooping it up after the game and in the background you could see a girl on someone's shoulders, too blurred to recognize. Peggy was plenty scared while she ate her breakfast so I told my mother I wanted to keep the picture and I cut it out before I went to work and put it in my room, but Peggy and I both knew my dad had gone over the paper with a microscope before we were up.

Sid was gabbing with a rich-looking guy in the front of the store, and I picked off another case of whiskey. I wondered how long it would be before he noticed his inventory slightly short, but since Luttermann had come after me with a carving knife, I was ready to do anything to get that rat. After I shut the back door on the truck, I tiptoed to the doorway between the storeroom and the front, figuring I could take another case.

"The kickback on the track will be thousands," the man said.

The word *track* caught my ear, and I eased a little closer.

"Nothing to stop it now. You're a rich man, Sid, the first new buses are sitting over on University. You can give up peddling hooch and move to Florida."

A wobbly old guy came in, and I whipped through the storeroom, out to the truck. I drove away and thought about what I'd heard, and I knew it had something to do with the streetcars. My dad kept saying the whole deal was the work of crooks, but I thought he was exaggerating like he did when he was mad and I didn't know if I should tell him and, even if I did, what could he do? Anyway, I didn't want to mess up things with Sid until I had enough liquor to do the job, but I suspected that my dad knew what he was talking about after all.

I stashed the case with the other two in the deserted garage, and with it, the old rusted crowbar from the boiler room. I knew it would get harder as more and more liquor disappeared, but I didn't feel so bad about it since I was just borrowing it and Sid would get it all back anyway.

All day Sunday I bounced off the walls thinking about Gretchen. In church I prayed like crazy and I slept most of the afternoon, but by evening I was going bananas. I found my dad in his upholstered chair, studying the newspaper like God was giving a final on it. I was so worried over Gretchen I wanted to tell my dad all about Otto Luttermann and how he chased me with a knife, but I was afraid he'd call the cops and Gretchen's father would get her. I settled on the edge of the sofa and tried to swallow the bird's nest in my throat and my dad was so busy with the paper he didn't seem to notice.

"Dad, could I talk to you for a minute?" I said.

"Hmmmm." He didn't move. Then he lowered the paper and looked at me with a make-it-quick-I'm-memorizing-the-newspaper expression.

"What did you say?" he said.

"Could I talk to you for a minute?"

"What about?"

"Ah . . . something that's been bothering me lately."

"You in trouble at school?"

"No, nothing like that."

"You know I've told you a thousand times how important it is for you to do well at school."

"Yeah, I know."

"Are you doing anything to hurt your grades?"

"No, no, I'm doing okay."

"I never got to college and now it's up to you to see that *you* do. You can't let anything get in the way or you'll end up like me, at the mercy of those with money and power. They can brush me off like dandruff, they can buy and sell the

Company like one of those little red hotels on your Monopoly board. You want to end up like that, a little red hotel on their Monopoly board?"

"No, I won't, I'm doing okay in school, I'll graduate fine."

"Well let's not hear anymore talk about trouble with school," my dad said as he pulled out his pocket watch.

"It isn't anything about school. It's something—"

"Lurine!" he called, "the news is coming on."

He reached over and snapped on the big Philco, and with Cedric Adams about to start yakking about the atom bomb and the Communists, I knew I might as well be talking to a stump.

"Have a nice talk with your father?" my mother said as she passed me in the dining room.

"Yeah." I ducked into my room where I could bounce off the walls in peace.

On Monday I ran the last few blocks to catch Gretchen at her locker if she showed up and she looked relieved to see me.

"How are you?" I asked, checking her for any bruises. "Did he hurt you?"

"No, but he's acting strange after Thursday night," she said excitedly. "Something happened and I heard noise and the back door slammed and I went to the window and saw him run through the yard. Then it was quiet. He didn't come back for a long time."

"He was after *me!*"

"*You?*"

"Yeah. He found me in the house, and he chased me clear over to St. Clair and a streetcar saved me, but I dropped the baby."

"The *baby!*"

"Yeah, I had Little Jacob, and I knew if I could show him to the police, they'd take your father away and—"

"*Oh, nooo,* not the *baby,* you can't, you can't!"

"I dropped him, I'm sorry, I lost—"

"Where's Little Jacob now?"

She was starting to panic and my heart was pounding like I was running from Luttermann all over again.

"I don't know, I'm sorry, your father has him, I lost him."

"Did you tell the police?"

"No, I didn't tell them anything, I was going to take the baby to them."

"You can't *do* that, don't you see! He'll tell them *I* killed Little Jacob, and they'll *hang* me! You promised, you promised!"

"I won't, I can't, he's gone," I said, trying to calm her down because I noticed kids looking at us. "I just thought . . . listen, tell me what happened at your house?"

"Nothing happened. He kept me home Friday and I helped my mother house clean and do laundry."

"Didn't he say anything to you?"

"No, just that I had to stay home and help my mother."

The first bell rang.

"Golly, I was afraid he'd beat you," I said. "I thought sure he'd figure you told someone about the baby." I took hold of her arm. "Are you sure he didn't hurt you?"

"Yes, but I don't know why he didn't figure it out."

Gretchen gathered her books and closed her locker.

"I gotta run," I said. "Maybe he thinks I was just a robber and I thought I had a ham or something."

The look in her eye scared me, and when she hurried away in the jammed corridor, I legged it to my locker, suspecting that she felt her father knew more than he'd let on. I figured he didn't hurt her because after I saw the baby he was afraid the cops would show up any minute. How long would he hold off when they didn't?

Monday the pairings for the district playoffs came out, and luck seemed against us. Central was paired with Monroe in the first round and I knew how tough that would be after playing our guts out to upset them only a few days ago. With loser out, I hoped we could finally play up to our potential and take the first step up the ladder toward the State Tournament.

"They warned us at work that some stupid kids have started a new fad," my dad said as we ate supper. "Pulling trolleys isn't enough for the delinquents of St. Paul. Now they're jumping on the fender! A motorman on the St. Clair-Phalen line had a kid jump on his the other night."

"I didn't know streetcars had fenders," Peggy said.

"People call them cowcatchers," my dad said.

"Why do they call them cowcatchers?" Peggy said, "there aren't any cows."

"Isn't that awful dangerous?" my mother said.

"If they miss, the wheels would slice them up like bacon," my dad said. "What kind of upbringing has a hoodlum like that had?"

I had a hard time swallowing, like someone had run a vacuum cleaner down my throat, and I wondered what my dad would do if he realized he was eating with that very hoodlum?

"I'm glad you're past that foolish age, Cal," my mother said.

"Yeah, so am I," I said.

Chapter 30

The snow was melting all over the place and running down sewers and I loved to see spring come. Lola and I were spending more and more time together, but Gretchen was going down hill and I tried to buck her up by telling her I'd get her away from her father soon. She'd been absent early in the week, but on Thursday, she sat behind me. I was trying to memorize a stupid poem for Bellows' class when I glanced up and saw Otto Luttermann come in the side door of the auditorium and walk toward Miss Whalmen's table. He was *here, in school,* the one place I felt safe! I slouched in my seat and peered from behind my book, trying to decide what to do while he stood there talking to the teacher.

"It's my father," Gretchen whispered.

Luttermann turned and came to our aisle and headed right for me. I wanted to jump out of my seat and blast out the back of the auditorium but I couldn't move. Had he found out I was the kid he chased all over the neighborhood? I bent over the desk top and put my head down on my arms like I was sleeping, hoping Whalmen didn't spot me because sleeping in study wasn't allowed and she'd holler my name. It felt like I was under water, holding my breath and expecting a butcher knife plunged in my back any second. Under the seats, I could see his black shoes stop at my row, leaving only two kids between me and the madman. Sweat was showing up all over my body and I just about made a break for it when Gretchen picked up her books and joined her father in the aisle.

She followed him out the side door and I straightened in my seat and I was breathing like I'd run from Chicago. Did he recognize me? I vowed to swipe two or more cases on Saturday. I had to get him before he got me.

Thursday night we took on Monroe in the District Tournament and we played like we were running in wet concrete and had sawdust for brains. Mulligan jerked Jerry when he threw a bad pass and he pulled Scott for traveling. Instead of our first step toward the State Tournament, it was really embarrassing, and the coach began playing juniors, as if to say To heck with you lousy seniors!

Once during a timeout, I looked into the stands out of habit and I almost swallowed my Adam's apple! Luttermann was sitting there with his eyeballs trained on me. Jeez, he knew who I was! I couldn't think and I couldn't concentrate on the game and I found myself sitting out most of the fourth quarter with the game still in reach.

After the game I stuck to Jerry and Scott like body guards and I kept an eye peeled for Luttermann when we left the field house with the girls. We all felt pretty lousy for the way the game turned out and we headed for home. Lola and I didn't talk much on the way and I just held her and I figured she thought I was feeling bad about the game and I wanted to tell her the truth. After we took Lola home, I had Jerry drop me in the alley and he didn't seem to think anything of it. I slipped in the back door and felt relieved to be home. When I was in bed I kept seeing Luttermann staring at me out of the bleachers and I got up and peered out my bedroom window.

Gretchen wasn't in school Friday and I was really scared for her. Why did he come and get her in the middle of study hall? Was he going to hurt her now that no cops showed up at his house? I wondered what I'd do if Gretchen never came back to class, like Helga? When the last bell rang, I ducked out the locker room door behind school, avoiding my buddies, and I legged it over to University, a way I'd never gone. I took the University streetcar to Snelling and transferred there. Like a spy I got off at Portland and bombed through alleys all the way home.

Lola and I walked to the Highland theater that night and saw *The Lady Takes A Sailor.* We sat in the back and necked during the movie and Lola snuggled up to me so cuddly that sometimes I'd realize my hand was up against her breast and I'd forget all about the movie. Criminy, once I almost jumped out of my seat when I thought I spotted Luttermann off to one side in the theater but it turned out to be only my imagination drawing bogeymen in the dark. I tried to forget about Gretchen and her father for a while and I put my tongue into the nectar of Lola's mouth.

Back at Lola's apartment it was a different story. Mary Muldoon let us know she was up and on duty while Lola and I sat on the sofa in the front room. It became a game with us, adding to the excitement. I'd cuddle with Lola and linger with a long kiss, expecting her mother to appear at any second with a phony excuse to go to the kitchen. We had untangled and bolted up two or three times when she pulled that, and everything we did seemed more exciting under the nose of Lola's mother.

"You're funny," Lola whispered.

"I am?"

"Sometimes you look at me like you've never seen me before, like you're going to eat me alive."

"I like looking at you, your little ears." I squeezed her ear. "And your bunny teeth."

"Oh, don't look at my teeth, they're dumb."

"No they're not, they're cute . . . like they're peeking at me."

I looked at those two protruding teeth and her warm, wet lips and I kissed her. The radio covered our sounds, and for the first time, right inside her mother's barricades, I moved my hand over Lola's sweater and caressed her breast. I don't think I'd have dared if it wasn't for the goofy mood we were in with her mother acting like the FBI. Jeez, Lola let me hold her breast for a minute and then pushed my hand away.

"My mother," she whispered.

Holy cow, I was so excited I couldn't remember my name.

With one eye cocked on the hallway, I was blowing fuses right under Mary Muldoon's nose. I had my hand under Lola's sweater on her bare back when her mother's voice came marching down the hall.

"Time to come to bed, Lola."

I wanted to ask, Can I come too? but instead I caught a streetcar for home. I realized I'd forgotten all about Gretchen for a while and I didn't understand why, but to touch Lola's breasts was the most wonderful thing I'd ever imagined, and I hoped I wasn't some kind of pervert or something but I wanted to fondle them, to memorize them, to sleep with my head nestled against them.

On the way home, I dared sneak halfway up Goodrich from Fairview to spy on Gretchen's house and yard. Everything seemed normal and the black Plymouth was parked at the curb. I shivered as I peered out of the shadows, and I hoped that Gretchen was all right. Then I turned and raced for home.

Chapter 31

On Monday, Gretchen slid along the row behind me in study hall and settled in her seat. I turned and whispered.

"What was your dad doing here?"

"He was sick, he got off early and didn't want to come back for me."

"Did he recognize me?"

"I don't know."

"He was at the basketball game Thursday night," I said.

"Basketball game? What time?"

"Oh . . . around eight-thirty, nine."

"I think he was home," she said with a puzzled expression. "Are you sure—"

"I saw him staring at me," I said. "Does he still go for walks at night?"

"Yes . . . but sometimes he goes out the front door now."

"Maybe he went out early Thursday night."

"No . . . I think he stayed home, he was sick."

Jeez, now I was more confused than ever, like I couldn't believe my own eyes.

I felt like The Shadow or something, ducking Luttermann all week. I rode the streetcar to school and back instead of hitching, and I bombed home right after school. I didn't go to the Hi-Y or sorority meetings Tuesday night, and on the phone, I told Lola I was feeling kind of sick and we didn't go out Friday night. I zig-zagged all over the neighborhood getting home so he couldn't find out where I lived, and I stayed out of sight in our apartment.

On Saturday I took a roundabout way to work, through alleys and yards, worrying that Luttermann recognized me as the kid in the truck behind the bakery. At work there were no orders to pick up liquor, and I slammed a box of groceries into the back of the truck with the darn luck. I had named my plan Rat Trap in honor of Gretchen's father and I knew I had to get it done.

I decided to stop behind the liquor store anyway, figuring I could ask Sid if there were any deliveries, like I'd forgotten to check with Mr. Finley. When I got there, Sid was waiting on some customers up front, and I didn't hesitate. I grabbed a case of Schenely Whiskey and hauled it to the truck. Jeez, every pore was seeping sweat and my heart was pounding, but I blasted up the concrete steps of the loading dock, back into the storeroom. I snatched a case of Old Grand-Dad bourbon and stumbled to the truck like a guy saving stuff from a house fire. Without looking back, I careened up the ice-rutted alley rather than out onto Prior where Sid might spot the truck. I shouted. Two cases, and Sid didn't know I'd been there.

When I got to the hideout, three grade-school kids were dorking around in the alley and I waited about five minutes until they finally headed for the railroad tracks. When they were out of sight, I stashed the two cases in the deserted garage. With every week, I knew the chance of some kid finding the booze went up and I hated to think of coming for it in the middle of Rat Trap and finding the liquor gone, like trying to light a stick of dynamite with a train roaring down on you and finding you'd lost your matches. With cardboard, old shingles, and rags, I covered the six cases under what looked like a worthless pile of junk, and then I took off, knowing it would be a disaster if anyone spotted me around the old garage.

I'd finished dressing for the hay ride when my mother stepped into my room with one roller in her hair and a sadness in her eyes.

"I know you must be disappointed that your father didn't go to your games, Calvin."

"Yeah, it's okay."

"Do you know *why* he didn't?"

"I don't know," I snapped. "He was tired, he wasn't feeling good, there wasn't time without a car."

I pulled on my jacket and zipped in my anger and I wanted to get out of there.

"I think he's jealous," my mother said quietly.

"Jealous!" That was the dumbest thing I'd ever heard.

"Not so much of you as what you were doing."

My mother stepped into the doorway, blocking my escape. Jeez, I hated talking about stuff like that.

"I gotta go."

"Did you know that he went to Central, too?"

"No-o-o, he never told me that."

I couldn't believe it, my dad went to *Central!*

"He did, and every day after school he walked downtown and worked for three or four hours, the whole time he went to high school. He never got to play sports, and he wanted to so badly. He once told me that he could always outrun and outhit his boyhood friends. He was a natural athlete." She paused for a minute. "So, I think it was just too hard for him to go and watch you and remember all that he missed out on. Do you see, Calvin? It wasn't *you.*"

"Yeah, I guess so." My voice was choking up.

"Don't blame him," she said.

"I don't blame anybody. " I slid past her in the doorway. "I gotta go."

It was getting dark when the eight of us crept up the bank towards the porch of the spooky house like little kids, shoving and tugging and laughing nervously. I told Steve I had to run an errand for my mom and had him pick me up over at the drugstore on Selby after I sneaked out of the apartment and made my way through yards and alleys.

We were dressed for a moonlight hayride, and they all

wanted to tempt fate and thumb their noses at the Terror of Summit Avenue one more time and I wished I could tell them who'd been chasing me.

We pussyfooted onto the porch and you could see a faint light from behind the drapes.

"Isn't this mean?" Lola asked on her first trip to the porch.

"Naw, it keeps the old guy going," Steve said. "He loves chasing us."

Steve was with Jean, a veteran of this game, along with Jerry and Sally, and Scott and Katie were bouncing up and down like they wondered if they weren't tempting fate once too often.

Inches from the large wood door we milled and pushed and nudged one another and no one had the guts to knock, like we knew that the scary time just before it happened was as much fun as being chased. Steve couldn't stand it and he pounded on the door like a bill collector. Sally and Lola broke for the steps, but Jerry and I grabbed them and held them on the porch.

"I'm scared," Lola said.

"That's what's fun," Jerry said.

All eight of us stood there quietly laughing, expecting the Runner to come blasting out the door any second. Nothing happened.

"Knock again," Steve said, "he didn't hear us."

Jerry stepped up, dragging Sally with him, and pounded again while we all braced ourselves with one eye on the door and one foot pointed toward the street.

The latch clicked and Steve and the girls flew off the porch like a covey of partridge while Scott and Jerry and I retreated to the wide concrete steps with our eyes riveted on the door. It opened slowly, and a small woman showed up in the doorway, alone. We hung there like dorks, trying to think of what to do next, and then Scott, always one with the manners, stepped toward the door.

"Hello, ah . . . does Mike Birt live here?"

"No . . . not here," the woman answered softly.

Jerry and I moved up beside Scott, and I looked past her into the house. In a wheelchair, with the left side of his face slack and droopy and an Afghan over his lap, the Runner slumped like he'd been shot.

"Sorry to bother you, ma'am," Scott said. "We must have the wrong house."

We turned and started down the steps.

"He'd chase you if he could," she said.

Holy Moses, we were bayoneted by her words, and we did an about-face.

"Yes, ma'am," Scott said. "We're sorry."

We drove out Lexington for the Circle "S" Ranch and jabbered about the times the Runner had scared the noodles out of us, about Sandy's famous dash, already exaggerating like crazy. Under a railroad bridge, everyone held a hand on the roof, making a wish, as Steve leaned on the horn and the Chevy yodeled a two-note song and blasted our secret hopes out toward the moon.

We actually had moonlight, and while we snuggled in the hay under the skidding clouds, all we could hear was the hooves of the horses and the harness bells. I'd made off with two cases of liquor that day, and the accumulating stash, like a can of gasoline on a stove, reminded me that I would have to come up with the guts to finish it.

"Do you ever feel lonesome?" Lola whispered.

"Yeah, sometimes."

"I don't when I'm with you," she said, pressing her warm lips on my ear. "I feel happy when I'm with you, like the world's a good place." She sounded sad.

"Is your mom still mad at you?" I said.

"Yeah . . . she thinks I should be going out with Tom."

I rode through the sharp spring air under the silver clouds and I cuddled with Lola and I felt alone and I couldn't quit thinking about Little Jacob and Gretchen and I hated Otto Luttermann's guts and I prayed I'd be brave enough to do what I had to do. The temptation to give it up came gliding out of nowhere like an owl, coaxing me to turn away from Gretchen and her insane family and cling to Lola, to enjoy my final days at Central with the girl I'd always love.

After we'd taken the girls home, I bombed out of the back-seat when Steve dropped off Scott and told them I wanted to walk. I cut through yards and alleys as if the Runner was right on my tail and when I hit my block I knew no one could have followed me. At the alley I stopped and I was breathing pretty hard. I crouched by McCluskey's wood fence and studied the distance to the back door of the apartment. A light wind whispered in the bare branches and everything seemed normal and the neighborhood shadows looked familiar and safe. I was about to sneak down the fence when a funny feeling stopped me, like I could feel someone watching me. Jeez, I stood there sweating and I couldn't make myself move and I was scaring myself sick.

McCluskey's wood fence on one side, a bare lilac hedge and garage on the other, twenty yards of alley, my alley, where I shot buckets and played for years. Cripes, I snapped out of it and forced myself to leg it, holding my breath, telling myself I was imagining things. I tried to move quietly but it sounded like I was walking on broken glass. When I passed the garage and the telephone pole with my backboard on it, I started breathing again and the good old apartment building stood there solid in the night like a castle welcoming me home safe.

Before I reached the door his arm locked around my neck. Instantly every muscle in my body fought him, elbowed, twisted and kicked, but he was really strong. Pain gagged in my throat. I tried to yell but couldn't and his iron grip crushed the strength out of me. He was dragging me back-wards and I thought he'd break my neck. There was no more air in the world. I couldn't fight him anymore, spiraling down, down. Everything went black and splintering daggers shot into my skull and I knew I was dying and I remember thinking, He got me, darn it, he got me!

Then, like out of a dream, I heard Peggy's clear young voice.

"We've called the police! The police are on the way! We've called the police!"

Instantly I *was* falling and my head hit the asphalt but there was air in the world again, sweet, precious air, and breath. I found myself lying in the dark by the corner of the neighbor's garage, sputtering and gasping, and I saw Peggy tooling down the alley with a handful of lettuce and stuff. She never saw Luttermann or me, figuring she'd cleared the alley of evil without a clue that this time she had. I sat up and my throat felt like it was on fire and I coughed up blood and my windpipe seemed to be caved in. I was woozy but I had to get up and get into the apartment, Luttermann might be back any second. Then it hit me, he wouldn't be back, hauling his scrawny ass for home, thinking someone had actually called the police. I knew it was funny but I couldn't laugh.

Peggy hustled back through the alley and I picked myself up and walked out of the shadows, a little wobbly.

"Hi, Cal, how was the hayride?"

"It was fun," I said with a very strange voice.

"What's the matter, you been cryin'?"

"No, I think I'm getting a cold," I said as we slipped quietly in the door to the back stairway.

"You probably got cold on the hayride," she whispered as we opened our apartment door.

"Yeah. Did you see Hot-foot?"

"No, but I left him lots of food. Good-night, Cal."

"Peg . . ." I said and I reached out and hugged her.

"Don't," she said and pulled away. "I don't want to get your cold."

She tiptoed down the hall and I wished I could thank her for saving my life and I hoped that some day, when Luttermann was in jail, I could tell her what she'd done. But for now, no one but Gretchen could know I'd ever heard of Otto Luttermann. I thought of calling the police and telling them he tried to kill me, but I never saw him and his wife could lie and say he never left home and he'd get out of it and then he'd get Gretchen. Now I believed her; he'd kill her.

I got a drink of water at the kitchen sink and tried to calm down but I was shaking so hard I thought my teeth would rattle out and I couldn't get over how my little sister had spooked Luttermann and made him let go while there was still a few seconds of life left in me.

I was breathing hard and sweating and my heart was thumping, and I was still plenty scared of him, but I hated the guy, and now I knew I could do it and there'd be no more putting it off and I couldn't wait to nail him. I wanted to punch him in the face for trying to kill me, I wanted to hammer my body into him like madman Fred Walker in tackling drills, I wanted to bury him.

It was hard to swallow but I drank a little more water and I was calming down some and I sat at the kitchen table in the shadows and it dawned on me that in the crazy way life works out the little cottontail I'd saved last fall had just saved me—the bunny and my wonderful sister.

Chapter 32

On Sunday I tried to cover the bruises on my neck with the collar of my shirt but my parents spotted them in about two seconds. I said I'd been wrestling and goofing around on the hayride and Peggy said I probably got them from all the necking and we all laughed, even my dad.

I don't know why, but we always celebrated birthdays at breakfast in our family. I don't think it had anything to do with being Norwegian, but we had our sliced bananas earlier than usual Monday morning so my dad could be at the party. My parents gave me a swell double-breasted brown suit to wear at graduation.

"That will be a red-letter day for our family," my dad said. "Our high school graduate. I'm already getting proud."

"I can't believe he's eighteen," Peggy said. "Doesn't seem that old."

"You'll have to register for the draft now, Calvin," my mother said with worry in her face.

"I'm a grownup now," I said to Peggy, "and children have to mind grownups."

"I don't have to mind him, do I Mom, do I?"

She sprang from her chair, pigtails flying, and put a hammerlock on me.

"Let's spank him, let's spank him!"

I pretended to fight them off but I let them get me down on the kitchen floor and spank me, eighteen times each, and a pinch to grow an inch. Peggy and I had learned not to whack very hard or we'd get it back when our turn came. I made a wish and blew out the candles on my cake.

"What did you wish?" Peggy asked.

"I can't tell, or it won't come true."

None of them in seventeen hundred years could have guessed.

My dad had to be at work early. They were shuffling drivers around in their schedules so they could train them to drive buses.

"I'm a streetcar motorman, not a moron bus driver. I wouldn't drive one of those stinking machines . . ."

He pulled on his jacket and picked up his lunch box.

"They think the people of this city are stupid, that they'd rather ride on one of those filthy diesel contraptions than on a clean, quiet streetcar. The streetcars have been good enough for fifty years and they'd be good for fifty more."

He went out the back door, steaming like a radiator.

The way Gretchen'd been going through Nut Goodies I figured the Pearson Candy Company would have to build another plant, but when I gave her one before the bell in study hall, I realized she wouldn't last much longer. She'd given up, with no sign of hope in her hollow eyes, and the strong little light in her that always surprised me had gone out. I didn't tell her about her father trying to kill me; I thought it would really upset her and she might snap and go crazy, but now we both had his scars and I'd never doubt her again.

"Just a few more days," I told her, "and he won't be able to hurt you anymore."

Gad, I was tired of hearing it myself. My words didn't seem to register with her and her glassy stare said Fish stories, only more fish stories. She mumbled something about moth balls and I didn't get it at first but I knew they were poison and then it hit me that maybe she was thinking about killing herself. The bell rang and the assembly hall got quiet, and I wished I could convince her that it wasn't just talk anymore. Her face told me; if I didn't do it quickly, something terrible would happen. All week I went to school and came home with one or more of my buddies and I didn't stick my nose out of the apartment after dark.

When Mr. Finley said, "Stop at the liquor store," my body
turned into a gigantic goose bump. I'd prayed there would be
a liquor order and Mr. Finley's words seemed to whack me
on the back and send me across the starting line. I slammed
the door of the loaded truck and headed up Grand.

Spring was popping out all over; I loved it; it always
reminded me of Uncle Emil. I planned to wear the green
cashmere sweater Lola had given me for my birthday to the
dance that night, The Fool's Frolic. That morning, April Fool's
Day, I'd been on guard, but my dad, more and more gloomy
over the wrecking of the streetcars, hadn't tried to hoodwink
me as usual. Peggy was so gullible it wasn't much of a chal-
lenge to trick her, but I'd sliced a hot dog on a bowl of
Wheaties and set it in front of my mother at the table with
her coffee. She laughed some of the worry off her face and
tried to tickle me like she always did.

When I pulled in behind the liquor store I tried to calm
down by thinking of Lola and the dance. I'd settled on the
number ten to be sure it was enough to make it a big-time
crime, and if I could pick off two today, I'd have ten. Inside
the storeroom there were two cases with the yellow order
slips stuck on them. I loaded one in the truck, Ridels down
on the River Boulevard, and then went to the front of the
store to find Sid. Darn, there were no customers, but Sid was
sweating over a pile of invoices at the counter.

"Just the two orders today?"

"Oh . . . yeah," Sid said, glancing up, "just the two."

He was really busy so I hustled back and heisted a case of
Walker's DeLuxe and hauled it to the truck. Then, in a cold
sweat, I came back for the other real order. When I had that
in the truck, my instincts told me to get the heck out of there,
but one more would make it ten, maybe four or five hundred
dollars worth. I was so scared I could feel my heartbeat in my
eyeballs, but I hurtled the steps and grabbed a case of Old
Fitzgerald. I had slammed the door on the back of the truck
and piled in to gun away, when Sid showed up at the back
door with a bottle of vodka in his hand.

"Cal, hold on! I forgot a vodka for Ridels."

If I could do it over I'd just drive away like I didn't hear, but I hesitated, a split second, I couldn't think, I couldn't move, and I was lost. Sid was at the back of the truck, opening the door. I jumped out and rushed back, in hopes I could distract him from noticing the two extra cases in with all the grocery boxes.

"Here, I'll take it," I said, reaching for the bottle but he hung on to it and tried to open a carton I'd stolen, thinking it was one he'd filled with an assortment of liquor. It was sealed, and his eyes were zigzagging all over the place. I stood there like a stump, trying to make up my mind to run while he looked at the other Old Fitzgerald box with Ridels' order sticking out. My legs turned to rubber and my body quit breathing on its own.

"What the hell's going on here?"

I couldn't tell which eye was looking at me but I knew one of them was.

"You stealing from me . . . you god damn stealing from me, you little bastard?"

"Nooo, those were all together, I thought they were part of the orders."

Sid grabbed me by the neck and dragged me into the storeroom.

"Why you dirty little crook, you been stealin' me blind."

He whacked me on the ear and dragged me toward the front of the store and I could hear a ringing sound in my head. I thought of breaking away, slugging him and running, but what good would it do? He had me red-handed. He shoved me in the corner behind the counter and reached for the phone.

"It was just an April Fool's joke," I said. "I was going to bring them back."

He dialed and I was in a daze, like it wasn't really happening, and I didn't hear much of the call or the cuss words Sid was shouting at me, and I tried to shake myself out of it and use my head.

"I know you're in on the streetcar deal, and I won't tell the police if you let me go."

He straightened his stooped shoulders and looked surprised.

"What are you talking about?"

"You know, you know, the streetcars, and all the money you're making with the other crooks."

"You been reading too many comic books," he said.

"Bringing in the buses, ripping out the track, you know, with Firestone and General Motors."

I hoped to make him think I knew more than I did, and for a second, Sid's wacky eyes narrowed and he looked scared.

"You don't know what you're talking about, you little snotnose. Your crazy stories won't get you out of this."

A squad car pulled up in front and two policemen got out and headed for the front door. I could feel porcupine quills in my throat and I thought about Gretchen. I'd failed her. She'd go crazy now, or kill herself. I could hear Uncle Emil's matter-of-fact voice. "Bit off more than he could chew."

Handcuffed like a dangerous criminal, I rode in the back of the squad car. Off the top of my head, I told them I'd taken the liquor for some friends and Sid cried bloody murder that I'd probably been robbing him blind all winter. They drove down Grand Avenue and I slumped in the backseat, figuring everyone in St. Paul would know about it in eleven seconds. We passed a streetcar coming from downtown, and I thought about how I'd gotten into this, how I'd screwed it all up, and what I'd give to be riding that Grand-Mississippi home.

Chapter 33

Downtown they hauled me into the city jail like I was going
to make a break for it or something. I shuffled around the
police station in a daze, hardly knowing what was going on,
papers and questions and waiting in grubby rooms. It was
like I'd thrown up on myself and I'd never be clean again and
people would screw up their faces and hold their noses like
they did when I had the bean soup all over my jacket.

"How old are you?"

"Eighteen."

"Sorry, kid, you're not a youngster anymore, you're into the
big time now."

They called my parents. Cripes! What would my dad think
about me, and my mom, and Lola? I couldn't think straight
and I tried to decide what I'd tell them, and I thought of
Gretchen. If I told the truth, what would happen to her? If I
told them about the stash it would only get me into a lot
more trouble, and even if it wouldn't, would I give up on
stopping Luttermann? I could almost laugh at how screwed
up everything was; they snagged the wrong guy.

In a small room, I sweat with my bawling mother. They
took off the handcuffs but I couldn't think of anything to say
and she sat beside me on a wooden bench like she'd been
run over.

"I don't know what I've done wrong, Calvin. We did the
best we could. What did we do? What did I do?" she sobbed.
"I give up the ghost."

"It wasn't *you*, Mom, you didn't do anything."

"How could you *do* such a thing? How could you *do* this to
us? I did the best I could. Didn't we do the best we could? I
tell you, I'm hoodooed."

"It'll be all right, don't worry, Mom."

"Don't worry? Don't *worry!* You're in *jail.* You've been

arrested! You'll have a criminal record for the rest of your *life,* and you say Don't worry?"

"How's Dad?"

"He doesn't know what to do. He refused to come to a jail to see you, said If Calvin's been stealing liquor, let him stay in jail, that's where he belongs."

We sat there like strangers and my mother sobbed and kept blowing her nose into a soaked hanky.

"They say a public defender will help you if we don't have a lawyer," she said. "I don't know what to do; should we get a lawyer?"

"Gosh, no, Mom, I don't need a lawyer. Cripes, I stole the stuff. What good would a lawyer do?"

Finally a policeman came to the open doorway and told her she had to go. I stood awkwardly.

"Will you call Lola? I had a date with her tonight."

My mother struggled to stand, like she'd turned a hundred and thirty-seven years old in the last ten minutes, and it really bothered me to see her like that.

"What'll I tell her? That you're in *jail?*"

Criminy, I didn't know what she should tell her, or if it would make any difference.

"Tell her I'm sick, that I have the flu."

They were holding me over the weekend until I could see a judge on Monday. My mother would ride the Grand-Mississippi home alone.

When the iron door to my cell slammed shut, it echoed like I was in a huge dungeon or something and I could still hear it even though I'd been sitting there thinking for a long time. I tried not to panic but I was really scared and I thought I might go nuts any minute. I stood up and steadied myself against the cold iron wall. Spit on it, I told myself. Spit on it!

The cell was only big enough to take about two steps and you had to turn around. It had a metal toilet without a lid and two bunks that folded from the wall. Jeez, when you had to go to the can, anyone walking by could stare at you, like an animal at Como Zoo, and I figured I'd wait until it was dark to go.

There were guys in the other cells, but I couldn't see them. The cells faced a corridor that had high windows on the opposite side. I hoisted myself onto the upper bunk and tried to ignore the strange voices and sounds around me.

When it got dark and they finally turned off most of the lights, I couldn't sleep. I could see Lola's face and her bunny teeth and I remembered how she laughed. I escaped through the barred window on the wings of my memories, across the sky, north, and I thought about Uncle Emil and the time I rode the moose.

We were cutting across a large lake in the Old Town canoe when my uncle spotted a bull moose swimming from an island to the far shore. We paddled like crazy until we caught up with it. I didn't know they could swim and it was kind of dog-paddling along. Jeez, it was huge and its antlers looked like two big sails and it was snorting at us, but it was pretty helpless because it had to keep swimming or it would sink. My uncle told me to ease over the side of the canoe and get on its back. By that time—the third summer I'd spent with him—I'd do anything he told me.

I slipped into the water and swam up on the back of the moose and hung on to the hair on his neck. Uncle Emil stayed back a ways in the canoe and he clapped.

"Thata boy, thata boy, ride 'em cowboy!"

I started to think that maybe this wasn't such a good idea and the bull kept looking over his shoulder at me with a big, black eye and he was saying Wait until I get you on shore, you little twerp. My uncle had taught me that a moose was more unpredictable and cantankerous than a bear, that just for the heck of it he might come over and stomp you. I yelled at my uncle.

"What do I do now?"

"You climbed on, now you gotta ride it out."

My uncle laughed and I didn't dare get off because I was afraid the moose would turn around in the water and slice me up with his front hooves. I hung onto his neck and rode it out and even though I was in the cool lake I was sweating like mad.

When the moose was almost to the shore my uncle told me to slide off. Jeez, easy for him to say, but I did, and I started swimming to beat the band, out into the lake towards the canoe. The moose hit bottom and walked out of the water and looked back at us. He shook his black coat and snorted, like he was saying Come on over here and try that. My uncle told me that there weren't many people in the whole world who had ever ridden on the back of a wild moose and for the rest of the summer I felt pretty good about myself.

But as I thought about it in my little bunk in the dark cell, I felt like I was riding that moose again, scared to death at what I was doing, and I could hear my uncle's words, "You climbed on. Now you gotta ride it out." I *had* climbed on, but I didn't know if I could ride it out and I didn't know how to get off.

I'd never been in a courtroom and it felt like a funeral parlor, though I'd never been in a funeral parlor either, but with all the dark woodwork and dim lights and everyone quiet it was like someone had died. I stood in front of a high bench like a murderer and the sad-looking guy who was the public defender stood beside me, too fat for his suit. When I'd talked with him in my cell the day before, he told me to plead guilty at my arraignment because it was my first offense or something. At the arraignment I was in and out of a much smaller room in about three seconds and the guy told the judge *we* pleaded guilty. Jeez, it sounded like he was in on it with me.

My mother and father huddled in the first row and a

bunch of gloomy-faced people were there—I didn't know who the heck they were—hanging around to watch the Gant family's public humiliation. The scrawny, white-haired judge looked like he'd died five years ago but he stared at me like he ate nails for breakfast.

"Don't you love your parents?" he said.

"Yes."

"*Look* at your parents!"

I turned, but my father, in his Sunday suit, wouldn't lift his head. My mother glanced at me for a second like I was an orphan and then she turned her crying eyes to her lap.

"Do you see what you're *doing* to them?" the judge said.

I turned back to face him.

"Well, *do you?*"

"Yes."

I hated the judge for what he was doing to all of us.

"I don't know what's getting into you youngsters. You think you can go out and break the law whenever you please. You usually don't get caught the first time, so I assume you've been doing this right along. Your crime falls under Minnesota Statute 622.06, Grand Larceny, Second Degree. Do you know what the penalty is, son?"

"No."

"Up to five years in the state prison. What do you think of that?"

It's funny, but right then I thought: Darn, I didn't have to swipe ten, *two* would've been enough, but I couldn't tell the old bugger that. Behind me, I heard a sob fall from my mother's lap.

"I don't know," I said.

"It's not so funny, now, is it. I'm giving you thirty days in the workhouse as a good lesson. And one year probation. And, son, you better keep your nose clean. Anymore trouble, if you get so much as a traffic ticket, I'll ship you to St. Cloud for a year or two."

The judge pounded his gavel once.

"Thirty days!"

A hardboiled-policeman took my arm and led me out a side door. At the last second I glanced back at my parents. They were sitting there like statues, staring at the floor.

Chapter 34

They hauled me to the workhouse, only a couple miles out Lexington from Central. The sad-looking brick building crouched in the middle of a huge lawn, and I remembered the times I passed it and pitied the poor guys inside. The days took forever, living with winos, con artists and petty criminals, and the old guys kept asking What's a kid like you doing in here?

I thought I'd be breaking huge rocks with a sledge hammer all day—they called it the workhouse—but most of the time I spent twiddling my thumbs in a cell, although for a part of each day I did have to mop floors and clean latrines. Jeez, you should've seen the toilets. I thought I was in an institution for the blind! The smells and filth turned my stomach, but I did the kind of job my dad would be proud of and I swallowed my anger with the crummy food. I tried to sleep as much as possible and do my time in that outhouse, but sometimes at night, I cried into my mattress and I wanted to tell someone that they had the wrong guy.

There was a friendly old palooka who kind of took me under his wing, like what I needed was the advice of a bum in the workhouse. Spence had the eyes of a sawed-off shotgun and he smoked cigarettes down so far his fingers were yellowed and scorched and his face was so wrinkled and leathery it reminded me of an old catcher's mitt. He'd talk quietly for hours, and a lot of it was gibberish, but I couldn't help liking the guy, and I told him about Lola, and my dad, and a little about Gretchen.

"Homo sapiens is a mammal species that needs physical, skin to skin, touching and affection to *survive*," old Spence told me one gray afternoon. "Caressing and kissing and effing are not frivolous pleasures, the fancy frosting of life, but *necessities*, like air, water, and food. It has been demonstrated—"

He coughed like he'd choke to death, wiping phlegm on his sleeve, and he caught his breath.

"It has been demonstrated that infants of this species who aren't loved in this manner *die.*"

Spence paused and squinted out of his crimped face.

"Same goes for adults. They don't fall-down-and-quit-breathing die, but they *die.*"

"What do you mean?" I said.

"They substitute material things for love and hoard them; they use alcohol and drugs to numb the pain; they hide in the sterile world of the intellect; they escape by slipping off into insanity; or they strike out in rage, stealing and destroying and killing. But without physical love, they *die.*"

Spence nodded at a fat prisoner hauling his three hundred pounds to the lavatory.

"See that poor soul."

"Yeah," I said, watching the huge, baby-faced inmate.

"He thinks food is love, and he's trying to fill the emptiness in his heart and soul with mashed potatoes and gravy."

Spence told me he'd gotten a Ph.D. in philosophy from Northwestern University, but I found it hard to believe. What would a smart guy like that be doing in here? But I had to admit that some of what he said made a lot of sense and I figured he turned to booze when someone didn't love him and I wondered if Steve felt so bad about his brother that he was doing the same.

Sunday finally arrived, Easter, and Steve was the first waiting to see me. I got so choked up when I saw him, I couldn't talk for almost a minute, and right then I felt so close to him I knew we'd be friends for the rest of our lives. We sat facing each other on the wooden benches in the grubby visitors' room, knee to knee.

"How are you doing?" Steve said, forcing a smile over the lousy circumstances.

"I'm learning how to clean toilets."

"Looks like you're in one."

Then we just sat there like we were afraid to talk about it, but Steve had more guts than I did.

"Did you really do it?" he said.

"Yeah."

"I don't believe it, I just don't believe it." He shook his head. "What in the heck for?"

Jeez, it was hard to come up with a reason that made sense.

"I don't know . . . to sell," I said.

"You're lying, you stupid peckerhead, you'd never do that."

I could see the anger and disappointment in Steve's eyes and I wanted to tell him the truth.

"Is that why you wanted to hot-wire a car?"

"No . . . that was just to use Finley's truck a few times."

With things on a sour note, Steve handed me a letter from Lola and I looked at it for a second and shoved it in my pocket until I could read it alone.

"Cripes, we've got to break you outta here," he said, and he smiled like old times. "Central's not the same without you. We had D.B. going crazy on Thursday, Bellows nailed Jerry's butt with a poem, and Sandy's in Kirschbach's seventh period for a month."

He sprayed the depressing room with his laughter and I don't know why but it really made me feel good, it really did, but it seemed like Steve was there about two minutes and his time was up.

"Only twenty-one days to go," I said. "Thanks for coming."

"I always wanted to know a convict I could visit in jail."

We stood and almost bumped heads and without thinking, I hugged him. He hesitated at first, but then he bear-hugged me back. I don't know where the words came from but I heard them falling out of my mouth.

"I'm glad you didn't jump off the Ford Bridge."

"So am I," he said and he punched me on the shoulder.

Lola's note said that she was really sorry, but her mother had forbidden her to see me anymore. *She* was sorry! Jeez, I tore up the note and flushed it down one of my polished toilets so none of the jailers or outlaws could read it and make fun of me. It was almost funny: a Dear-John letter into the john and I could see Lola's mother running a victory flag up her mast. At least someone was happy with the way things turned out.

They called me to the visitors' room again, just before visiting hours were over. My mother had come, alone. In better control of herself, she began with small talk about food and toothpaste and how the screens needed to be put up. Then she told me I'd been expelled, that I couldn't graduate with the class and with several arrow shafts still dripping blood from my chest, I wondered how many more were in the air.

"Why did you do it, Calvin?"

"I didn't, I mean . . . not really. Oh, I can't explain it."

The question hung in the room, unanswered, like in Bellows' class, and I wished one of the inmates or visitors would raise a hand and come up with an answer.

"I can't understand it, Calvin. You've always been such a *good* boy."

My mother was really confused and she tried to under-stand what only I could explain. Jeez, I wanted to tell her about Rat Trap, but I couldn't give up on Gretchen.

"I told Pastor Ostrum. He said he'd come to see you."

Holy smoke, the whole world would know. I wondered what Mr. Finley would think, and my friends and teachers? My mother got up to leave.

"Say hello to Dad for me," I said.

"You'll never know how bad you've hurt him," she said with a different worry in her voice. "Awful bad."

She faked a hug and then limped over to the big iron door and disappeared.

Chapter 35

When what had happened finally sunk in, I was really ticked off, and I scrubbed and polished latrines like I wanted to kill someone. Darn it, that wasn't the way it was supposed to turn out. I'd blasted my parents, lost the girl I loved, thrown away my chance to graduate with my class and just about been choked to death, and after all of that, Otto Luttermann hadn't a scratch on him and I was locked up and couldn't do a thing to help Gretchen.

I could save myself, some, by explaining my plan to my father and mother, and to Lola, and they'd believe me. They might think I was stupid for trying something like that, but at least they'd know I wasn't a lousy thief. But if I told them, I'd be giving up on Gretchen just so they wouldn't think I was a jerk or something. In court the cops could make them tell what they knew and Luttermann would get away, but they couldn't tell what they didn't know and maybe I could tell them later, when Luttermann was locked up and Gretchen safe. Until then my family and friends would have to think I was a bad apple, because I just couldn't get back in good with them and save my reputation with Gretchen's only chance.

I found out later that on Wednesday afternoon, my dad was driving his streetcar through downtown St. Paul on Fourth Street, probably worrying over me and not paying attention, when he pulled up behind a driver who was trying to back his four-hole Buick into a parking space. The bald man shook his fist and honked, motioning for my dad to back up, but my dad wasn't about to back up for a stupid automobile. Let him go around the block and try again. The driver got out and shouted at my dad, motioning him back, but my dad held his ground as another streetcar pulled up behind. The guy locked the doors on his car and stomped off, leaving the streetcar blocked and my dad steaming. The streetcars and cars began stacking up and honking and ringing their bells like it was a Fourth of July parade.

After several minutes, the driver came back with a policeman, explaining what happened and pointing at the streetcar. The cop marched over and told my dad to back it up. Holy cow, how could he back up with half the streetcars and cars in St. Paul lined up behind him. The traffic jam now piled up three blocks back to Wabasha with drivers shouting and leaning on their horns.

The cop walked behind my dad's streetcar and motioned the next car back. Foot by foot and minute by minute, they made enough room so the smirking driver could back his Buick into the parking space. Twenty-eight minutes behind schedule, my dad pulled the plug from the dam, heading out north on Mississippi Street. The next day my dad had a fit at breakfast when he saw the whole thing reported in Thursday morning's *Pioneer Press*.

Every day it rained like crazy, and the sweet smell of greening grass drifted through the high barred windows. I kept out of sight as much as possible through the next week, did what I was told, and polished the toilets to a shine. Spence came in the can one day and leveled his shot-gun eyes at me.

"You mad at the toilets?"

I stopped attacking the hardened stains and sat back on my heels while the old guy stood at the urinal.

"This isn't the way I thought it would turn out," I said.

"Life's a surprise, a pin-the-tail-on-the-donkey surprise. When you think you've stuck it on his ass, you find out you've stuck it in your ear."

He shook off his dong and turned to face me.

"I've been thinking about how brave we all are." The

worn-out old man staggered slightly and braced himself with one arm against the crummy wall. He peered into the daylight streaming through the high glass-cubed window, talking in a whisper like the light was a vision from God.

"We keep on trying, we go on and on and on without love, searching, hoping . . . carrying on another hour, another day . . . You know what?" He turned and looked at me squatting on the floor. "Here's the kicker. We keep wanting someone to love us, our mother or father, the woman in our life . . . friends, or God." Spence coughed and blew his nose into a urinal, one nostril at a time. "Surprise, surprise. I think, finally, the love we need the most is our own . . . we never learn to love ourselves."

He shuffled out of the lavatory with his fly open, and I sat on my haunches for a minute, confused. I thought you weren't supposed to love yourself; you'd turn out conceited and selfish. I guessed Spence had never felt loved, and I wondered how my life would turn out? Could I possibly end up like Spence, alone, unwanted, left at the city dump like a worn-out shoe?

My mother came on Sunday and told me some friends were waiting to see me. She was a lot better and she tried to act her old self and make everything happy. What I'd done still confused her, but it wasn't the end of the world, and she was sure that I'd learn some great lesson, like the judge said, and never again disgrace them like that. She tried to cheer me up, and I tried to return the kindness, and we parted on a high note.

"Only fourteen more days," she said as she hugged me.

"Yeah, only fourteen."

Sandy came next and I was really embarrassed to have her see me there. She sat next to me on one of the benches along the wall with the grubby room full of women visiting their husbands and boyfriends and it felt strange with Sandy there.

"I know you didn't do it, Bean, I just know you wouldn't."

"Thanks."

She yakked about school and told me that Scott was going with Katie and she tried to smile but I could tell how bad she felt.

"Have you seen Lola?" I said.

"Yes . . . she's . . ."

"I figured she'd be back with Tom," I said.

Sandy nodded. "I talked to Gretchen the other day."

I hadn't dared ask, but as long as Sandy brought her up I figured it wouldn't hurt to find out what I could.

"How is she?" I said.

"She came up to me in the hall and asked about you. When I told her you wouldn't be back to school, that you were in jail, she looked like she was going to be sick. She just said Oh, no, oh, no, and walked away like I wasn't even standing there."

"Would you do me a big favor, Sand?"

"Sure, anything."

"Get a Nut Goodie and give it to Gretchen and tell her it's from Cal."

"A *Nut Goodie!*"

"Yeah, but don't tell anyone else about it. Will you do it?"

"Sure, Bean, but why a Nut Goodie?"

"Just say it's from Cal; she'll understand."

The candy bar was the only way I could think of to let Gretchen know that I was still on her side and that I hadn't given up on her or on stopping her father.

When Sandy left, Jerry and Scott showed up, and I was starting to wish they didn't allow visitors.

"This is a mickey heaven," Jerry said as he eyeballed an old wino, and I could tell he was trying to avoid it by joking around. "I could go crazy in here."

"So could I," I said.

"Are you getting out soon?" Scott said.

"Yeah, two weeks."

We were really uncomfortable, fumbling for words, though both of them tried to show they were on my side. I thanked them for coming to visit their convict friend, and their laughs were hollow, but I was steaming that they could actually believe what they'd heard about me. Didn't they *know* me after all the years together? Didn't that *count* for something? Doggone it, I wanted to shake them by the ears and shout You dumb jerks, do you really think I'm a crummy thief? When they left I realized that Jerry didn't punch me on the shoulder . . . not once.

On my hands and knees, I was scrubbing out the marble latrines the jailbirds had so much trouble hitting and thinking they should be given Norton bombsights, when a guard said I had a visitor. Wednesday morning? There were no visiting hours on Wednesday. Could it be Lola, skipping school when her mother wouldn't know and persuading them to let her see me? I washed my hands and tucked in my shirt and hustled to the visitors' room with high hopes. What I got was Pastor Ostrum.

Jeez, I was ashamed to see him. It'd been pouring rain again, for days, and when I walked between the wooden benches toward him, I caught something in his face that warned me to turn and run. He stood there in a dripping raincoat and looked more like an undertaker than a preacher. He kind of sagged onto a bench like he was tired or something, and as I reached him, he nodded for me to sit too. I squatted on the edge of a bench and I felt my throat going dry and someone was unloading bricks in my stomach.

"Cal . . . your father died last night."

Chapter 36

They let me go home for two days to be with my family and attend my father's funeral. Even though it rained most of the time, I hung the screens on the apartment my first day out and I didn't have to worry about my father finding a window with a streak or smudge.

That night, and into the day of the funeral, I looked for any chore that needed doing because I knew I'd be gone another ten days and my mother and Peggy would be alone. Uncle Rudy and Auntie Sister were there most of the time, as well as other friends, and as the black sheep of the family, I kept busy and, as much as possible, out of sight.

I couldn't believe my father was dead, like he was just away for a few days. I couldn't understand that I'd never be able to talk to him again, explain what I'd done, tell him how much I loved him. It felt like something in my chest had torn loose and would never be connected again. People tried to make me feel better but it didn't work.

They buried my dad in Roselawn Cemetery out on Larpenteur. I'd gone there lots of times with my mother to put flowers on the grave of my grandmother and hear stories about my mother's childhood. I stood beside my mother and sister, who sat in folding chairs for the short service. Like it would be giving in to it, I refused to sit, and I could hardly breathe or swallow and I wanted to scream and punch something in the face. I held back my tears like my father always taught me and pretended I was strong.

After causing trouble that looked bad for the Company—at a time when they were doing their best to stay out of the newspapers—my father was fired on Friday. On April 18th, the following Tuesday, he ate a bowl of ice cream while he listened to Cedric Adams with the evening news and then went to bed and died from a heart attack. I knew the doctor had it all wrong.

Pastor Ostrum read from the Bible, and I was standing beside the grave like Steve, knowing his parents blamed him for his little brother's death. No one said anything, but I knew they figured I killed my dad when I went to jail. The only thing that kept me from going nuts was my hope that one day, when my dad stood in glory, he'd know why I'd done it.

It had stopped raining but the sky was overcast with black clouds. I helped my mother to Uncle Rudy's car. Jerry was there with Steve and Scott, and Sandy stood back a ways with Sally and Jean. I felt shame for thinking about Lola with my dad lying back there in that fancy box. Uncle Rudy and Auntie Sister, with all the cousins, came back to the apartment to help with the food and kind of run things. Most of the time I hid in my room, while all sorts of people milled through our apartment, talking and eating and carrying on as though my dad still drove the Grand-Mississippi line.

When the dishes were washed, the leftovers put away, and the last relatives had gone home, I sat with my mother and sister in the kitchen. The apartment seemed empty, like some stinking beast had ripped all the life out of it, and though I didn't know its name, I darn well knew one of its henchmen. Wham! All of a sudden, right between the eyes, it came out of the sky, and I saw that the butcher's time had come. It was perfect, I was supposed to be in jail.

My mother was beat out from the last three weeks, and my dad's death seemed like the final blow. Our doctor left pills to help her sleep, and I saw to it that she swallowed them with warm milk. I tucked her in before nine, sitting on the edge of her bed.

"You be sure and get right down there now. We can't have any more trouble," she said.

"I will, I'll change and take the streetcar. Don't come on Sunday, I'll be all right, a little over a week and I'll be home."

"You're going to be my good boy, aren't you, Calvin."

"Yeah, Mom, don't worry about a thing. I'll get a full-time

job. I'll take care of you. We can stay right here in the apartment, you'll see."

I put my hand on her shoulder and kissed her on the cheek, but she looked so small and so alone in that big double bed. I checked on Peggy and found her in bed in the dark. I stepped into her room with only the light from the hallway.

"You awake?" I said.

"Yeah. Are you going to stay here tonight?"

"No." I moved to the foot of her bed. "I'm going now."

"When will you be back?"

"In ten days, it won't be long, you and Mom will be okay."

"Can't you stay, just for tonight?"

"No, I can't. I'll get in trouble."

"Oh . . ."

I couldn't see her face in the shadows, but she looked smaller to me, a little bundle under the covers.

"You want me to stay awhile?" I said.

"Yeah."

I crawled onto the bed beside her and we didn't say anything for a few minutes.

"I would've come to see you in jail, but they said I was too young."

"That's okay. I'm glad you didn't see me in there."

"Why did you steal that stuff?"

"Oh . . . it's hard to explain. Maybe some day I'll be able to tell you," I said, trying to find words to make her feel better. "It was kind of like taking carrots for the cottontail."

"It was?" she said with some relief.

"Yeah."

Peggy lay quietly for a minute.

"Do you feel real bad, Cal?"

"Yeah, real bad."

"Just spit on it," she said.

"Yeah, spit on it."

My sister was so darn brave, trying to make me feel better,

but I was going to do more than spit on it tonight. With a very strange piece of cheese I'd sucker the filthy rat into the crunching jaws of the trap.

"Can we feed Hot-Foot next winter?" she asked.

"Sure. Everything is going to be okay. You'll see."

She didn't say anymore. I lay still, listening to her breathing, and before long, she fell asleep. I wished I could lie there all night, safe and warm, but I had a promise to keep and I peeled myself off the bed and tiptoed to my room. I had to hurry, change my clothes, get the wire, screwdriver, and leather work gloves from the cellar. It was nine forty-two.

I jogged along Fairview and knew a lot of things could screw up my plan. When I reached Goodrich and turned west, I prayed that Luttermann would take his usual walk that night. Across the street from the house, shadowed from the streetlight, I crouched beside a parked car and caught my breath. Low, dark clouds sealed off the sky and reflected the city's glow. I hadn't run in awhile, and I felt the sweat trickling off my forehead and down my back, but to my relief, the black Plymouth was parked in front of the house like always. With my heart pounding, there was nothing more to do but wait. I pulled on the gloves.

Right on time, Luttermann appeared out of the shadows so quietly and suddenly, I almost jumped out of my skin. He crossed Goodrich and headed south on Howell. I waited a minute and then crept behind parked cars to the corner. Far down Howell I caught a glimpse of him, striding into the night. He probably found out I was in jail and figured I was out of the way. Boy, did I have a surprise for him.

I hurried to the car, opened the door, and slipped it into neutral. I leaned my shoulder into it, slowly moving the car west on Goodrich, steering with my right hand. Luckily the street was level, and before long, I had it rolling quietly through the intersection. In the middle of the next block, in a dark space between streetlights, I turned the car into the curb and stopped.

In a second I had the hood up and attached the wire to the coil. When I jumped the starter with the screwdriver, the straight six 95 horsepower engine I knew so well kicked over a few times and started. I shut the hood and drove away without turning on the lights for another block.

I stayed away from thoroughfares to be safe, meandering my way toward the deserted garage. I imagined I could smell Luttermann in the car, and even through the leather gloves, feel his clammy fingerprints on the steering wheel. Had kids playing in the alley found my stockpile and reported it, or stolen it? I carefully drove the side streets and thought about riding the moose. It was too late to turn back, I'd have to ride it out, and I was glad.

Chapter 37

I doused the lights and turned down the alley and my heart was going faster than the engine.

"Be there, be there," I prayed out loud.

In the shadows I coasted to the garage and left the engine idling while I dragged the sprung door open. I fumbled my way over the junk in the pitch black and brushed against something hanging from the rafters that scared the zippers off me. But I found the stash just the way I'd left it and I was really happy.

Jeez, I tripped and stumbled in and out of the garage and loaded the liquor as fast as I could, two cases in the trunk, five in the back seat, and one case of Old Grand-Dad in the seat beside me. I didn't forget the crowbar, and with my face covered with sweat, I drove away. Grand and Summit were too risky, so I took Portland, driving past our apartment where my heart-broken mother and sister were sleeping. If my mother could've seen me, she'd have had her own heart attack.

I had to hurry; time was running out on me and I pulled in behind the liquor store with the lights off and waited as a car passed on Prior. I left the engine running and carried the crowbar to the back door. I took the liquor ahead of time so I'd only be at the store about two seconds and not get caught. In the dark I slid the crowbar in place and pried with everything I had. The door groaned, the crowbar slipped. I kept jamming it into the crack like a madman but I was so jittery I missed half the time. I kept prying and then an alarm went off, clanging bloody murder like a fire drill at school and it was rattling me and I could hardly breathe. I strained on the bar until I could feel my face bulging and then the door finally broke free. I slid it open and hustled into the storeroom, shoving cases around and making it look like a robbery. I could hear the grainy voice of the old judge pronouncing sentence on me, *Five years in the state penitentiary*, while the jangling alarm was waking everyone in North America.

I bombed out of the storeroom and into the Plymouth and when I shifted into first and let out the clutch, the car lurched forward and stopped dead. I'd killed the engine. Criminy, the clanging bell drove spikes into my brain. I pushed the starter. Jeez, I forgot, it wouldn't work without a key. I was blowing it; they'd catch me again. *Bit off more than he could chew, bit off more than he could chew.* Sweat ran off my forehead. The screwdriver! Where was the screwdriver? I fumbled in the dark and found it on the floor. The burglar alarm was driving me nuts, and I started to panic. I opened the hood and jumped the starter. The engine caught and idled. I slammed the hood, slid into the car, and gunned the engine while I carefully let out the clutch. The Plymouth roared away like I was drag racing on Lake Street.

I hoped someone who heard the alarm would see the car as I swung up Grand, two blocks to Lacher's Drugstore. Headlights appeared down Grand, and I slowed, waiting for the car to stop at Fairview and then drive on. Jeez! another car came along Fairview and stopped at the intersection. Where were they all coming from on a late Thursday night? I swung around the block for another run at it and this time Grand was empty and as I got near the corner, I checked the rearview mirror. The cops would be coming any second, but I had no idea from what direction.

At about ten miles an hour, I turned up over the curb and rammed Luttermann's Plymouth halfway through the drugstore display window. Jeez, the shattering glass sounded like the whole building'd come down on me. The jolt of the sudden stop surprised me and I smacked my nose on the steering wheel. I had to get out of there fast.

I grabbed the screwdriver and the crowbar and tried to open my door. It was jammed. I bashed my shoulder into it but it wouldn't budge. The right side of the car was wedged against the wall; that door would never open. I reached over the seat, trying to open the back door, but with the pile of liquor boxes there wasn't room. I could see headlights coming up Grand. I rolled my window down and slithered out and as I raced across the street, somehow I remembered. The hot-wire! With the oncoming headlights only a block away, I scrambled back to the Plymouth. The hood had popped open and I jerked the hot-wire from the engine. Then I beat it across Grand, into the shadows between Smart's Texaco and an apartment building.

When I crossed the alley, I heard a siren in the cool night air. I bombed around a garage, high-hurtled a hedge, and came out in a front yard on Summit. I tried to figure the direction of the siren as I sprinted up the boulevard where the Runner had chased me so many times. I felt good. I had no way of knowing what would happen back there, but son of a gun, the police would be looking for Otto Luttermann, and I thought enough law had been broken to put that maggot behind bars for a year or two.

I ditched the crowbar and other stuff in garbage cans and sewers while I legged it through quiet neighborhoods all the way to Dunning field and Central. The school stood there dark and gloomy, and I realized I'd never be going back, never again sit in D.B. Sanderson's physics, Tony Kirschbach's seventh period, Miss Whalmen's study hall. I tooled over behind the stadium and gazed through the wire fence and I could hear voices cheering and the sounds of contact on the field, I really could, but the stands were empty as an east wind blew over the deserted field, and I turned and ran from the memories.

I hurried down Dunlap, alongside Lexington ballpark where I'd shagged foul balls to get in free. When I crossed University and headed out Lexington, I felt like I did when I'd rode the bull moose across the bay.

I hustled over the shadowed lawn of the workhouse and made it back before the deadline of midnight. The bald-headed jailer who checked me in asked how I hurt my nose. Jeez, I touched the swelling with my fingers and was surprised. I'd forgotten all about it. I told him I'd stumbled when I got on the streetcar. He was yawning and could hardly keep his eyes open. He picked up a pen and started to write in a big ledger.

"Your dad died, huh?"

"Yeah."

"That's tough."

"Do you have to write the time I got here?"

"Yeah."

"Could you put me down for making it around ten, so my mom won't worry if she checks on me. I could've been here by then but I went to see my girl for a while and then I stopped at the White Castle to load up on gut bombs. I knew I'd be in here another ten days and—"

"*You* like White Castles, too? I love those little sinners. Yeah, sure, let's put you down for nine-fifty."

He worked his tongue as he jotted in the time.

When I crawled onto my bunk, I couldn't sleep. What if Luttermann had an alibi, a friend he visited on his night walks? Or what if he got home before the cops got there? His wife would lie and swear that he'd never left the house. Golly, all the things that could go wrong buzzed around in my head like horseflies. I was afraid my trap would never work the way it was supposed to, and if it did, if by luck it caught the rat by an ear or a foot, would it be enough to set Gretchen free? I kept waking up and worrying like crazy all night.

I got up long before they rattled my cage, in hopes of overhearing some word about Gretchen's father during the day. I kept my ears peeled for any bits of information about arrests and stuff from the past night, but I didn't hear anything. I had no idea what happened after I bombed away from the drug store and I didn't dare ask any questions. New faces showed up with their crimes in the last twenty-four hours, but Luttermann's wasn't one of them. When I thought about all that could've gone wrong, I tried to escape by sleeping, but I kept thinking about my dad and Gretchen and Lola. It scared me when I saw how fast everything I loved could be lost.

The next day, Saturday, I spent part of the time degreasing a big iron cook stove in the kitchen and listening for crumbs of information that might fall from the jailers' tables. On Sunday I about went nuts waiting for a visitor, anyone, but the visiting hours were slipping by.

When a guard finally called me to the visitors' room, I thought I'd find my mother waiting but it was Steve who showed up. Criminy, was I glad to see him and we talked about school and things and stayed away from stuff about my dad and it was almost like we were pretending that I wasn't in jail. After a few minutes, I couldn't stand it any longer.

"Have you seen Gretchen in school?"

"Gretch the Wretch? Haven't you *heard?* Her dad stabbed a cop, they caught him breaking into a liquor store, he's in jail."

Holy Toledo, it had worked! But stabbed a cop. It was like I'd been hit in the chest with a sledge hammer. I wanted to jump up and shout, but I was scared stiff at what I'd started and how I might be in big trouble. Jeez, I tried not to look too excited.

"How's the cop?"

"Going to be okay they say. Gretchen's father must be some kind of a nut."

"What happened to Gretchen?"

"I don't know. Haven't seen her. I suppose she feels terrible."

I bet she didn't, but I still couldn't believe it. I never figured he'd stab a cop or anything like that, but it worked! Gretchen was free, she wouldn't go crazy. But now it was her turn to finish the rat by telling them how he murdered Helga's baby.

"How long is Gretchen's dad going to be in jail?" I said.

"Don't know, is he in here?"

"Could be, I've never seen the guy."

I kind of shivered. They'd have to keep Luttermann in jail for two or three years for stabbing a cop wouldn't they?

"You got something going with Gretchen's dad?" Steve said.

"What do you mean?"

Jeez, I held my breath; I must've left some big clue.

"Well, you're both hitting the same liquor store so I thought you might be in the same gang."

Steve sprayed the room, and I started breathing again, wishing I could tell him how close he was to the truth.

My mother came for the last fifteen minutes, and Steve gave up his place to her. I thanked him for coming though I'd never be able to tell him what terrific news he'd brought. My mother had read about it in the papers and she'd seen Lacher's Drugstore window all boarded up. She'd absent-mindedly left the one curler in her hair, and I didn't have the heart to tell her, knowing how embarrassed she'd be.

"Wasn't that terrible, a stabbing right in our neighborhood. The paper said one of the girls of the family went to Central. Maybe you know her, Cal. Luttermann?"

"Luttermann? No . . . I don't think so."

When my mother left, I sat on my bunk and I was so excited I couldn't think straight. I couldn't believe it! Luttermann was in *jail!* It had worked better than I'd planned. Then dread blasted me. When all she had to do was tell them what he'd done, would Gretchen be able to beat back her fear and slam the bolt on her father's cell, or would she be too scared to finish him?

The last week went on forever and I worked hard, asking for more to do when I ran out. Nights were the hardest. I could hear all the gross noises of the derelicts and rummies and I fought back memories and regrets, seeing my father's face and hearing Lola's laugh. But Sunday morning came, and I'd paid my debt to society. I told Spence I'd come and visit him. No you won't was all the old guy would say.

They opened the steel-barred door and I walked into a gray spring drizzle like I was in sunshine. It felt good and my whole body let out a sigh like I'd been holding my breath too long under water. The spring rain felt clean, and when I'd walked a block I glanced back at the soggy-looking work-house. I'd learned what it was to be locked up and I remembered Spence's words and I knew how brave they were, Spence and all those lonely men, and I caught the Como-Harriet for home.

When I stepped off the streetcar on the corner at Fairview, it had stopped raining and I looked kitty-corner at Lacher's Drugstore where the front window had been fixed and the new brick in the wall below the glass was the only sign of the smash-up. Little by little I would pay back every cent for the damage I'd done, but I didn't know how yet, without some-one finding out I did it. My father taught me to pay for what I broke and I figured all along Sid would get his liquor back. But, darn it, I didn't want to pay for the damage to the car, like I wanted to smash something of Luttermann's if I couldn't smash him.

I wished I could go to Gretchen's house and see her, but I knew that was out. I glanced across at Finley's Market and I wanted to explain it to him, but I didn't know how. A Grand-Mississippi car came the other way and when I caught myself checking to see if it was my dad's, I turned and ran for home.

Chapter 38

My father had ten thousand dollars in life insurance from the Army and some money coming from the Company retirement fund so we weren't going to starve or anything, but my mother couldn't peel the worry off her face, like she'd have to go through the Depression all over again, only this time alone, so I tried to work on the happiness stuff whenever I could. I helped her sort things out and kept telling her everything was going to be okay, but it was hard because I kept thinking about my dad. Mr. Shaw, the apartment owner, would let us stay on as custodians as long as I was there. My mother hadn't told him I was in jail.

Early Monday morning I hitchhiked to school to catch Gretchen at her locker. I kept an eye peeled for Lola, though I knew her locker was on the other side of the building, and I ached inside when I realized I didn't belong here anymore.

Gosh, Gretchen was so glad to see me I thought she was going to hug me, and I actually blinked when I saw her. Wearing a light green sweater and a plaid skirt, and with her hair cut short and all fixed up, I hardly recognized her. She looked kind of relaxed and happy, basically, but I could see in her eyes she was still afraid and it reminded me that it wasn't over.

"Gee, do you look great," I said.

"I've wanted to see you for so long, my father's in jail, the police came to the house and started asking my mother questions and I came downstairs to see what was going on and then my father came home and when he saw the police he got really mad and he thought I'd told on him and he started shouting at me."

"What did the police *do?*" I said.

"One of them tried to calm him down and my father knocked him flat and ran into the kitchen and the other policeman ran after him and my father stabbed him and then the first policeman hit my father with a billy club and knocked him out and I was so scared and I had to hold a dishtowel on the policeman's bleeding chest while the other one ran out to call for help and I told them what my father had been doing to me and they put me and my sisters in a foster home and they're so good to us."

"That's swell, that's great. Did you tell them anything about me?"

"No . . . nothing, but *you* saved me, Cal."

"What do you mean?" Could she have figured it out?

"I'd decided to kill myself. I was going home Monday and swallow the moth balls I'd hidden and when they found me in the morning I'd be dead and he couldn't do me anymore. But then Sandy came up to me in the hall and gave me a Nut Goodie and she said it was from Cal. I couldn't believe it, it was like a note from you coming out of the sky, telling me not to give up, that you were still going to help me. I saved the Nut Goodie in my locker and every day it reminded me and gave me hope and then, like a miracle, the police came to the house."

The first bell rang and I knew there wasn't time to explain.

"I'll meet you here for lunch," I said.

She reached out and touched my arm for a second and then took off down the hall, blending in with the other kids. Holy cow, Gretch the Wretch had vanished from the halls of St. Paul Central.

At the drugstore on Dunlap, I studied the help wanted ads in the *Pioneer Press* for most of the morning and I met Gretchen at her locker at the lunch bell and gave her the penny loafers I'd kept in my locker, and the baby doll, too, but I wrapped it in the newspaper so no one would see me with it. She looked at the doll kind of sad like and set it carefully in her locker.

Out on the lawn there were twelve million kids eating lunch and I kept hoping to see Lola. Gretchen wanted to know why I was in jail and I figured she had a right to know. I knew I could trust her. After warning her that I'd go back to jail if anyone found out, I told her how I nailed her father. I had to keep it down with kids all around us and she listened with her mouth hanging open and her teeth about to fall out. She thought her father had been doing bad things when he went out at night and that they'd finally caught up with him. She told me she never believed I stole anything and she couldn't understand what I was doing in jail.

"Oh, Cal, I'm so sorry, I bet you wish you'd never met me."

"Gosh, no, it's okay, I just never thought it would turn out like this, that anyone would get stabbed or anything."

"And now you can't graduate, Cal. I'm really sorry."

She didn't seem to know about my dad and I didn't want her feeling bad about that, too, so I figured I'd tell her some other time when things were better.

"How many years did they give your father?" I said.

"Nothing yet . . . they don't—"

"*What?* Didn't you tell them about Helga's baby?"

"Yes, I told them."

My stomach started going queasy.

"You mean that after you told them how he killed a baby they still might not lock him up?"

"Yes, that's why I made you promise to never tell anyone, it isn't enough, it's like they don't *want* to know."

"Did they find the baby?"

"I don't think so, it wasn't in the freezer."

"Didn't your mother tell them?"

"She's too scared, she lies for him, she said there was no baby, they think I'm making up stories because I'm crazy."

"Doesn't *anyone* believe you?" Jeez, I had to lower my voice because I noticed other kids glancing at us.

"I think Mr. Brown does. He's the County Attorney, but they have to have a trial."

"And your father could get *out of it?*"

"Yes . . . the killing, what he's done to me and Helga. They told me I'd have to tell it all to the judge and a jury with my father sitting right there watching me . . ." She looked scared like she used to. "I don't know if *I can.*"

"You *have* to!" I said. "They've got him for stealing and stabbing a cop, that ought to keep him for a year or two, but for murder, he won't get out for a long long time, maybe never. You have to, otherwise . . ."

"You don't know him."

Her voice changed and she nailed me with her eyes and I knew why she was so afraid of her father; like McCluskey's dog, she believed he could get her no matter what the cops did, and I was starting to believe it, too. She stared off across the housetops on the other side of Lexington and said it like it was one of D.B.'s laws of physics.

"If he ever gets out he'll kill me."

She promised me, like I had promised her, that she'd never tell what I'd done as long as she lived. It would be a secret between the two of us that would kind of hold us together in a crazy way. I still couldn't tell her how her father tried to kill me because it might scare her even worse and then she wouldn't dare testify against him. The bell rang, and I stayed on the lawn, watching Gretchen and all the kids swarm back into the school.

When I was alone in the sunshine, I don't know why but I sat there a minute with my stomach churning and remembered the first day we'd come to Central. Gosh, I could hear the sounds, I really could, and I could remember how I felt, and it was like all of a sudden I was back there and a huge sadness came up around me out of the grass and I had to get out of there fast. I headed for downtown, I had to find a job. When I was almost to Selby, I stopped and looked back, one last time.

At the department stores where I applied—The Emporium, The Golden Rule, Schuneman's—one of the things they wanted to know was if I'd ever been arrested. I hitchhiked home like a criminal, really scared and wondering if anyone would hire a jailbird. A guy picked me up in a new Lincoln with a 152 horse V8 engine and I didn't even ask to see it. He dropped me at Summit and Lexington in front of St. Luke's Catholic Church, and while I stuck out my thumb, I noticed a building under construction next to the church. On a hunch I walked over and found the labor foreman for the Hagstrom Construction Company.

"Do you belong to the Hod Carriers Union?" the tall guy said.

He was looking me over and I tried to puff up a little and flex my muscles.

"I will tomorrow," I said.

"Okay, we'll give you a try."

Holy cow! I had a job on a construction crew. I took fifty dollars out of my savings to join the union, but I'd make a dollar fifty-two an hour, an unbelievable amount when I'd been working for fifty-five cents.

The work was harder than I thought it would be and I fell into bed like a zombie every night. We ate all our meals at the kitchen table, staying away from the dining room like my dad's memory hovered over his empty chair. We were sitting at the table one night when Steve and Jerry pounded at the back door.

We bombed over to the Flat Top for Cokes and fries in Steve's Chevy and I really felt good, like they weren't afraid of doing stuff with me or they didn't care what people thought. We yakked about all kinds of stuff and they brought me up to date with the social scene at Central, careful not to say anything about Lola and Tom. But something had changed that none of us could do anything about. I felt older than them, somehow different. I was no longer a schoolboy.

Chapter 39

I missed Lola so much I tried not to think about her but the harder I tried, the worse it got. I'd heard that she'd gone to the Spring Swing with Tom and for days I about went crazy trying to figure out if I should call her or not. Then one night I couldn't stand it any longer, but her mother answered the phone.

"Is Lola there?" I said, trying to disguise my voice.

"Who is this?" Mrs. Muldoon said.

"It's Cal."

"I thought as much. Lola will no longer be answering your calls, so please don't bother us anymore."

"I just want—"

The line went dead, and my stomach kind of flipped over, and I don't know why but I remembered standing in the bus stop on the North Shore and looking through the smudged glass of the phone booth and feeling like I'd just been kicked out of the human race. After two weeks of misery, I got off early on a Friday afternoon because we started pouring concrete at seven in the morning. In my grubby work clothes, I hiked to Central. I kept an eye out for any of my teachers, and I cornered Lola in the hall after her last class, figuring Tom would be playing baseball. She looked surprised but she acted like she was glad to see me.

"Hi," I said and I was really nervous.

"Hi." She gave me kind of a timid smile. "It's good to see you, what are you doing here?"

"I came to see *you*."

After stopping at her locker, we left school and hoofed it up Dunlap.

"Are you all right," she said.

"Yeah . . . I guess so."

"I'm sorry you can't come back to school."

"Yeah, I always worried about Steve and Jerry, with Bellows after him." I laughed halfheartedly. "And I'm the one who won't graduate."

I couldn't think of what to say. Seeing her, I just wanted to sit on someone's lawn and take her in my arms and have her love me because she was the only person in the universe who could make me feel better. Instead, she made it worse with her acting like we were just friends or something. She was singing that night in the operetta *Joan of the Nancy Lee*, the big deal of the year for the choir, and she yakked about how the girls in the cast take over the pirate ship and all that stuff without ever talking about us.

We were almost to Selby when she said, "I still care for you, Cal. I miss seeing you and talking to you."

I love you had been changed to *I care for you* by way of the city workhouse.

"I miss you," I said and the darn tears came flooding into my eyes and I didn't want her to see.

"Why did you do it, why?" she said and I could tell she was plenty mad. "Everything was perfect . . . we were so happy, and then you go and ruin it by acting like a hoodlum! How could you! How could you rob a liquor store and—"

"I did it for someone else," I said and we stopped short of the corner where other kids waited.

"I thought I knew you." Her face was twisted like she was going to cry and her chin was trembling. "I'm all mixed up. Maybe my mother is right; I don't know anymore."

"Will you see me tonight?"

"I want to see you, but my mother won't let me, I promised her."

"If you loved me, you'd see me anyway."

"That's where we're different. I *obey* my parents."

Her words ripped the scab off something bleeding inside of me, and as the Selby-Lake streetcar glided up the hill, she moved away to get on. She turned.

"I'm sorry about your dad, Cal."

"I'm sorry about *you*, you're dying on me, too."

She got on the streetcar.

"You said you loved me!" I called.

I stood there watching it carry her away. Then, before I knew it, something inside me just took off running after her, like it was my last chance ever with Lola. I had to dodge the cars behind the streetcar and they must have thought I was nuts, sprinting down the street to beat the band because the conductor was really taking off, but I grabbed the rope and jerked it and the streetcar died on the tracks. Then I pulled a Groucho Marks, running along the left side of the streetcar, because I knew the conductor would come piling out the door on the right and hustle back to fix the trolley. Another streetcar was coming the other way and I just about got mangled between them. I bombed in the front doors and everyone was buzzing about what was wrong and I spotted Lola about halfway back, sitting with a white-haired old woman. I worked my way back to her and got down on one knee in the aisle and she almost swallowed her gum.

"Please see me tonight," I said, and the old lady and every-body started gawking at us but I didn't care. "Please, if you don't I'll *die*."

Lola didn't know what to do and she started blushing and I wanted to kiss her like mad.

"Not so loud," she said. "I can't, I promised my mom."

"Please, just once."

"You're crazy."

"I'm crazy about you. Please, just tonight."

Everyone was looking at Lola like they were wondering what she'd say, and the old woman elbowed her and nodded.

"I can't, I'm going with Tom."

"Tom doesn't love you, I do."

Jeez, the conductor had the trolley connected again and the air brake motor was thumping and I knew he'd be back in front in a few seconds.

"Please," I said, "just tonight, then you can throw your life away with Tom if you want."

"No . . . I can't . . . oh, I'm all mixed up."

Tears filled her eyes and started running down her cheeks and I got off my knee as the conductor came in the front doors.

He spotted me and yelled, "Hey!"

People groaned like they were disappointed when I slipped down the aisle and ducked out the back doors. I stood on the curb and watched the streetcar roll away and I thought maybe she'd get off and come running back to me but when it stopped a block up, Lola didn't get off and I stood there, waiting, until it went out of sight. It felt like my heart had been smashed. I'd never get to figure out the color of her eyes.

I got used to the hard work and I was proud of myself that I'd learned how to steer a buggy with hundreds of pounds of wet concrete across the narrow planking and dump it right where the finishers wanted it. I helped around the apartment building with the stuff we were responsible for, brought my paycheck home to my mother without taking out a nickel, and reported to my parole officer right on schedule. The high-strung, wiry little guy talked like he expected me to hit a bank within the week and I figured it was the company the poor guy kept. Seeing this character twice a month for a year would straighten out the most hardened criminal or turn him into a stark-raving ax murderer.

I had dumped the ashes from the incinerator in the alley when the idea hit me like a falling clinker. I bombed over to Summit and it felt strange to hike up onto the porch in broad daylight and knock. The little woman opened the door with worry in her eyes.

"Hello, I'm Cal Gant. I live just over on Portland and I wondered if I could see your husband."

She hesitated like she was thinking. "He's not well."

"I know, I want to tell him something."

I gave her a big smile and she studied me with her crinkly eyes and then backed into the house, motioning for me to follow. I closed the door and searched for starting blocks carved in the hardwood floor. She led me into a sunroom where the Runner was slumped in a wheelchair and the left side of his body was limp. He was staring out the window and she stepped in front of him.

"There's someone to see you, John."

The phantom of the neighborhood, who had scared the pants off us so many times, was *John*. I moved around in front of him and squatted so that he could look in my eyes.

"He can't talk," she said.

"I'm Calvin Gant, John. I used to knock on your door, and you'd chase me and my friends all over the place."

I smiled and watched to see if the guy understood but he didn't act like it, just sitting there looking right through me. "Once you chased me across the Ramsey playground and almost caught me and I jumped over a fence and landed in some fresh dog shit, got it all over my clothes."

Normally I'd never cuss like that, but on the spur of the moment, I thought it might get some kind of reaction out of him, and it did. His face changed like he was remembering.

"You sure could run fast, and I'm sorry if I made you mad, or caused you any trouble."

"Oh, it wasn't any trouble," she said. "He enjoyed it."

I plopped back on the carpet like I'd been hit with a frying pan.

"What do you *mean?*"

"Oh, he loved chasing you boys. Some nights he'd peek through the drapes in hopes you'd come and pound on the door."

"I don't get it," I said.

"One night some cute boys ran up and pounded on the door. I suppose they'd been going from house to house looking for some excitement. Well, John happened to see them, and he burst out the door and chased them all over the neighborhood. When he got back, he felt wonderful. He could remember when he was a boy and what fun it was to be chased and to be frightened. So, the word must have spread, because it wasn't a few weeks later when they were back. And for years, John has chased the neighborhood kids. It was his way of playing with them."

I couldn't believe what I was hearing.

"But what if he caught them?" I said.

"Oh, he'd never catch them. He'd run fast enough to scare them good, but always stay just behind them. Then, when he was bushed, he'd sneak off in the dark, work his way through the alley where they couldn't see him, and come back to the house. I'd have a cold drink waiting for him, and he'd tell me all about the fine boys he'd chased."

Holy cow! The terror of Summit Avenue had been playing with us! But he was right, if we'd known, all the fun would have gone out of it.

"I noticed your yard hasn't been raked. I was wondering if I could do that for you, for free. I'd really like to," I said, looking into the Runner's watery eyes.

"I was going to look for someone to do the raking," his wife said. "John loved to do it."

"Where's your rake?" I said.

I raked the lawn in about four hours and she kept coming out with cookies and lemonade and all kinds of stuff until I had to wave her off. Before I left, I went in to say good-bye to John. He made a deep gurgling sound that I couldn't figure out.

"He said, 'Thank you,'" she said.

Jeez, I put a hand on John's shoulder and squeezed a little and I had to get out of there. She came to the door with me.

"I'll be back Saturday," I said. "Keep a list of things you need done. If you need me during the week, just call. My number is Midway-1932."

I bombed down the steps and stopped in my tracks.

"Oh . . . what's your name?" I said.

"Jeanette."

"I mean your last name, so I can call you."

"Conley, John and Jeanette Conley," she said. "We never had any children."

"You've got one now."

I waved and took off for home. I had to get to bed early. Gretchen and I were taking the bus to Fergus Falls in the morning to see her sister Helga, but all the way home I thought about the Runner. Gad, who would believe it. I couldn't decide if I should tell my buddies or let them go on remembering the mad dashes in the dark with a crazy man creaming right behind you.

Chapter 40

The night before, I told my mother I was going out in the country with a friend and on Sunday I left before she was up. I planned on telling her all about Gretchen but I was still plenty scared at the trouble I could be in.

At the corner of Lexington and Selby I met Gretchen at six in the morning, figuring it was best if people didn't see us together for a while. Her foster parents, who lived a few blocks from Central, offered to drive her to Fergus Falls, but she told them she had to go alone. She couldn't wait to see Helga and tell her that she didn't have to be crazy anymore. I didn't want to let on but I was pretty skittish about going up there with all those loony people, afraid that some nut would grab me and strangle me or something.

After taking the Selby-Lake downtown, we caught a Greyhound going north and had our pick of seats because there were only a few other passengers. Riding out of the city in the silver bus, I remembered my first ride in one to meet Uncle Emil in Grand Marais. I settled back into the cushioned seat and I was really tired, like for the first time I could relax. So much had happened so fast that I couldn't catch up. The motion of the bus made me sleepy, and I thought it would be nice to take my mom and sister to the North Shore that summer. I promised myself that when I got older and made enough money, I'd buy back Uncle Emil's cabin beside that wild lake with the loons and lily pads.

Out in the country everything was growing like crazy and the corn looked like little green soldiers marching in perfect rows, and heat waves made puddles on the highway that danced off just when the bus was about to splash through them. Gretchen dozed most of the way to Little Falls, and at that stopover we ate a big breakfast. She was gaining weight, filling in some of the hollow places and learning how to laugh.

"I have to go to the doctor tomorrow," she said when we were settled back on the bus, "and I hate to."

"What for?"

"So he can be a witness at the trial . . . and tell them . . ." She gazed out the window as her words trailed off.

"Tell them what?"

"Do you think Little Jacob went to heaven?"

"Yeah, sure I do," I said, caught a little off-guard.

"I'll never see him again."

"What do you mean?"

"I'm going to hell."

"Oh, gosh, no you're not. Why do you think that?"

"I killed him."

"*What?* I thought Helga—"

"He was *my* baby, *my* little boy." She kept looking out the window. "And my father made *me* do it. He held my hands under the water on Little Jacob and I couldn't let go, and my baby kicked . . . and splashed . . . and . . ."

She covered her mouth with her hands, trying to hold the horrible stuff inside. I couldn't speak, like she'd ripped out my tongue, and I glanced around, afraid someone might hear us but the nearest guy was two seats away and he was sleeping.

"I tried, Cal, I screamed and fought him," she said. "I pulled my hand free and dug my fingernails into his face and then everything went black. I think he socked me; I came to on the bathroom floor. He jerked me up by my hair and made me look at my baby. Little Jacob was underwater and he wasn't moving anymore but he looked so alive and his mouth was open like he was still trying to breathe. My father said that if I ever told anyone about him, he'd tell them I killed Little Jacob and they'd hang me."

It was so terrible and sad I thought my heart would break. I felt so sorry for Gretchen and I hated her father and I wished I'd been brave enough to turn around when he was chasing me and fight him, beat his head into the ice.

"He said we had to kill the baby." She shoved words between sobs. "That it was the only way we could be saved. I knew it was a lie, I knew it. *No* mother should kill her baby, no mother should *ever* kill her baby. I'll go to hell for it. I'll *never* see Little Jacob again."

"Yes you will," I said when I could finally talk. "God knows what really happened."

She huddled quietly by the window like she wanted to be alone, wiping her dripping face with her hands.

"Why did you tell me it was *Helga's* baby, that *she* killed it?" She wouldn't look at me.

"I thought you'd hate me. I didn't think you'd help me if you knew I murdered my own baby." She glanced over at me and her face was all smeared. *"Do* you hate me?"

"No, golly . . . I don't hate you." My voice was cracking.

"That's why the doctor has to examine me, to tell them I've had a baby." She sighed. "I wish they'd just believe me. I hate having him examine me."

"How could you have a baby when you were going to school?"

"I got big during the summer. I stayed in the house, never went out. I knew it was a boy. I sang to him, all the hymns I know, and I told him I'd take care of him and protect him."

She couldn't talk for a minute.

"I didn't keep my promise to him, I didn't—"

"Gosh, you did as much as you could," I said. "You can't blame yourself for—"

"I had him on the sixteenth of September; my parents kept me out of school, said I was sick. My mother got my books and assignments and no one said anything when I came back."

"Didn't you go to the hospital to—"

"My mother delivered my baby, it really hurt and I was screaming and my father turned the radio way up so no one would hear me. When Little Jacob came out, a march was playing real loud and I remember thinking he'd be a soldier."

"Gosh, you're brave."

I put my arm around her gently and pulled her toward me.

She felt stiff as a board, like she'd never had anyone hug her before, and she awkwardly let her head rest on my shoulder. I felt her shudder, and we rode north like two orphans looking for home.

The huge stone building looked more like a prison, with high towers and bars on the windows and nurses that seemed like jailers. On a women's ward, some of the ladies were only half-dressed and some were worse, one stocking up and the other down and their buttons weren't all buttoned and their hair was all over the place and a skinny old lady had her shoes on the wrong feet. I watched one woman with scabs all over her head squat in a corner and then a puddle ran out from under her dress, and Jeez, I looked the other way and I wanted to get the heck out of there.

A big nurse I'd hate to face in tackling drills told Gretchen they had little hope for her sister; they'd tried everything, even electric shock, but Helga hadn't improved. Another nurse brought Helga from some back room and she looked like she was sleepwalking. They set her on a wooden chair and Gretchen sat facing her. In a green dress that looked like it'd been washed a million times and black hightop tennis shoes with no socks, Helga looked like Gretchen used to.

"You don't have to be crazy anymore, Daddy's in jail," Gretchen said. "He can't hurt you anymore, you can come home."

She stared off into space no matter what Gretchen said like she'd locked the door to her heart so no one could ever hurt her again and it didn't matter what Gretchen tried.

I sat on a wooden bench along the wall and watched the pitiful women on the ward. They seemed to be lost, like they'd run off into another world. I don't know what death smells like but I think that's what someone had tried to cover up with Pine-Sol or something. The raggedy women shuffled around like corpses without graves and I wondered if Spence was right, that they went crazy because they couldn't stand living without love? From the corner of my eye I watched a nervous, stooped woman sitting by the window in the hot sun, pulling black hairs from her chin and putting them in a little pile on her lap.

It was really sad and we left Helga sitting on that lousy ward without her ever letting on that she recognized Gretchen. Gretchen knew she'd lost her sister, but I felt glad that at least Gretchen wouldn't end up in that death house. Neither of us talked much on the trip home. We got hamburgers at Little Falls, and she only nibbled at hers, though she cleaned up her chocolate malt.

"Do you think crazy people can go to heaven?" she said.

"I don't know, but after what's been done to them, I'd think they'd be the first ones in."

She reached over and took hold of my hand. It was getting dark and she turned her head to the window and the passing countryside and I held her hand all the way home.

The following week I noticed I was getting used to the hard work of the construction crew, and when I'd finished around the apartment on Saturday, I checked with the Conleys. Mrs. Conley had some boxes she wanted down from the attic. That was all she asked, until I wheeled out of her a bunch of stuff that needed doing around the place. I spent the afternoon mowing the lawn and pruning lilac bushes and she kept hauling out food and I didn't have the heart to turn her down. I ate peanut-butter cookies and drank lemonade for all the kids they'd never had and then I sat a few minutes with John before I left.

I didn't know why I was doing that stuff except since my dad died I felt like I owed something back for my life, like I figured my dad could see what I was doing and he'd know he raised me right. When I walked home, I could see the Runner on some lousy men's ward in that big state hospital, but he had someone who loved him, and Jeanette was hanging onto him with both hands.

Chapter 41

Across the street from the construction site I sprawled with my back against a big elm, eating the lunch my mother packed in my father's lunch box. That first morning she handed his box to me I just about told her no, but then I took it without saying anything.

I was chomping away and trying to relax when I noticed a guy with an arm in a sling crossing Summit, coming from the construction shack straight for me.

"Are you Calvin Gant?"

My stomach tightened. "That's me."

"Could I talk to you for a minute?"

"Yeah, I'm about done eating."

He didn't look too hot, a solidly built guy with a receding hairline, a nose that looked like someone slammed a door on it, and curly reddish hair. He squatted gingerly, like it hurt, and I started to get a bad feeling.

"My name's Sergeant Riley. I'm a policeman."

Cripes, I couldn't swallow or breathe and I could feel my face turning gray.

"Don't worry, I just want to meet you, to talk a little."

"Why?"

"Well, I've had a lot of time to think, nearly killed about four weeks ago, a suspect stabbed me. I was stupid, dealing with a man I should've been ready for, didn't see it coming. Lucky for me, he was left-handed, been right-handed, he'd have stuck it in my heart."

The guy stared at me with a funny look on his face.

"Like to run something by you, if it's okay with you?"

"Okay . . ." Jeez, what else could I do, and I was trying my darnedest to look calm.

"Well, this guy is a real cuckoo. Come to find out he'd been beating up his family, sexually assaulting his daughter, maybe killed her baby, his own son, and drove another daughter crazy. Fits the description of a Peeping Tom we've been trying to catch in the Highland neighborhood for over a year. His wife is a helpless soul, mentally screwed up herself by this lunatic. Awhile back I get a call from some kid, tells me there's a guy like this, beating his daughter, but he can't tell me who unless I'll lock the man up."

Riley stopped for a minute and made a face like his arm hurt him or something. He shifted his position and I didn't dare look him in the eye.

"Any of this sound familiar so far?" he said.

"No."

I shook my head and tried to look like I'd never heard any of that stuff and, at the same time, swallow the rest of the tuna-fish sandwich that had turned to sawdust in my mouth.

"Well, this kid calls me several times and then one night, tells me he's going to bring me a body. I try to tell him I'll come to the body, but he insists. Then I don't hear from him anymore. Nothing. Now this psycho is a brutal bastard that should be castrated, but he's also a religious nut. Checked him out pretty carefully, and from what we've learned, stealing liquor would be the last thing this guy'd do."

Riley cleared his throat and I felt my face flushing. Darn, I'd never thought of that.

"Just doesn't fit. Hurt somebody, rape them, but he wouldn't have anything to do with booze, and why would he crash into a drugstore with his car? No rain that night, no one chasing him, and the man wasn't drunk. Smelled fishy. Come to find out that about three weeks before, some high school kid got nailed stealing a case of whiskey from the very same store. This little fact only came to my attention accidentally when a detective casually pointed it out to me—that the Prior Liquor Store had been robbed twice that month. Am I tweaking your interest?"

I glanced at my watch and kept my eyes away from his.

"I only have a half hour," I said.

"Okay, won't keep you, but the more I thought about it the more I thought it was too farfetched." He stood carefully and winced. "And too beautiful."

He held his bad arm with his good one and looked down at me with a real friendly expression on his face.

"System works pretty well for most people, but it didn't for Gretchen. Has gaps that allow some people to be brutalized, people who are scared to death and unable to free themselves, and I don't know what we do about that."

He squatted down on one knee right beside me.

"But *you* did. I think *you* called me, I think *you* nailed that filthy sonofabitch, and I think you're one helluva kid . . . one helluva kid."

The policeman looked me in the eye and I had to look away.

"Listen, Cal, if it was you, we're going to need you to finish him. That pig is where he belongs, hope they lock him in a cell at Stillwater until his guts rot."

I was tempted to tell him, to shout what I'd done, but my instincts warned me. Never, for as long as I lived. It was Gretchen's job to finish him, I'd done enough, for crying out loud! No, I'd never tell, or *I* could be the one in jail.

"Will the guy go to Stillwater?"

"Don't know, but the County Attorney probably won't go for murder unless we get something more. If they don't nail him with murder, if all they have is the stolen goods and the assault, could be out in a year or so."

I got to my feet and picked up my work gloves with my father's lunch box. Riley stood up beside me.

"I don't know anything about it," I said. "I had some friends who wanted the booze. It was just a crazy, spur-of-the-moment thing with me. I made a dumb mistake, a really stupid mistake."

I turned to go back to work. Riley took hold of my arm.

"Sure, kid, I understand, but I wish to hell I had a kid like you."

I hurried across the street and beat back the tears. I wished my father could say those words, but my father's mouth was closed forever and he died thinking I was a cheap hoodlum. I stowed my lunch box in the labor shed and got in line with a buggy to wheel away the heavy concrete.

In my work clothes I sprawled on my bed, trying to get up the energy to take a shower, when I heard the phone. Why did I always think it would be Lola?

"It's for you, Cal," my mother hollered from the kitchen.

My instincts wanted to tell her to say I wasn't home, but I knew she wouldn't. I felt a knot in my chest as I stumbled barefoot for the kitchen. My mother sauntered into the living room with her coffee.

"Hello," I said.

"Cal? It's me, Gretchen."

"Oh, hi . . . how are you."

"I'm scared, Cal, I'm really scared. Mr. Brown doesn't think he can prove my father killed the baby without someone else's testimony. He's going to get out of it, Cal, and he'll *get* me."

"Wait a minute, calm down, did you tell them there was someone else who saw the baby?"

"No, no, I didn't want to drag you into it. Mr. Brown hoped my mother would help, but she's more afraid of him than I am, she only says what my father tells her to say. I'm scared, Cal."

With the phone to my ear I looked out the window into a sunset. I was mad and scared and all mixed up and I could see Luttermann slipping the trap, strolling out of jail in six months or a year, and I asked myself if I was willing to go to jail again to kill the rat?

"Cal. . . . are you there?"

Gretchen's voice was pulling at me like a lunatic from that other world, that crazy, insane world, and I could hear another voice in my heart, *Hang up the phone and run, run north, to the Shore, where they can never find you, where you can live like the owl and the otter.*

"Cal. . . . will you tell them? Will you tell them you *saw* the baby?"

Criminy, I knew I'd feel lousy no matter what I decided, and I hated the police and the law that would let this butcher get away with it.

"Will you, Cal, please, please."

"Okay."

Chapter 42

I was sweating in a leather chair in Mr. Brown's office—he was the County Attorney and a pretty big wheel. He looked like Jimmie Stewart but with more guts and I would've guessed he was a farmer or something. The place was piled with all kinds of books and tablets and paper like he'd been going to school since the Civil War. Basically I felt good about him, like he wanted to get Luttermann as much as I did, but it seemed I'd been answering questions for a month. He sprawled behind a big desk and asked me lots of stuff like he kept forgetting what I'd just told him. A short, chubby woman, perched on the edge of a chair, scribbled notes, and a sweet-smelling pipe tobacco filled the place.

"And that's the last you saw of the baby?" the guy said.

"Yeah, under Luttermann's arm. He still had the knife."

"Did the streetcar motorman see him?"

"No . . . I don't think so."

"Did the motorman see you on the cowcatcher?"

"Yeah, when I got off and ran."

"When you talked to Sergeant Riley on the phone, did you tell him you would bring him a dead *baby?*"

I thought for a minute, watching the stenographer's pencil dance across the notebook. "No, I didn't dare say baby . . . I said *body.* I'd bring him a *body.*"

I could tell that disappointed him and he kept kind of gritting his teeth when he wasn't talking.

"Can you think of anything more?"

"Well, one night I watched Gretchen's bedroom window, I watched lots of nights, but one night I saw Gretchen was naked and Mr. Luttermann was in the room with her."

"What were they doing?"

"I couldn't see."

"Why were you looking in her bedroom window?"

"She wanted me to . . . she wanted me to *see* something so I could tell the police. She said they wouldn't believe her."

"And did you *see* something?"

"No . . . I never could see anything."

He picked up his pipe and shuffled around the jumble in his office and he looked plenty worried. He stopped and stared out one of the tall windows like the lady and I weren't there. Then he came over and sat in the chair next to me. He held his hand up to the young secretary like he didn't want her to write anymore.

"Cal," he said, looking at me real serious like, "Gretchen told us her sad and terrible story and something inside me believes her. I was hoping her mother would corroborate Gretchen's story, but she didn't. Like her husband, she claims Gretchen is a sick girl, that she made it all up. My instincts tell me that the mother isn't telling the truth, but I can't go to trial with only my instincts. Your testimony becomes crucial. If you want to help Gretchen, you have to tell me everything you can about your involvement with her. If you go on the stand, they'll do everything they can to discredit your testimony."

"Okay," I said and I knew right then I was a goner.

Mr. Brown's hair was kind of mussed and he put both hands on his knees and leaned towards me.

"I'll ask you the kind of questions you'll have to answer on the stand, all right?"

"All right," I said and my Adam's apple was trying to get out.

"Why are you here?"

"I don't know what you mean."

"Why are you here? Why are you involved with Gretchen Luttermann? What business is this of yours?"

Jeez, it was like he'd switched sides and now I was sweating bee-bees.

"She asked me to help her . . . and I knew what her father was doing to her."

"Are you involved with Gretchen romantically?"

244

"Am I *what?*"

"Are you two sweethearts?"

"No." Cripes, what a lousy question.

"You haven't kissed her or . . . touched her?"

"No, I have a girlfriend," I shot back. Then I thought. "At least I *had* one."

"Why did you steal two cases of liquor back in April?"

I didn't answer right off. I looked at my hands in my lap and felt the sweat trickling from my armpits. It was all coming unraveled. I was being trapped, and this time I'd be sent to jail for years.

Leaning closer to me, Mr. Brown smiled slightly.

"You're not on trial here, Cal, but I have to know."

"Will I go to jail?"

"No . . . I have a great deal of weight with the court. If you help us get this man, I'll get any further charges against you dropped. What do you say?"

I looked into the guy's big friendly eyes and I don't know why but I figured I could trust him.

"I stole it to frame Luttermann."

"And the car?"

"Yeah . . . I smashed it into the drugstore."

The guy looked like he'd just lost his job or something and he stared at me like he didn't know if he should scold me or congratulate me.

"You *stole* Luttermann's car, filled it with stolen liquor, and deliberately *rammed* it into *Lacher's Drugstore?*"

"Yeah. Could you find out how much it cost to fix?"

"Why?" he said and he scratched his head.

"I'm going to pay for the damages, little by little, maybe five or ten dollars a week. I have a good job."

Jeez, the room got as quiet as Whalmen's study hall and the lady and I just sat there and I was holding my breath. Mr. Brown shook his head from side to side like he couldn't believe it and then he got out of the chair. The wood floor creaked as he walked to a window and just stood there. I was getting more and more scared and I wished he'd say something. Darn, Luttermann had fooled me. He wasn't a rat after all. He was a porcupine.

"I want to get this man, Cal," Brown said while he kept looking out over the city below. "I want you to know that and trust me. I want to put him away for as long as possible."

Brown started walking around again, muttering to himself like we weren't in the room. He stopped in his tracks near the door and turned to me.

"I appreciate your willingness to help Gretchen. I'll need to know everything you did and anyone you talked to about her. Can you stay for a while and help us get this all down?"

"Okay . . . I guess so."

Brown turned to the wall and let out a big sigh, just standing there for a minute with his head in his hands. Then he smacked his hands together and spun around and looked at me and the chubby woman.

"I may be going back into private practice after this, but we'll go for murder in the first degree!"

I wasn't sure what that meant, but it sounded real serious for Luttermann and I felt good and I liked this guy and it was like I had someone in on it with me for the first time.

Steve picked me up first on the way to the powwow and he went stag, too, and I knew he did it so I wouldn't feel left out. After we'd picked up the rest of the bunch, we headed out Rice Street for Sucker Lake. Everything seemed normal. They played and sang and ate like I'd never been in jail or kicked out of school. Only the ache in my chest kept me from feeling like one of them. Tom and Lola were there, but I avoided them as much as possible.

"Would you like to go to the Junior-Senior Prom with me, Cal?" Jean said when she handed me a hot dog.

It wasn't until then that I knew what I'd do.

"Thanks for asking me, but I'm going with Gretchen."

It would be nice if Gretchen knew anything about it. I was no longer eligible to go, but Gretchen was, and she could darn well invite anyone she wanted. I couldn't wait until tomorrow to talk to her.

My mother acted confused when I steered her into a back pew Sunday morning. We were breaking tradition, but it felt like everybody was staring at me, and sitting in our usual spot, with my father not there, would only make it a lot worse. The three of us had taken the streetcar, but I didn't stand up front and talk to Andy Johnson. The guy tried to smile when we got on, but he couldn't keep the sadness out of his eyes.

During the service, I had all I could do to keep from bawling, and I couldn't find anywhere to hide my face. We stood with the congregation at the right time and held the hymn book at the right page, but neither Peggy nor my mother nor I could sing two words. Every hymn reminded me of my father and I had to keep looking over next to my mother to make sure he wasn't there.

After church I called Gretchen and met her on the Summit boulevard that afternoon. She balked.

"Thanks, Cal, but I don't feel much like it."

"It'll be good for you, get your mind off your father and the trial."

There had been nothing in the news about Luttermann since his arrest, and she was afraid that all they'd try him for was stabbing the cop.

"The closer it gets the more scared I am," she said.

"Then the dance is exactly what you need, to have some fun."

When she said she'd have nothing to wear, I told her I'd get some money out of my savings for a new dress. She only agreed if I promised she could pay me back when she got a job in the summer.

"I don't know how to dance," she said, like she was excited and petrified just thinking about going.

"Neither do I, and I've been going to dances for years."

That settled it. She had a week to shop and get ready for the Junior-Senior Prom, her first social outing ever.

I don't know why, but when I went up onto the porch and rang the bell I was really nervous. Mrs. Wallace let me in—she was the lady taking care of Gretchen and her sisters for a while—and she asked me a bunch of questions about the dance and how late we'd be out, but basically she was real nice about everything. Mr. Wallace was a balding guy and he just smiled and listened. Then Gretchen showed up in a light pink formal and I thought my glasses were lying to me. Jeez, no one in the universe would believe that was Gretch the Wretch. Her two little sisters stood around watching kind of bug-eyed and didn't let out a peep. Everyone was nice and all, but I was relieved to get out of there, figuring they'd heard all about me.

At the car, Steve and Sandy treated Gretchen like she'd been doing this with us all the time, and off we went. It was kind of screwy and sad when you thought about it because I knew Sandy wanted to be with Scott and Steve wanted to be with Katie and I wanted to be with Lola and here we all were, going with someone else, and I just hoped that Gretchen would have a good time.

I could tell that she felt strange and out of place when we walked into the ballroom of the St. Paul Hotel, but so did I. For never having danced, she had little trouble moving her feet in step with me since I only did the slow dances anyway. Most of the kids looked like they had no idea who I was with and I'd catch them staring. We drank Seven-Up and watched the other couples, and when Steve gallantly asked Gretchen to dance, she hesitated and looked at me for a sign, like she didn't know if she was supposed to or not. I nodded and

smiled, and Steve escorted her to the dance floor like Errol
Flynn or something. I had to laugh.

"I can't believe that's Gretchen Luttermann," Sandy said.

"I know," I said, "I can't believe it either."

Sandy watched Scott and Katie dancing lovey-dovey.

"I'm really sorry about Lola, Cal, I know how you must feel."

"Yeah, well . . . I'm sorry about you and Scott."

I could see she was about to cry and I wished I hadn't said
anything.

When Gretchen and Sandy were off to the biffy, Steve said,
"Are you in love with Gretchen or anything?"

I watched the dancing couples.

"No," I said, and I thought that loving Lola was like having
polio—you end up with a limp.

"Do you think it would be all right if I asked her out?"
Steve said with a sappy grin on his face.

"Yeah . . . sure . . . but be awful nice to her."

After the dance we hit the Hasty-Tasty on the other side of
Minneapolis and Gretchen ate two cheeseburgers, besides
fries and a chocolate shake. Steve dropped her off first, and I
walked her to the door.

"Thanks, Cal, I never thought I'd go to a dance. I had fun."

"You can do lots of things now," I said in the shadows of
the porch.

"Maybe," she said, and I could tell she was still plenty scared.

Steve dropped me next, and when they drove away, I don't
know why but I started bawling like crazy, just like that. Jeez,
tears came gushing out of my eyes, and I tried to muffle the
sounds as I walked around to the back, afraid I'd wake up the
whole neighborhood. If I had to guess, I'd have figured it was
losing my dad that was making me cry but maybe it was Lola;
I couldn't be sure anymore. I didn't know if it was a sign of
growing up or proof that I was Norwegian, but somewhere
deep inside the dreads had seeped in and had a stranglehold
on my heart.

I hated crying.

Chapter 43

I waited until the night before the trial to tell my mother. I found her rooted in her favorite corner of our beat-up brown sofa, listening to the evening news. When I spilled it out, she sat up like someone tossed a cherry bomb under her and she snapped off Cedric Adams in the middle of a sentence.

"A dead baby in the *freezer!*"

"Yeah, and if I hadn't dropped it, Luttermann would be in Stillwater right now."

"Oh, Calvin, oh that's so terrible . . . and he tried to *stab* you?"

"Yeah, he was plenty mad because he knew if I got away with the baby he'd go to jail."

"Whose baby was it?"

"Gretchen's. He drowned it."

"Oh, that poor girl, that poor dear girl."

"After that I had to sneak around because I didn't know if he knew who I was or not and then the night of the hayride he almost strangled me and Peggy saved me when she came out the door."

"Oh, Calvin, right here in our alley, oh, Calvin, that's what those marks were on your neck, oh, why didn't you tell us, tell the police?"

"I couldn't," and then I told her about my plan, Rat Trap, the whole thing. Her mouth hung so wide open I thought she'd dislocate her jaw.

"*That's* why you stole the liquor, *that's* why you went to jail?" She caught her breath. "Oh, Calvin, oh, Calvin. Why didn't you *tell* us, why didn't you tell your *father?*"

"I wanted to . . . I tried." I squirmed in my father's favorite chair. "I couldn't or it wouldn't have worked. Dad would've told the cops or something and Luttermann would get away."

She looked at me like I'd just flown in from Mars.

"How on earth did you ever *think* of such a thing?"

"I don't know . . . the police wouldn't do anything unless they had evidence and there wasn't any after I dropped the baby, and I *had* to do *something.*"

"Well you certainly don't have to get mixed up in the trial. You've done enough, Calvin, more than your share."

"If I don't, the man will get away with murder, Mom, and he'll come back and kill Gretchen."

"Let the police take care of him. They certainly—"

"That's why they need me, to tell about the baby."

"Calvin, your father told you a thousand times to leave well enough alone, and if he was here—"

"Remember what Dad did for McCluskey's dog."

"That's different, that was a dog, he felt sorry for it."

"Gretchen's more than a dog."

My mother moved her lips like she was going to say something but she couldn't come up with anything and then she sagged back into the sofa and sighed.

"Oh, Lord, I'm hoodooed, I'm just plain hoodooed."

In my new brown graduation suit, my perfectly ironed white shirt, and my wide red tie, I waited nervously on a wood bench outside the courtroom, watching people in the courthouse hallway. Footsteps on the marble floor sounded like we were in a cave and except for the cops in uniforms I couldn't tell the crooks from the good guys. The longer I sat there the more I felt like *I* was on trial, but Mr. Brown promised me he wouldn't ask about the liquor or the stolen car, taking the chance that Luttermann's lawyer hadn't figured that all out. But I knew I had to tell the truth no matter what they asked and I was shaking in my boots.

Jeez, I saw Mr. Rogers, the school counselor, coming along the hallway in his baggy tweed suit, looking like he was lost. When he saw me, he smiled and came bombing over to the bench.

"Hi, Cal, this the right place?"

"Yeah, this is it."

I felt embarrassed to see him and he just stood there with his hat in his hand.

"How's it going?" he said.

"Oh, I don't know. I think Gretchen was first. I haven't gone in yet."

"Cal . . . I wish I could have been more help to you—"

A policeman pushed through the swinging doors and looked at us. "Calvin Gant?"

"Yeah," I said and I got up. "That's me."

"Come with me."

The cop held the door, and I took a deep breath and shrugged at Mr. Rogers and forced my legs to walk.

I followed the policeman down the aisle between empty rows of pews and it felt like I weighed five hundred pounds. The people in the courtroom turned their heads and looked at me like I was going to be hung. Because of all the bad stuff that Luttermann did to Gretchen and her family, the judge had agreed with the County Attorney to a closed trial.

Tom Brown looked kind of nervous at a table on the right and a bunch of people sat along the far wall in the jury box and I was really glad to see that the black-haired judge wasn't the old codger who'd given me thirty days. The policeman led me through a low wooden swinging gate near the front and my stomach knotted and I sucked for air. Otto Luttermann was sitting at a table to the left not six feet away. I could smell the guy breathing down my neck, and I turned to Mr. Brown's friendly face.

"Relax now, Cal. They'll swear you in," he said as he held my arm for a minute. *Relax?* The guy must be a comedian on his day off.

I had to walk right in front of Luttermann on the way to the witness stand, and a guy there had me put my left hand on a Bible and raise my right hand and I never heard what he said but I said I do. My heart was thumping and I sat in a chair like I was in a pulpit, higher than everyone but the judge, and all the faces looked at me like they were expecting a sermon or something. I tried to look at Mr. Brown on the other side of the courtroom but Luttermann's face was like a splinter in the corner of my eye. Before I could force a swallow down my throat, Mr. Brown was standing by his table and asking me questions. I got the first one right; I did remember my name.

I told them how I'd talked to Sergeant Riley and Mr. Rogers without letting on that it was Gretchen I was talking about.

"Gretchen showed me bruises on her legs two different times," I said.

When I told them I'd found a baby in the freezer and how the man chased me with a knife, Mr. Brown surprised me.

"Cal, do you see the man who chased you with the knife in this courtroom?"

"Yes."

"Would you point him out to the court."

Holy Toledo, I didn't want to look at him, but I did, looked right into his rotten face and pointed.

"There."

Luttermann stared at me and his eyes were like a rat's and they said I'll get you.

"I have no further questions for the witness, your honor."

The judge looked at the young blond guy sitting next to Luttermann.

"Mr. Moss, do you wish to cross-examine the witness?"

"Not at this time, your honor," he said, "but we request the right to recall him at another time."

"So granted," the judge said and turned to me. "You may step down."

I hurried past Luttermann, afraid he'd grab me, and Brown smiled and nodded toward the center aisle. I pushed through the swinging gate and high-tailed it for the door, feeling pretty good that I'd done it, but when I got out in the hallway, a policeman said I'd have to hang around in case the defense recalled me, and it felt like he'd knocked the wind out of me.

We ate supper in the kitchen, and my mom and I tried to keep most of the details about the trial from Peggy but she'd picked up a few things by always hanging around.

"Why did that man chase you with a knife?" Peggy asked wide-eyed.

"I took something from his house, something that would help Gretchen," I told her.

"What did you take?"

"Some evidence."

"Good for you, Cal. Gosh, wait till I tell Anita," my sister said.

"You'll tell *no one*," my mother said. "Your brother could be in a lot of trouble if you tell *anyone*, he could go to jail for a long time. This is private family business."

"I'd have done it, too, if I knew someone was being beaten by their father," Peggy said.

"You learn to mind your own business and stay out of trouble," my mother said. "Look where it's got your brother."

The ring of the phone cut into our safe kitchen, and some-how I knew I shouldn't answer it. My mother felt the same dread because she let it ring four times before she lifted the receiver.

"Hello." She paused. Then she handed the phone to me. "It's for you."

Gretchen's voice came at me like a firing squad.

". . . and they had lots of people tell what a good man my father was: a Sunday school teacher, his boss at the post office, our pastor," she said breathlessly. "It was scary, Cal. I watched the faces of the jury. They *listened* to those people, they *believed* them."

"Didn't Mr. Brown ask them questions?" I said.

"No, he didn't. I don't know why. Then they put my mother on the witness stand. She said nothing I told them had ever happened, she said I lied, that I made up stories. They're turning it all around, Cal, twisting it. They're trying to make it look like *we* did something wrong, like you're my boyfriend and we tried to get my father."

The *we* did a flip-flop in my stomach and I wanted to join the foreign legion.

"What did Mr. Brown do?" I said.

"He seems worried. After my mother talked he looked awful disappointed. I was praying she'd tell the truth."

"How much longer is it going?" I said.

"I don't know, but Mr. Brown was sure they'd call you back tomorrow morning."

When I got off the phone I thought about running away.

"What did she say?" my mother asked.

"Her mother wouldn't tell the truth."

Gretchen's words had oozed out of the phone like a thick black goo and fallen in a lump on the table. No one knew what to do with it.

"Finish your supper, Cal," my mother said.

"I'm not hungry."

I was sitting on my bed and worrying about tomorrow when Peggy came to my door on her way to bed.

"Did that man murder someone?" she asked and I figured she'd overheard my mom and I.

"Yeah, a little baby."

"Oh, how wicked. I'm glad you're not going to let him get away with it."

I looked at her for a minute, and I remembered when I was young like her. "He may get away with it anyway," I said. "Maybe he already has."

"How can he *do* that?" she said with her face all screwed up.

"I don't know. Sometimes they don't believe you when you tell the truth."

"They'll believe *you*, Cal. Good night."

"Good night."

I had to go back tomorrow and sit there in front of everyone and hope that Luttermann's lawyer hadn't found out about the stolen liquor and the frame. If I started hitchhiking that night, I could be in the north woods by morning.

Chapter 44

The hot and humid courtroom smelled of old varnish, and I
felt a little light-headed in my graduation suit and knotted tie.
A meek-looking woman in a black dress hunched in the row
behind Luttermann and I figured it was Gretchen's mother
and they were trying to show the jury what a swell family
they had. Mr. Moss, Luttermann's lawyer, a younger jock who
had eyes that really nailed you, kept zipping around like he
had ants in his pants. In a double-breasted gray suit and
polished black shoes, he looked pretty snazzy.

"What is Gretchen Luttermann to you?" he said from
behind a table and his voice sounded like he knew what he
was doing.

"She's . . . a friend."

"A girlfriend?"

"No . . . a friend," I said, trying to look the man in the eye.

"She's a girl and a friend. Doesn't that make her a girlfriend?" The guy smiled at me and he seemed pretty cocky.

"No. A girlfriend is someone you love."

"Do you love Gretchen Luttermann?"

"Ah . . . no . . . well sure, but not like that. She's a friend."

"Okay, we've established she's a girl . . . friend, and you
love her.

"Objection," Mr. Brown said. "Counsel is badgering the
witness."

"Sustained," the judge said.

"Now, Cal . . ." Moss moved in close, like we were buddies
or something. ". . . do you feel responsible for Gretchen
Luttermann?"

"She needed help."

"Do you generally go around helping people?"

"Ah. . . . no. . . . sometimes."

"Do you think you're supposed to save people, rescue people?"

"No . . . I don't know . . . if they need help."

"Did you choose Gretchen as someone to help?"

He walked over by the jury with his back to me.

"She asked me to."

"Did you know that Gretchen's father was strict with her?"

"Yes, he would–"

"That he didn't allow her to go on unescorted dates with boys?"

"Yes, but–"

"Objection!" Mr. Brown called out. "The witness has a right to answer the questions."

I wanted to know if the witness had the right to run.

"Sustained," the judge said. He looked over at me. "You may answer the question."

"Her father wouldn't let her go anywhere alone," I said. "He didn't even let her *talk* to boys."

Moss spun around and stared at me. "Did she talk to *you?*"

"Yes."

"Did you watch the house to see when her father might not be home."

"Yes . . . no."

"Well, Cal, which is it?"

"I watched until he went on his walk; he went somewhere every night at ten."

Moss wheeled to the table and snatched a paper from his stuff. He looked at the jury.

"Now, Cal, I have a police report here that says you were arrested on April first of this year for stealing two cases of whiskey from the Prior Liquor Store."

"Objection, your honor." Brown stood. "This is irrelevant. The witness is not on trial here."

"Your honor," Moss said," I'm trying to establish the credibility and the motivation of the witness."

"Very well," the judge said, "but let's stay on track."

"Is this report correct, Cal?" Moss moved in close again.

It felt like the witness chair was tipping and sweat broke out on my forehead and one drop ran over my eyebrow into my eye before I could wipe it away. I gripped the arms of the chair and caught Luttermann smirking.

"*YES!*" I said kind of loud, surprising myself.

"Did you steal Mr. Luttermann's car?"

"Yes."

"Did you deliberately drive it into the drugstore window?"

"Yes." I could hardly breathe.

"Cal, are you in love with Gretchen?" Moss asked calmly.

"No."

He walked over and stood behind Luttermann and put his hands on Lutterman's shoulders like they were good old fishin' buddies.

"This conscientious father wouldn't let his daughter see you, would he?"

"No."

"And so you were mad at him, weren't you?"

"Yes, but not because he—"

"Just answer the question with a yes or no," Moss said and he moved out from behind Luttermann and his eyes were like bullets. "Were you angry at him?"

"Yes . . . but . . ."

"And you framed him so you could be with his daughter."

"No, I was—"

"Then you made up a story about a baby to get her father out of your way?"

"Objection," Brown said. "Speculation, the defense counsel is leading the witness."

"Sustained," the judge said like he was bored.

Moss looked at the jury. "Cal, did you frame Otto Luttermann?"

"There really was a baby," I said real fast, "and I did it to make him stop hurting her."

"Your honor," Moss said and he looked at the judge.

The judge turned to me. "Just answer the question with a yes or no." I nodded.

"If there was a baby," Moss said, "were you the father?"

"No."

My hands were sweating and I wanted to punch that creep.

"Cal, have you ever gone on a date with Gretchen?"

He walked across the courtroom and looked over at me.

"Ah . . . no . . . kinda."

"What do you mean?"

"We went to the Junior-Senior Prom . . . with friends."

Jeez, the courtroom was getting hot and my tie was too tight.

"But Gretchen was *your* date."

Moss turned and looked at me. I glanced at Mr. Brown and he nodded like everything was okay.

"Yes."

"Were there other times you went out with Gretchen?"

"No . . . well, we just went to Minneapolis once."

"On a date?"

"No, to get Gretchen away from everything."

"To be *with* you?"

"No . . . to be *away* from her father," I shot back and I was really getting ticked off.

"When her father was out of the way, did you take her on a date, to the Junior-Senior Prom?"

"No . . . I mean . . . yes."

Moss came zooming right up to the witness stand.

"Isn't the junior-senior prom the big event where you take your best girlfriend?"

"Yeah, but *my* girlfriend wouldn't go and—"

"Cal, do you expect the jury to believe your story about a baby when you've admitted framing this concerned father who is only trying to protect his daughter from getting into trouble, as so many young girls do these days?"

"Objection," Brown said and he stood up and I could tell he was getting mad, too. "Irrelevant, calling for an assumption."

"Sustained," the judge said, and I couldn't believe how bad that creep lawyer was making it look.

"Cal," Moss said, standing right in front of me, "did you and Gretchen plan to frame her father?"

"No, she didn't know anything about it."

"Were Gretchen's tales about her father, stories without a shred of proof, a part of this same attempt to get him in trouble and out of the way so you two could be together?"

"No, *nooo* . . . Jeez, you're—"

"Objection, your honor, that calls for speculation," Brown said.

"Cal, have you had sexual relations with Gretchen?"

"No!" Cripes, I hated this guy's guts.

"Did you and Gretchen have a baby? Is that what these God-fearing parents are trying to protect their daughter from?"

"No, no, you're changing it all around."

"Cal, don't you think you've caused Mr. Luttermann enough trouble?" He stood by the table and he was talking real friendly. "Do you expect the people on the jury to believe such a story?"

He waited, but I wasn't going to answer.

"Cal, don't you think it's time you tell the truth and let this God-fearing man *go home* . . ." He nodded at Mrs. Luttermann. ". . . *home* to his good wife and children?"

Holy cow, Gretchen's mother started chattering like a chipmunk, like her mouth just went off on its own, yakking so fast I couldn't understand what she was saying, and everyone was looking at her and I thought she'd popped her cork.

"Quiet, please," the judge said, like he was talking to a little kid. She stood up and she was really shaking and she was babbling something and Luttermann turned around and stared at her.

"Sit down and be quiet!" he said.

Moss looked like he couldn't decide what to do.

"Order . . . order in the courtroom, please," the judge said.

Gretchen's mother turned away from Luttermann and kept yakking, real fast, and finally I could understand what she was saying.

"There was a baby, there was a baby, there was a baby."

She kept saying it like she didn't dare but she was making herself do it anyway and Moss scooted over to her and said something.

"No-o-o!" she yelled and she pushed him away. "There *was* a baby. It was *his* baby." She pointed at Luttermann. "And *he* killed it!"

Jeez, everyone kind of gulped and held their breath and just sat there but Luttermann blasted out of his chair and leaped over the table and came for me.

"Son of Satan!" he shouted.

I was cornered in the witness stand and he grabbed me by the throat with both hands. I tried to pull his arms away but I couldn't and I couldn't breathe. In a couple seconds two cops and Henry Moss pounced on Luttermann and tore his hands from my throat and I was coughing and gasping and Luttermann, with his face right in mine, spit on me. I don't know what happened, but my fists started banging away on his face, for Little Jacob, for Gretchen, for Helga, hard, hammering shots that felt like I was slugging a cast-iron bell. His head whipped back and forth like a punching bag until the men holding him realized they had to protect *him* from *me*.

Everyone was shouting and shoving and a cop wrapped his arms around me and held me so I couldn't nail Luttermann any more, but I really felt good, I was flying. I'd wanted to punch him for a long time and my chest was heaving and my heart pounding like I'd been running for my life again. They dragged Gretchen's father away with hands cuffed behind him and his nose and face were bleeding like a butchered hog. Mrs. Luttermann stood in her tracks, hanging on to the back of a bench like she was standing in a hurricane.

The judge kept shouting, "Bailiff! Bailiff! Order! Order!" and banging his gavel but no one paid any attention and everyone was yakking like crazy and standing around like they didn't believe it. Mr. Brown shoved through the melee and began wiping the blood off my face with a hanky and I noticed my bloody hands and my splattered suit.

"Are you all right?" Brown said.

"Yeah, I think so," I said, holding one hand in the other. "I think I broke my hand."

Jeez, I felt weak and I slumped back into the witness chair.

"I think we broke the case," Brown whispered. "We drew the last wild card in the deck."

He was trying to wipe away the blood on my suit and white shirt, but it only smeared worse.

With Luttermann out of there, everything kind of settled down and Mr. Brown went back to his table and the judge, who seemed kind of shook up, apologized to the jury and to me for what happened. I started to shake and kind of shiver and I don't know why, but the judge told the jury to disregard what happened, and I wondered how in heck they could do that. I looked down at the smeared blood on my suit and remembered how mad my mother was when I got blood all over my jacket from the cottontail.

"Blood doesn't come out," she told me. "If you'd leave well enough alone you wouldn't be covered with blood."

Darn, she'd hit the ceiling again. I figured my suit was ruined but it didn't matter, I wasn't going to graduate anyway.

The judge turned to Henry Moss, who was sitting at his table like he'd just fallen out of an elevator.

"Does the defense have any more questions for the witness?"

"No, your honor." He wasn't cocky anymore.

"Mr. Brown?" The judge glanced towards the County Attorney.

"No, your honor, but the prosecution would like to recall Mrs. Ruth Luttermann to the stand."

The following day, I sat in the row behind Mr. Brown when the jury came in. I had on my old Sunday suit, and my right hand, which wasn't broken, had band-aids on two knuckles. Gretchen was sitting beside me and she really looked nice in a yellow dress with a yellow ribbon in her hair, but she was plenty worried and she held her breath and knotted her fingers. Luttermann didn't look so hot; his nose was bandaged and he had a fat lip and a puffed black eye and I felt pretty good about that. He kept staring at the jury like he was still trying to scare them.

"Have you reached a verdict?" the judge asked.

A short bald guy stood and said, "We have, your honor."

The judge turned to Luttermann. "Will the defendant stand?"

With a policeman on each side and his hands cuffed, Gretchen's father stumbled to his feet.

"Would you read your verdict to the court."

"We the jury, find the defendant, Otto Luttermann, guilty of murder in the first degree."

Jeez, it was like everyone let out a big sigh. Luttermann sagged into his chair like a zombie and Mr. Brown had a big grin on his kisser and Gretchen was looking at the jury with tears running down her face.

"Thank you, thank you," she was saying softly but they couldn't hear her. Then she turned to her mother who was sitting across the aisle and her mother gave her a timid glance and then looked at the floor.

"Will the defendant stand and face the bench," the judge said.

Two policemen lifted Luttermann to his feet and he just stared at the wall.

"Otto Luttermann, for your heinous and monstrous crimes against your own flesh and blood, I sentence you to life imprisonment at the penitentiary in Stillwater."

Luttermann never blinked, like he never heard a word the judge said.

Gretchen was crying all over the place as the policemen muscled her father out of the courtroom. Her mother sidled over to her and hesitated, like she wasn't sure what Gretchen would do. Gretchen studied her for a minute and then timidly put an arm around her. Stiffly, her mother put one arm around Gretchen, like two little kids who didn't know how to hug.

Chapter 45

Graduation came down on me like a ton of bricks. All day at work I thought about not going, but to see Gretchen walk across that platform would be worth all the hard feelings. I rode the Grand-Mississippi home from the job, and I just about jumped out of my pants when I saw an old woman walking her dog along Grand. I yanked the chord and grabbed my lunch box and scrambled for the rear doors. It was McCluskey's dog!

I bombed down the sidewalk in my heavy work boots, and I don't know why, but my heart was hammering, like finding McCluskey's dog would somehow bring me closer to my father. The shrunken woman and bowlegged dog toddled along ahead of me like old cronies who had survived the war together. When I caught up I hung back for a minute, to make sure. There couldn't be another dog like that, padding along beside the woman with his huge ears flopping and his baggy eyes shining, and when he noticed me he started wagging his tail to beat the band.

"Pardon me, ma'am," I said as I pulled up even. "I think I know your dog."

The woman stopped and McCluskey's dog sat at heel. She wore a gray wool watch cap and a long windbreaker that seemed way too warm for summer. Her gnarled hand held a leather leash.

"Why, Ambrose, do you have friends I don't know about?" she said to the dog.

"Where did you get him?" I said.

"From the Humane Society, he was my Christmas present."

I kneeled, and the mongrel wagged his tail like he was beating out a brush fire, slurping my face with his monster tongue.

"You old son of a gun," I said as I rubbed the dog. "Fell into hog's heaven."

"Ambrose was the name of my late husband, I've lived alone for nineteen years. Now Ambrose has come back to me. Do you believe in reincarnation?"

Jeez, the woman's face looked a little like the dog's, all wrinkled and saggy with watery brown eyes.

"I don't know what that is," I told her.

"How do you know Ambrose?"

"A man near us owned him, treated him awful."

I scratched the dog's side and one of his rear legs started pumping like crazy.

"That's what they told me, that he had been terribly neglected. All he needed was lots of love, they said, but I recognized him right off. Ambrose found his way back to me. He sleeps with me, you know."

"That's swell."

I wondered if that cute little lady really believed that McCluskey's dog was her dead husband, and if she did, so what.

"My sister used to feed him peanut-butter sandwiches."

"Did you call the Humane Society on that dreadful man?"

"No, my dad did."

I stood up and looked into her weathered face.

"Well, I may never have found Ambrose if he hadn't. Thank him for me, will you?"

"I can't, he died."

"Oh, I'm so sorry." The woman paused. "Your father must have been a good man."

My eyes and throat started filling and I had to look away.

"Yes, ma'am . . . he was."

They rambled down Grand at their own pace, and I watched them for a minute, leaking tears onto my dirty work shirt. I figured they were good for each other, and on the way home, I couldn't wait to tell my mom and Peggy.

"And she thinks the dog's her husband who's come back from the dead," I told them at the supper table. "She called it incarnation or something."

"How was he?" Peggy said.

"Jim-dandy, she sleeps with him."

"We don't believe in reincarnation," my mother said. "We believe we go to heaven when we die."

"I'm so happy he has a nice home," Peggy said.

"Yeah, so am I," I said. "She's a funny old lady, kinda looks like McCluskey's dog. I think she's daffy but the dog sure wasn't complaining."

"If we did believe in such a thing," my mother said thoughtfully, "Horace would come back as a streetcar."

She looked at us with a faint smile, and I realized I hadn't seen her face brighten like that since my father died.

"Yeah, he would," I said. "He'd be a streetcar."

We all began to laugh, and I thought my mother was going to be all right.

While I was putting on the finishing touches in the bathroom mirror, Peggy leaned on the door jam and watched me. I always had trouble knotting my tie so it would come out balanced. Somehow my mother got the blood out of my new double-breasted suit.

"You look good," Peggy said.

"Thanks."

"I wish you were graduating tonight."

"Yeah, I don't know what I'm dressing up for."

I finished with the tie and took a comb to my damp hair.

"Cal, do you think Dad loved us?"

I turned and looked at my sister for a second and I could tell it was really bothering her. "Gosh, yeah, sure he did."

I turned back to the mirror and finished with my hair.

"He never *said* so," she said.

"Well, maybe he showed us by what he did for us."

"Yeah . . . maybe, but I wish he'd said so."

I laid the comb on the sink and looked in the mirror.

"Yeah . . . so do I."

When I was ready to go, my mother called me into the living room. She was perched on the edge of the sofa and she nodded for me to sit in my father's chair.

"I have something I want to say to you, Calvin."

"Yeah, Mom."

Jeez, she had this real serious look on and I could tell she was kinda nervous and I wondered what was coming next and I swallowed a lump in my throat.

"Are you sure you want to go tonight? It will be very hard for you and I don't think you realize—"

"Yeah, I know, but I gotta go."

"Do you want me to go with you?"

"Oh, gee, thanks, Mom, but I'll do all right."

She kind of pursed her lips and her eyes turned sad.

"Calvin, you didn't kill your father."

Jeez, I looked at her and then at the floor. She was trying hard with the happiness stuff, but I knew I killed him, and I hated talking about it.

"I know you think your going to jail did it, and I think I let you think that to punish you for what you had done. But the Company killed your dad, the streetcar was his life, and when they took that away, he was lost."

"But he thought I was a juvenile delinquent or something."

"I know, I know, but I knew your father pretty well after all these years, and I can tell you for sure that he's mighty proud of you tonight."

Cripes, it was like something let go inside of me and I was crying and I couldn't stop.

"Somewhere tonight he knows what you did, and why, and he's prouder of you than if you graduated at the top of your class."

I was wiping my face with my hands and my mother handed me a hanky and I couldn't stop and Peggy came in.

"What's the matter with Cal?"

"Nothing," my mother said, "it's going to be all right."

My mother came over and sat on the edge of my father's

chair and put her arms around me and I was bawling like a baby and then Peggy came over and hugged me and I was getting my suit all wet.

I rode a Grand-Mississippi downtown and sat on the bench seat right behind the motorman, searching for some clue my dad had left, knowing he probably drove this car nine million times. For a second I thought I caught a whiff of his scent, a scent that still hung in his closet and sometimes haunted our apartment like a wild animal marking its territory.

I thought about how far I'd come since I started my senior year, how much I'd seen, what I'd learned, how much I'd changed. If I could go back I'd do a lot of things differently, I guess, and I don't know why, but I remembered what Pastor Ostrum had said one Sunday that fall: that love wasn't a warm feeling, something that just happens to you, but a decision you make, something you *do*. I didn't know if that was true, but if it was, then it wasn't Lola I had loved through it all, but Gretchen.

Chapter 46

When I got to the balcony in the St. Paul Auditorium twenty minutes early, I found a seat at the railing, on an aisle so I could bomb out of there. Thank goodness my suit had dried on the streetcar ride downtown. There were a few people hustling around on the main floor and the place was filling fast.

While I was sitting there I started thinking about that wacky little lady and McCluskey's dog and that incarnation stuff and I wondered how Uncle Emil would come back if he had the choice. Then I knew. He'd come back as one of the singing wolves and fling his loneliness at the moon, but we didn't believe that stuff. We believed we go to heaven, and all of a sudden this happy thought popped into my head. In· heaven there would be at least one streetcar with thousands of miles of shiny track and there would be no cars and everybody would ride the streetcar and my father would be the motorman and he'd take people wherever they wanted to go, and he'd be smiling and yakking and clanging the bell like mad.

The crowd of spectators stood and craned their necks and I kind of choked up when my class marched in while the band played "Pomp and Circumstance." They were all dressed real spiffy and the program said there were three hundred and fifty-four graduates. A few were missing.

Everything went fast. The class president, Randy Mayler, gave a short talk and the speech class and choir put on a musical drama. That kind of stuff usually dragged for me, but this was different, and memories of school with all my friends were crashing down on me. What I'd have given to be down there with them and my dad in the audience watching.

The Commissioner of Education told the class that they

had been preparing for life these four years, and now they were crossing the threshold into *real* life. Jeez, what planet had that guy been living on? Before basketball games we had time to warm up, but one thing I'd learned for sure: In life you don't get any warm-up, you're in it up to your eyeballs right off the bat and it all counts, there isn't any practice.

Then, what everybody was waiting for started, and each student was called to go up and get a diploma. I edged forward in my seat. Tom was one of the first and Jean accepted her diploma with a big smile even though she was wiping tears from her eyes. Jerry marched across the stage like he owned the auditorium and Steve swung his crippled leg like a six-gun, his graduating as unbelievable to him as it must have been to his teachers.

Then I heard her name. "Gretchen Luttermann."

She got out of her seat and started for the podium, and I figured a lot of kids would swear they'd never seen her before. She'd put on ten pounds and looked pretty normal but I could tell she was really self-conscious. When the Superintendent of Schools handed her the diploma, I stood up and cheered and clapped, whooping it up the whole time she crossed the platform and it was the only sound in the place and everybody was turning and staring at me but I didn't care because I wanted Gretchen to know I was there and people probably figured I was some kind of a rowdy.

"Sandy Meyer."

She bounced down the aisle and scooted across the platform, and I could see her running for her life up Wheeler.

"Lola Muldoon."

Lola stood and headed for the front, and I thought my heart was going to fall out. Whoever said dumb things like It is better to have loved and lost than to never have loved at all? They're either morons or they've never been in love because it would be a whole lot better if I'd never known the taste of her mouth, never heard her laugh, but I *remembered* how she smelled, the feel of her spine under her Angora sweater when we danced, and the color of her eyes when she said I love you.

I always thought Lola was my reward for trying to help Gretchen but it doesn't work that way. Steve was taking Gretchen to the Commencement Dance at the Calhoun Beach Club, and I was happy that she'd be there with her class. I hoped they could help each other; they were my good friends and they'd been wounded and scarred and crippled in what that jerk of a Commissioner called *preparing for life*.

They all paraded across the platform, and then it was almost over. Gretchen turned in her seat and threw me a little wave and I waved back. The choir formed on their tiered platform and I watched Lola take her place in the second row. When they started singing, I figured it was time to rip out of there.

"Cal," Sandy said, all out of breath, as she squatted in the aisle beside me.

"Jeez, what are you doing up here; you're in the choir."

"My mother saw in the paper that you went to jail and smashed the car into Lacher's to help Gretchen get away from her father."

"*That* was in the *paper?*"

"Yes, tonight's, all about the trial, is it true?"

I nodded.

"Ooooh, Bean." She leaned over and hugged me. "Oh, Bean."

Darn, I wasn't going to get my suit wet again. Sandy crouched back on the aisle step.

"Mother said that was the kind of boyfriend I should find."

"We've been good friends too long for that," I said.

The choir was singing and someone behind us said "Shhhhhh."

"I know," Sandy whispered, "and you love Lola and I love Scott. I wonder what will happen to us, Bean?"

"You never know, Sand. Scott and Katie could break up

any time, when you least expect it. Things like that happen all the time, they really do."

I stood up and slid past Sandy.

"I gotta get outta here, have fun at the dance."

"I'm going to make them give you a diploma, Cal, I'll *make* them," she said loud enough to hear in Duluth, and I ducked my face and headed for the exit.

After bombing down the stairs, I came out on the fourth street side. I'd catch a Grand-Mississippi home. With none in sight, I walked toward the corner, and I could faintly hear the class singing "Fare-well, Speed-well." The street was all but deserted, and I remembered the first time I noticed Gretchen.

I'd thought about it eleven million times, and I wondered *what if* I'd been sick that day and didn't go to school, or my last name was Swanberg or Tomlinson and I sat way in the back of the study hall? Or what if we lived in a different neighborhood and I went to Marshall or Monroe? But as I walked up Fourth Street, I was *glad* I wasn't sick that day, that my name was Gant, that I went to Central. I was *glad* I did what I did!

I heard something and I turned in my tracks. A shiny new GM diesel bus came rolling up Fourth with Grand-Mississippi on its destination sign. It glided to the curb and the doors opened with a swoosh. I stood there with my mouth hanging open and looked at the driver, Andy Johnson, my father's friend.

"Say, I know you," Andy said. "You're Horace's boy."

A cloud of sadness drifted across his phony smile.

"You riding the bus?" he asked.

"The *bus!*" I said. "I wouldn't ride one of these ugly, stinking, good-for-nothing contraptions if they paid me. They're going to ruin the city with their noise and fumes, wait and see. We'll all die of TB or something."

"What are you going to do, walk?" he asked.

"Yeah," I said, "until they bring the streetcars back."

Johnson shrugged and closed the doors and roared away,

leaving me standing in a little cloud of diesel fumes. I started legging it for home. I was kind of tired and there was a thunderhead building in the west and I wondered if I'd get home before the storm. Heck, I figured Lola and Tom could break up anytime, maybe that summer, you never know. Things like that happen all the time, they really do.

∾ THE END

Author's Note

Although the main plot and characters are fictitious, I have incidentally used the names of actual students who were present at Saint Paul Central in 1949. All public events, dates, scores, news items, and locations are historically accurate.

The plight of the streetcar in the Twin Cities is factually chronicled, even to the downtown traffic jam in April of 1950 when an irate automobile driver blocked traffic until a policeman backed up the streetcars to allow the driver to park. I fictionalized the incident by making Cal's father the motorman on that streetcar.
–Stanley Gordon West, January 1997

In 1950–"General Motors, Standard Oil Company of California, Firestone Tire, and other companies are convicted of criminal conspiracy to replace electric transit lines with gasoline or diesel buses. GM has replaced more than 100 electric transit systems in 45 cities with GM buses and will continue this program despite the court action [the company is fined $5,000, its treasurer $1]."
–*The People's Chronology* by James Trager

"The conversion [to buses] was completed in 1954 as scheduled, and as it turned out, was a pillage of the electric railway system for the purpose of illegal personal profit for Ossanna and his associates. Several years later they were indicted, tried in court, found guilty, and sentenced to prison terms. The Green-Ossanna group took only five years to reduce to scrap metal what had taken the Lowry group over fifty years to build: one of the finest street railway systems in America."
–*The Electric Railways of Minnesota* by Russell L. Olson

St. Paul Central as it appeared in 1949.

St. Paul Central no longer exists as it did in 1949. The building was demolished in the 1980s and a "modern" school building erected. All that remains of the past is the name . . . and the memories.